HANNA, I FORGOT TO TELL YOU

HANNA, I FORGOT TO TELL YOU

A NOVEL

ESTELLE GLASER LAUGHLIN

TEXAS TECH UNIVERSITY PRESS

This book is typeset in Imprint MT. The paper used in this book meets the minimum requirements of ANSI/NISO Z39.48-1992 (R1997). ∞

Designed by Hannah Gaskamp

Library of Congress Control Number: 2020939549
ISBN 9781682830680 (cloth)

Printed in the United States of America
20 21 22 23 24 25 26 27 28 / 9 8 7 6 5 4 3 2 1

Texas Tech University Press
Box 41037
Lubbock, Texas 79409-1037 USA
800.832.4042
ttup@ttu.edu
www.ttupress.org

For Chase and Brynn
For Luke
For Miles and Simon

Contents

Contents

PART ONE

Queenly Warsaw

More than bread we need poetry at a time when
we don't seem to need it at all.

Chaim Kaplan, Warsaw Ghetto historian

CHAPTER ONE

Karmelicka Street

Malka lived at 25 Karmelicka Street in queenly Warsaw. Her street had tall buildings with ironwork balconies and was abuzz with noisy people. An arched entry gate led to her courtyard enclosed by buildings on all four sides. In the center sat a small garden. The windows in her second-floor apartment had a panoramic view of the entire yard. On warm days, she could put her head out the window and listen to neighbors arguing or breaking into laughter and watch boys playing soldiers and girls jumping rope. The most wonderful sight from her windows came at the end of each day. When dusk rolled in and the street lanterns glowed, Karmelicka Street looked as if it wore a crown of golden lights.

In Malka's neighborhood, everything was new and filled with wonder. Passover arrived like a grand awakening. Snow melted into long puddles that reflected the sky, houses clamored with holiday preparations, and the world looked joyful. On the day of the First Seder, Malka's mother swept the rooms clean of the last crumbs of bread and completed final touches. As the sun inched down on its westward arch, a reverent serenity settled over her neighborhood and filled Malka with awe. Dressed in their holiday best, she and her parents boarded a shiny black *doroszka* (horse-drawn taxi) to carry them to Aunt Sonia's house to celebrate. Brightly lit rooms sang with loving voices; aromas of cinnamon and freshly baked cakes and cookies wafted in the air; aunts and uncles brought wine and even more cakes and cookies.

At sunset, her beloved grandfather, Isaak, took a seat at the head of a festive table. A graying beard lay flat against his wide chest. Behind his round glasses were eyes that were kind, witty, and wise. All the guests followed him to the table and the Seder ceremony began. Malka, the youngest child present, asked the customary four questions. The telling of the Passover story followed.

Malka loved listening to the tale of sadness and hope, of slavery and freedom, of cruelty and mercy, and of miracles. Her heart cried with sympathy: *How were the poor Jews in Egypt able to endure the harshness of slavery?* And gratitude: *Thank God the Pharaoh is dead, and we are free.* Little did she then know what lay ahead.

The celebration went on into the night. She beamed with pleasure to be allowed to stay up late while most of the children in Poland were fast asleep. On the ride back home, Malka admired the fairytale images of the slumbering city. The darkness felt enormous, the universe mysterious beyond myriads of stars, and there was she, a tiny creature securely tucked under her parents' wings. At the end of the ride, she hopped out of the doroszka, rang for the custodian, and held her breath to hear the ear-splitting clang of the shutting gate followed by a shower of jingling echoes bouncing off the sturdy courtyard walls. Her family walked softly to their apartment and laid themselves to rest in the glow of the Passover celebration.

On the night of the First Seder, everything was different and exceptional. It remained a memory Malka recalled during a time when her heart abided on dreams.

CHAPTER TWO

The Explosion That Shook the Earth

F riday morning, September 1, 1939, was serene. The sky
stretched blue to the end of the world. Malka's father took
off to see patients, her mother was busy with Sabbath preparations, and Malka went to visit her best friend Hanna who
lived in an identical apartment one level above. The girls, both
eleven years old, were inseparable. They walked to school
together, played after school, and shared innermost secrets.
Even the night could hardly keep them apart. Before drifting
off to sleep, Malka would holler, "Hanna! I forgot to tell you
...!" And Hanna would respond with a more subdued, "Malka,
are you still up?"

A nimbus of black curls framed Hanna's tawny face; her
dark eyes sparkled with vitality. She was small and as agile as a
gazelle. In contrast, Malka was tall; her auburn hair fell neatly
to her shoulders; her eyes were big, green, and serious.

"Is Ben home?" Malka asked with forced nonchalance as she entered Hanna's apartment.

"No," Hanna replied. "Why are you asking?"

"Just wondered."

Malka loved Ben, Hanna's older brother by two years. When he had nothing better to do, he would enchant her with farfetched cops-and-robbers' stories and exotic tales of African safaris — all "absolutely true" — while Malka gazed, completely entranced, into his mischievous face. Ben's nose and cheeks were sprayed with freckles; his hair and eyes were the color of chocolate.

Sometime on that day, a deafening explosion shook the earth. Then . . . a wake of silence followed, as if all sound were sucked out of the universe. Seconds later, air raid sirens howled.

Stunned, Pani Rotenberg, Hanna's mother, turned on the radio. An ominous voice blared: "Attention! Attention! German warplanes have dropped bombs on Warsaw. Germany has attacked Poland without declaring war. Poland is at war!"

Malka bolted home to be safe with her parents. Before she reached the last turn of stairs, the door opened, and her mother ran into her.

"I was just going to get you. Did you hear what happened?" her mother asked.

"How could I have missed hearing the bombs explode, Mama? Where is Tata? Why isn't he home?" Malka demanded, although she knew her father was seeing patients in the city.

Frightened out of their senses, the two stepped to the window to wait for Tata to come home. In the background, the radio blasted horrifying descriptions of the attack: "It was terrible. A deafening roar of airplanes suddenly rose above the city. All traffic froze. In a split second, planes dived out of the sky and dropped bombs. Buildings exploded in front of pedestrians' eyes. The planes were gone before the buildings finished falling."

Even on that dreadful day when the first bombs fell on Warsaw, the brutality of war for Malka remained distant. The reality of war for her began that night. In an instant, she stopped being a carefree girl and began to carry life's heavy burdens.

That night, she was awakened by a fearsome roar of airplanes that made the darkness shudder. Within a few heartbeats, the planes were above her roof. Hissing flares lit up the sky bright as day, making every building a clear target. A barrage of otherworldly detonations shook the earth. Throughout that night, the heavens burst open with blazes of light. Flocks of German bomber planes, Messerschmitts and Stukas, swooped down, raining bombs on the city. Buildings crumbled to the ground and gargantuan tongues of flames devoured entire structures and their contents: books, toys, furniture, and people.

No one knew what to do. Imagining greater danger to be on the higher floors, neighbors stampeded downstairs as if they would rather be covered by the warm earth than be crushed by collapsing buildings. The explosions were unrelenting, like a continuous drumroll of supernatural thunder, each succeeding rumble rolling into the next. In the millisecond of silence — as loud as what came before it — Malka would open her eyes in disbelief: *Am I still alive? Are Mama and Tata alive?* So grateful, and so exhausted. Although she shivered with fright, she did not complain. The seriousness of the moment gave her courage far beyond what she believed herself capable of.

It had taken eight devastating days for the mighty German forces to sweep through Poland and reach the suburbs of Warsaw. The city was under siege, but Warsaw continued to hold the line of defense.

For the next four weeks, bombs poured on the residents' heads. Even when the bombardment paused, a few hours during the day, no one went to work or to school. At night, a blackout cloaked the streets in dreadful darkness. The capital seemed to be holding its breath.

In the final days of battle, the enemy encircled Malka's city and barraged it with bombs. They destroyed the waterworks and electrical systems. Frantic neighbors hauled furniture from their homes to barricade the streets in hope of stopping advancing German columns.

Pani Rotenberg shrugged her shoulders and jeered, "Furniture to stop German tanks? Ha! Much good that will do!"

Terrifying images of Jewish children in Germany forbidden to attend school or to play with their Christian friends, innocent citizens being beaten and arrested because they were Jews, and homeless people wandering wretchedly flashed through Malka's mind.

"What will happen to us if the Germans invade Warsaw?" she asked her father.

"Darling, there are many wise people among us. They will do what needs to be done to protect our community. Mama and I will do the same. Let us do the worrying."

Tata and Mama were her pillars, but she knew they were no match for the Nazi tyranny. Malka understood that from then on, she would have to bear fate's burdens in silence and do her part to protect them from the unthinkable. She pressed the palms of her hands to her heart and prayed: *Dear God, keep Mama, Tata, and me safe and keep us together. Don't let any of us die.*

Then, a proclamation blasted from the radio: "Armistice! Poland has fallen."

After the horrors Malka had endured, she now waited with dread for Hitler's army to enter the city.

CHAPTER THREE

Boots That Reflect the Sky

German troops marched into Warsaw on the first of October. The day was dark with anguish. Malka, Hanna, Ben, and Pani Rotenberg joined a dismal crowd of people standing on the sidewalk to witness their unfortunate fate. The thunder of invaders' boots against the cobblestones, the clang of their rifles, and the rumble of tanks made the city quake.

From that day on, Malka's once peaceful streets were patrolled by foreign soldiers. Their boots were polished so perfectly that they reflected the clouds; shiny revolvers dangled from their sturdy hips; and from their belts hung wood-and-leather whips, which they snapped at innocent people.

"Malka, do you know what's the most impressive thing about the German soldiers?" Hanna asked and didn't wait for an answer. "Their uniforms! Most of their faces are as ordinary as pumpernickel bread. My father and Ben are much better looking than most of them."

"You may be right, but I'm scared to death when I look at them."

"So am I. Ben said we must stand up to them, though."

"I don't know how to stand up to them, but I know how to curse them really well. My mother says it's not nice to curse, but I do it anyway. Maybe God will hear me and smite them like he did the cruel Passover pharaoh. After all, they are doing ungodly things. Our rabbi says killing is the worst sin."

"I hope your curses will work. I curse them, too. I wish them cholera, the pox, and leprosy — like in biblical times — and typhus."

"I think typhus has the best chance to get them."

"I hope so. If it doesn't kill us first."

Surviving each day in Malka's neighborhood was a cat-and-mouse game. The instant a Nazi patrol made a sudden appearance, panic hit the street. People hunched their backs, looked away in hopes of becoming invisible, and ran for cover, leaving the street empty. Those who didn't run fast enough — or had the bad luck to be in the wrong spot — were dead. The impromptu patrols in the Jewish neighborhood left behind puddles of blood and dread in every heart.

The instant a patrol departed, Malka and her friends swarmed out of their hiding places to reclaim their right to be themselves. Hanna was always first to knock on Malka's door and call out, "Malka, it's safe! The Nazis are gone! You can come out now!"

Together, they joined their bored friends in the courtyard. Their voices rose above the rooftops; their young imaginations soared. To conquer their fears, they made up games in which the boys slew the Nazis left and right with torpedoes and bomber planes exploding and blood squirting everywhere; the girls were nurses frantically attending to the wounded heroes. To soothe their longings, they made up skits imagining themselves back in school and taking fabulous summer trips to the countryside. Sometimes, their skits were silly and made everyone laugh. For mischief, they rang neighbors' doorbells and bolted down the stairs before a door opened. Most neighbors were forgiving of the kids' boisterous play. Their clamor let them know that no Nazi patrol was visible. And, of course, parents smiled with contentment to hear their children a safe distance away.

Although Malka and her friends played with abandon, they always kept one eye open for a Nazi uniform. Hanna was a genius at spotting a soldier at the furthest street corner and flying home, faster than shrapnel, to alert her parents and neighbors, "Two SS men are at the corner of Nowolipki Street! I saw them with my own eyes!"

Like wings of death, the alarm flew throughout the neighborhood, spreading panic. Everyone rushed out of the way. Doors and windows slammed shut to leave the impression that no one was home. The homeless on stoops pretended to be dead.

Malka, too, learned to rely on her alertness and speed to sound an alarm. Before a soldier had a chance to notice her and reach for his revolver, she was darting home to join her parents. Then, she took a post at the window. If she spotted a Nazi at the gate, she helped her parents to hide all contraband, such as books, white bread, sugar, pencils, a gramophone, a wedding ring, or money. She helped them shove it to the bottom of linen drawers, under beds, into socks, pillows, and pockets, behind couches, under floorboards, into their sleeves and underwear. Mostly, they prayed for luck to protect them.

Each time Malka stood guard at the window, she wondered: *What will we do if they come to our house and try to hurt us?* She had no real answer. Varying scenarios played in her head. At one moment she scratched at Nazi faces, those faces that called to mind messengers of the Norse gods. The next moment she reasoned with them, trying to make them comprehend how kind and worthy her parents were: *Surely, they have human hearts hidden under their uniforms. Their faces, after all, look no different than ours.*

Several months of painful occupation had passed. Fall had given way to cold weather. Dark clouds bruised the sky and hung low above the city. German patrols continued to make impromptu appearances in the Jewish neighborhood and left festering wounds. So far, no German soldiers had entered Malka's courtyard.

Then, one early Friday afternoon, Tata said, "Malka, I need you and Mama to stand guard at the window. I got hold of a stash of medicine and need a little time to work on it." Like nearly everything else, possession of medicine was illegal.

"Don't forget to give me a signal when you see an unfamiliar face entering the courtyard," Tata cautioned.

"I know, Tata. I'll be very careful. Don't worry."

Malka knew to alert her father not only when she saw a German soldier at the gate but also when someone other than a neighbor entered. A stranger could be an informer.

Mama and Malka took posts at two separate windows with the best views of the street gate on the opposite end of the courtyard. Malka's eyes stayed focused. She knew the price Tata would pay if he were caught.

After forty-five uneventful minutes, Mama and Malka screeched in chorus, "David! Tata! Two SS men at the gate!"

Mama ordered, "Malka, stay where you are! I'll help Tata hide the medicine. Let us know if they are walking toward our staircase!"

Malka crouched under the windowsill, like a little animal hiding from hunters. She peered warily over the ledge, watching every step the SS men took, every gesture they made, and kept a running report. Her heart hammered wildly. First, she saw them stroll through the long archway underneath the front building. The beat of their hobnailed boots ricocheted against the domed ceiling and spilled into the courtyard like a drumroll.

They reached the edge of the courtyard and stopped with a resounding, "Clop! Clop!" For the next few eternal seconds, they stood starkly in the sun's spotlight. Their dark uniforms — bedecked with sparkling medals — seemed to draw in all the light in the yard.

"Tata, they're in the courtyard now."

"What are they doing?"

"They're standing at the edge of the front building."

The soldiers took a couple of steps forward, "Clop! Clop!" and came to a halt. They slapped their menacing crops against their boots, lifted their chins, and studied the rows of windows rising from the silent courtyard to the open light of sky. They talked loudly, "Ja, ja! Ach ja! . . . Hah, hah, hah!"

How can those monsters laugh while holding a noose over our heads? Malka wondered. *Dear God, let them go away. Please. Please.*

The SS men proceeded forward with a leisurely stride. Toward Malka's stairwell!

"Tata! They're walking toward our stairs!"

"Stay calm, Malkale. Everything is hidden. It will be all right," Tata soothed.

When the SS men were one step from the stairwell, they turned about-face and began to walk in the opposite direction. Toward the street.

"Tata! They turned around! They're walking toward the gate! Maybe they'll leave. Please, God!"

At the very moment the drama was drawing to a promising end, Malka and her parents were startled by a familiar pat-pat-pat of paws galloping down the stairs, past their door, and out the stairwell into the courtyard. They knew it was Fifi, their upstairs neighbors' cocker spaniel.

Malka's eyes opened wide with terror. *It can't be! Why can't they keep their damned dog in the house?!*

"Oh, no! Tata! Fifi is following the soldiers!" Malka reported.

The soldiers stopped to pet the capering dog.

"My God, they stopped! They're playing with her. Should I run upstairs to warn the Keinigsbergs?"

"No! Stay where you are, darling."

Malka continued to peer over the windowsill. Bewildered, she watched the dog lick the Nazis' boots, play with their crops, run circles around them, hop up and down, back and forth, drawing them ever closer to their stairs!

"Tata, they are following Fifi to our stairwell. They're almost there!"

Mama, peering through a curtain crack, echoed, "Yes, David, they are getting awful close!"

"They may never come to our door. Come, let's sit together," Tata tried to reassure.

"What if they do come to our house, Tata?"

"I will not let them touch a hair on your head! I'll burn their eyes out with acid if they try!"

Malka believed that she was safe — if only in his love.

"Just hold my hand, Tata," she beseeched.

Like other Jewish children, Malka was prepared, in some abstract way, for the worst to happen. The threat of death in the course of a single second was as real to her as the absolute power of a single Nazi brute's whim. Still, death remained unreal. She could not fathom herself not being. She had one overreaching wish and prayed every time a German soldier drew near and made her heart sink: *God, if I must die, let me make the transfer to death holding Mama's and Tata's hands.* Being separated from them was more frightening to her than death.

Frozen with fear, the family listened to the pat-pat-pat of paws and the tromping of boots pounding up the stairs, past their door, and stopping on the third floor where Fifi's owners, the Keinigsbergs, and Hanna's apartments were located.

"Mama, they are on Hanna's floor. I'll die if they hurt her!"

Frightened beyond words, they listened to Fifi scratching frantically on her door and yelping. The SS pounded with their fists, hammered with their boots, and shouted with the air of unchecked violence, *"Aufmachen! Schnell! Verfluchte Juden! Hunde! Aufmachen!"*

Their shouts resounded throughout the silent courtyard. Malka had never heard men screaming like that before. Finally, the door groaned and flung open with a loud thud. Malka could hear the SS men storming into the Keinigsbergs' home, shouting, *"Verfluchte Juden! Hunde!"* as if the victims were deaf and devoid of feelings. She heard doors and drawers slamming and surmised: *They're looking for loot, like common thieves.*

Next, she recognized Pan Keinigsberg's frightened voice trying to explain something. Perhaps pleading? Then — God!

Could it be?! Two sharp revolver pops, "Tat! Tat!"

Malka's lips moved without a sound. A mournful sigh seeped into every household in the building.

As if their Übermensch standards had been stretched beyond tolerance, the two Nazis stormed out the door and down one flight of steps, stopping on the second floor. In front of Malka's door! Malka felt the taste of death on the tip of her tongue.

Mama murmured, "*Laleczko*, we must be brave." Then she added under her breath, "I hope they burn in hell for what they are doing to us!"

Malka shivered as though an earthquake was shaking through her body. She clenched her fists and resolved: *I'll not give the Nazi demons the satisfaction of seeing my fear. Or a single tear. Never! I hope they die.* She desperately wanted to protect her parents from the knowledge of her dread.

Then . . . like boulders falling from Malka's heart, the boots began to draw away from her door, pounding down the stairs, clop, clop, clop across the courtyard, and fading in the distance.

When the SS men were out of earshot, Pani Keinigsberg exploded with anguish and rage. Her two teenaged daughters, Ala and Tamara, yammered, "Mama! Oh, Mama!" Their laments ricocheted through the stairwell and trickled into Malka's apartment. Malka remained mute. She allowed herself only a soundless scream into a void — fathomless and terrifying.

Tata reached for his medical satchel, bent over Malka, kissed her on her head, and said, "I must go upstairs to the Keinigsbergs. They need me."

"I know, Tata."

Mama and Malka stepped out on their balcony and faced a ring of scared faces staring down from rows of windows into the courtyard. Some neighbors began to gather in the yard to collectively absorb the senseless murder. The Nazis shot a fellow human being for the crime of possessing a loaf of white bread! One bullet to the head, one to the heart. The head, as Tata saw when he arrived, lay splattered on the floor like pieces of cauliflower in red vomit.

Mama said, "All this for the glory of the Third Reich! What is happening to twentieth-century civilization?"

CHAPTER FOUR

A Gift of Hope

That Friday evening, after death had brushed against Malka's door, she curled up on the ottoman and felt herself falling into a gorge of despair. *What will happen to us? No one hears our cries; no one comes to our aid. Even God is sitting on his hands and is just looking on.*

Mama's voice broke her melancholy.

"Let's go upstairs to the Rotenbergs. It will be good to be together."

Malka charged ahead and tapped on Hanna's door. A timid voice asked, "Who is it?"

"It's me, Malka."

The door opened barely wide enough to let them step in. Malka thought, *Even the door is scared.*

The Rotenbergs greeted them with open arms: "So glad you are here!"

They pulled chairs up close to the tile floor-heater standing at the far corner in the living room. The fire was long out; a few dying embers glowed faintly in the burner. Pan Rotenberg lit a ball-shaped carbide lantern standing on a table. A small orb of light formed around them; the rest of the room was in semidarkness. Pani Rotenberg served lukewarm tea brewed that morning. Soon the room prattled with sympathetic voices going over the tragedy at the Keinigsbergs' household and discussing how to help Pani Keinigsberg and her daughters. The intentions were heartfelt, *but how can drowning people help a fellow man from sinking?* Malka wondered.

Then the conversation turned to hope. Pan Rotenberg said categorically, "The *Judenrat* must appeal to the Germans to curb the senseless killings."

Malka knew the Judenrat had accomplished great things for the Jews for many centuries; her grandfather Isaak had told her that. But how much power did the Judenrat have to influence the Nazis? The answer was obvious: not much. Still, the fact that the adults didn't give up trying gave Malka the illusion that they were not totally helpless.

When the conversation turned to rumors about Hitler's inevitable demise, Ben got up from his seat, pulled out a thick volume from a drawer, and left the room.

Malka whispered in Hanna's ear, "Let's go see what Ben is doing."

"He's reading. Can't you tell?"

"I know, but we can make him talk to us. He's more interesting than listening to empty speculations."

The girls tiptoed out to find Ben sitting on his bed in a cold room, bent over the weighty book, a heavy blanket draped around his shoulders.

"What are you reading?" Hanna asked.

"A book."

"Da! What is it about?"

"About two important men you know nothing about."

"How do you know that? Maybe Malka knows."

"That's right, Ben. Who is it about?" Malka chimed in.

"Jabotinsky and Herzl."

"Two Zionist visionaries," Malka said, hoping to impress Ben.

"See!" Hanna gloated.

"My grandfather told me they were dedicated to the creation of a Jewish homeland from where we'll no longer be chased. If you ask me, I think it's high time for another Moses to come to our rescue," Malka said in one breath.

"What do you know?" Ben said with admiration. "You're smarter than I thought."

Malka felt a smile spread across her face.

Ben declared, "If I'm not killed before the war is over, I will clear out of this bloody Europe. I'll join other Jews in Palestine and build our own state. I'll no longer be called '*Żyd.*' I'll no longer need to hide in fear. I'll roll up my sleeves, become a farmer and till the land, and make the desert bloom. We will live as free men on our own soil and die peacefully in our beds."

The girls listened to Ben's dream as if they were receiving a gift of hope.

Malka said, "Ben, you remind me of what my grandmother said, 'Paradise was invented by people who live hell on earth.' I didn't understand what she meant then, but I do now."

When the remaining embers in the heater turned to ash and the apartment grew as cold as their hearts felt that night, Malka and her parents tiptoed into the pitch-black stairwell to stumble to their apartment. The night was moonless, the streets deserted and blacker than black. Every so often the tat, tat, tat of rifle shots startled the dark vastness and reminded them: *The hunters are still awake.*

To combat her deathly fears, Malka turned her attention to the sounds seeping out of door cracks: a soft conversation, a sigh, a clink of a cup, a scoff, a sneeze, a bitter chuckle. She consoled herself: *We aren't alone. We have neighbors.*

CHAPTER FIVE

No Need for Copernicus or Galileo

Throughout the entire year of 1940, ominous news about German victories trickled into the neighborhood and compounded Malka's fears. The news filtered in via secret short-wave radios, screamed in underground newspapers, and wept by word of mouth. April through June, people lamented the German invasion of Denmark, Norway, Luxembourg, the Netherlands, Belgium, and France. Later that year, news of Germany, Italy, and Japan signing the Tripartite Pact went through the streets like dark prophecies. Although Malka did not grasp the full magnitude of the news, she got the gist: Hitler's power was expanding. She read panic in her parents' faces and she grew even more circumspect.

One misty October morning, Malka was awakened by a din of mutterings rising from the courtyard. She flung her blanket off, walked across the room, threw open a blacked-out window, and saw Tata standing in the courtyard with a group of agitated men. Their faces looked stricken. *What now?* she cringed.

She ran out the door of her room to find Mama leaning over the balcony's banister and listening to the stir below.

"Mama, what's going on? What are Tata and the men doing in the courtyard? What's happening?" Malka wondered.

"A decree is posted on the walls."

"What does it say?"

Mama drew in a deep breath.

"All Jews must move into a tiny ghetto, darling."

"What will happen to us? Will we have to leave our home, Mama? Where will we go?"

"We don't know yet. Maybe our street will remain in the ghetto."

"How I want to rip their heads off, tear their hearts out, Mama! Pound them to death!"

Mama caressed Malka's hair and said in the voice of a true believer, "Malkele, anyone who has as much hate in his heart as Hitler cannot own the world. Wait 'til the world hears about this. The world has a conscience."

"I don't see much conscience in this world, Mama."

Mama insisted, "You will see. If we survive this madness, you will see that the Nazis' children, and their children's children — for generations to follow — will be asking, 'Where was your conscience?'"

"Oh, Mama, I hope you are as good a prophet as you are a dreamer." Malka was young . . .

They remained standing on the balcony, watching the circle of neighbors grow larger and more animated.

"Can I go downstairs?" Malka asked. "I want to hear what they are saying."

"No," Mama answered. "Stay where you are. Tata will be back soon."

Tata entered the house, muttering in disbelief, "I cannot understand! How can anyone who loves his children and wife and parents carry out such barbaric edicts? I simply cannot understand it."

He paused, as if he were trying to absorb the full impact of the edict, then listed the draconian orders:

"Jews have two weeks to clear out of their homes located in the designated Christian sector.

"We are strictly forbidden to remove our possessions. We are allowed to carry away with us only a few personal hand-held items.

"Orders must be strictly obeyed. Violators will be shot on the spot."

"Where will our people live, Tata?" demanded Malka.

"We are allowed a tiny area. People will have to live on top of one another — multiple families in one dwelling. I hate to think how many will end up homeless."

Panic spread throughout the city. Rumors of doom and despair — and prayers for miracles — circulated in street corners, courtyards, and homes. Some said, "Twenty people will have to share one room." Others said, "Did you hear the latest news? Hitler is dead."

Malka's cute neighbor friend, Moniek, asked her, "Malka, where do you think you'll move if we're made to leave Karmelicka Street? Maybe we'll never see each other again."

Malka shrugged helplessly. "How should I know where I'll end up living? Maybe in the street. In any case, you won't have to be a Copernicus or a Galileo to find me. The ghetto will be no larger than a yawn."

The following dawn, a map of the ghetto streets was plastered on walls. Miraculously, Karmelicka Street was within its bounds.

Both Jews and Christians were in a frenzy to relocate. Jews ran for their lives from their homes in the Christian neighborhoods and into the designated ghetto streets. Christians abandoned their homes, businesses, and churches in the tiny ghetto to relocate to areas cleansed of Jews. The move threw the city into chaos.

Malka's Grandma Ester and Grandpa Isaak were forced to abandon their apartment on Miodowa Street near Krasinski

Park and leave their possessions, accumulated over a lifetime, behind. Every nook and cranny in their house held precious memories and shaped Malka's dreams—much like beloved fairy tales mold one's thinking in some magical way. There was her favorite corner armchair where Grandpa used to read to her while she sat on his lap. There was the big grandfather clock with its monotonous tick-tock and jarring hourly "Dong!" that almost made her jump out of her skin. The clock stood smack in the center of the most prominent living room wall, like an old tree with deep roots. Most unbearable was the indignity her grandparents were made to suffer.

Yet, Malka did not forget that things could have been much more tragic. In the thick of night, when fear closed in on her from all corners, she repeated to herself—over and over—*If Karmelicka Street had not been included in the ghetto, then all of us, including Grandma and Grandpa, Mama, Tata, and I, would have ended up in the street, without a roof over our heads, destitute, abandoned!*

At that tragic time, if you had a roof over your head, you had everything. Without it, you were lost.

As soon as the order was slapped on the walls—and before they had time to adjust to the shock—Mama rushed to her parents' house to help them move to Malka's apartment.

"Mama, I'm coming with you. Grandpa and Grandma need me," Malka insisted.

"Yes, of course you can come with me. Nothing will calm them more than your presence," Mama replied.

Grandma greeted them at the door looking disheveled, disoriented, stunned. "Thank God you are here. I don't know where to start!" Then she muttered as if to herself, "What's the use? Who knows if we'll see another sunrise?"

"Don't talk that way. You are scaring the child," Grandpa said.

"I'm not a child, Grandpa. I see what's going on. You and Grandma mustn't be so unhappy. I'll miss this house, too. But you'll live with us. We'll see each other every day."

Grandma's eyes brimmed with tears. "Such a wise girl, my Malka."

Mama warned, "Enough talk. We've got to get you packed and out of here before we run out of time."

"What do you think I've been doing? Maybe you can tell me: How do you choose a handful of items to last until you die? And how in the world can you fit all these 'essential things' into one allowable hand-held bag?" Grandma pointed to the objects around her. "I ask you, would I have kept all of this in my house — dusted and polished for all these years — if they weren't essential?"

The house was in complete disarray. Closet doors and drawers were open wide. Things lay scattered on chairs and floor.

Malka perused the clutter and concluded: *Actually, one can get along without much of this stuff. Although, I must admit, I'm attached even to the chipped cup sitting in front of me.* She remained silent.

"You'll be fine without most of it, Mother. You'll be comfortable in our house," Mama said.

Grandpa chimed in, "My beloved, I tried to tell you the same thing. Don't worry about these scraps. We don't need all this. We'll be with the children. We must be grateful. Most people will end up sleeping in the street."

Mama made Grandma sit down. Together they made a list of absolutely essential things to take: a few dresses, scarf, warm hat, sweater, wool stockings, change of underwear, toothbrush, and comb.

Malka suggested, "Grandma, you can wear a few pairs of underwear, a couple of dresses, a sweater or two under your coat when you leave. This will save packing room for other things. You can also stuff some of your jewelry into your pockets."

"Thank you, Malkale. And what will we do with the rest of the things we must take?" She turned to face Mama and Grandpa and insisted, "We must be practical and take some of the beautiful linen, silver, and other valuables. Mark my words, we will need them to trade for bread." Indeed, her foresight later proved to be correct and her pluck and tenacity warranted.

"How will we move all this without getting killed for it?" Mama asked patiently.

"We might get killed even if we don't schlep all this to your house. Don't be naive. If you cannot survive on what is allowed, you live on what is forbidden. You'll see. No one with a grain of common sense will stick strictly to the orders. We'll find a way. Borrow a cart somewhere."

Malka watched Grandma agonize over each item. She smiled a tearful smile when she heard Grandma say in all seriousness, "I must not forget my lipstick and rouge. My life may depend on looking my best. You never know these days."

Grandma, who looked as if she were made up of spheres piled pleasingly on top of each other, was always pretty, even when life was sad. Her wavy dark hair — now turning silver — was neatly brushed back. Among her morning tasks were to put a dab of powder on her peachy cheeks, run a stripe of red over her lips, slip on a pair of neat pumps, then prance off with the lightness of a dancer to tackle the day. Her blue eyes always twinkled with love. Of course, on this unfortunate day, all of Grandma's glow was snuffed out.

Grandpa was more decisive and less complicated. He took several favorite books out of hiding, picked out a few changes of clothes — as if he were going on an overnight visit — and declared, "This should be enough to serve my future under the Nazis."

Malka asked, "Grandpa, is this all you're taking?"

"Actually, I'm not quite done yet. Now, you must get off the chair you are sitting on, but stay close and watch."

Malka watched him fetch a screwdriver, detach the padded seat from the chair's wooden frame, and remove a large envelope from its location under the cushion. He placed the envelope on the table and withdrew from it a wad of złotys. He divided the money into several smaller stacks, tucked them into a few clothes pockets, and packed the clothing carefully on the bottom of his suitcase. He gave Malka a sad wink. "That should be reasonably safe. They'll probably not look there."

Malka said, "That's the first place I'd look, if I were a Nazi."

Next, Grandpa unscrewed two electrical outlets on the wall and carefully removed a couple of small cloth pouches. The hiding place was perfectly safe since electricity had been cut off in the Jewish neighborhood. He placed the pouches on the table, spread a small towel alongside them, and said, "Come here, Malka, sit down beside me. You'll enjoy seeing the tiny treasure I hid from the Nazi thieves."

Grandpa moved slowly, with silent despair and forced concentration.

"Grandpa, what is it?"

"See for yourself. Empty the pouches gingerly. Don't let anything roll off the table and get away from you."

"I'll be very careful, Grandpa."

Painstakingly, Malka removed small stacks of the shiniest, the most beautiful gold coins she had ever seen. She spread them carefully on the towel Grandpa had placed in front of her. She admired their perfect roundness, their artfully engraved surfaces and rich color. Their perfection seemed like visions from an intact world she once took for granted and now missed so much. The coins reminded her of holiday walks with Tata on tree-lined Królewska Street, stopping in front of Bracia Jabkowski Department Store windows to admire the most magnificent Christmas displays.

"They are beautiful! How will you carry them to our house, Grandpa?"

"Good question. I'll have to give it some serious thought."

"Maybe I can think of a way. Tata always asks me for ideas when he needs to outsmart the Nazis. He says kids are the most imaginative, most original thinkers."

"Your dad is right. What do you think I should do?"

"Well, if you carry it on yourself and the Nazis search your pockets, you're cooked."

"Right!"

"If they search your suitcase and find it tucked into pockets or socks — like you did with your złotys — you'll be equally kaput."

"Where should I hide it then?"

"Under the lining of your shoes. Or, maybe in the lining of a suitcase."

Malka paused and added, "But pick the shabbiest suitcase not to tempt the thieves. And put it on the bottom of the cart. That is, if we're lucky enough to find a cart."

"That is smart. How did you think so fast?"

"Grandpa, believe me, the Nazis give me plenty of practice at being sly — even if I'm only a kid."

"I know, my darling. No child should be subjected to such challenges." Grandpa embraced her and held her close.

In the end, Tata hired a wagon at a prohibitive price. The whole family made repeated trips to move Malka's grandparents' things. Pan Rotenberg and Ben helped. Just as Grandma foresaw, most people ignored the strict orders. They hauled chairs and cribs through open windows and carted them across the city. Ravenous thieves cruised among the swarming crowds like hungry sharks. Ben took on the role of security guard. When a suspicious-looking person neared their wagon, Ben squared his shoulders and assumed a slugger's face. The suspect got the message and looked elsewhere for loot.

Blessedly, Malka's grandparents moved in with her family before the deadline overtook them. They were among the lucky minority who had families or friends willing to share their homes with them. Most people were less fortunate. The day by which all Jews had to move into the ghetto, the streets were a sea of gaunt, bewildered people pushing carts piled high with furnishings, clothes, dishes, pots, silverware, and bedding. The pathetic throng trudged from house to house looking for lodging, calling up to windows and asking if there was room. Carts collided; thieves grabbed scattered possessions before the owners had time to pick them up. People bartered shoes, bread, whatever, for a corner on a floor inside a house. The clamor and shouts were deafening. On every street, lost children cried pitifully. When curfew closed in on them and guns rang out in all corners of the city, the homeless curled up on stairwells and against courtyard walls. Far too many remained without a roof over their heads.

Did the Nazis shoot anyone for disobeying orders and taking with them their own furniture or pillows? Yes, they killed plenty. But those who got away — including Grandma and Grandpa — had a few vestiges of material security to hang onto. Mostly, the German soldiers looked on the bedlam much amused and feeling vastly superior. They probably thought, "We'll kill them soon enough. We are the mighty Third Reich." The more sadistic ones found "creative" ways to exploit the tragedy for their entertainment.

Once, right in front of Malka's building, four pink-cheeked SS men picked out of the crowd the tallest woman in sight. Next, they grabbed the shortest, scrawniest, most famished-looking man. They forced the couple to dance together in the middle of the street. The brutes laughed uproariously at the pitiful couple and snapped pictures with their Leicas to send home to their wives and *Fräuleins*.

Malka's parents gave up their large bedroom to Grandma and Grandpa and moved into Malka's smaller room. Malka slept on a sofa in what was now her grandparents' room. Sharing a room had a small drawback: She gave up her privacy. On the other hand, having her grandparents' attention to soothe her fears — even before she gave words to them — outweighed any sacrifice a millionfold.

At night, when fearsome darkness hung outside her windows and the air flinched with distant gunfire, Grandpa would speak to her with swaddling comfort. He would say things like, "Malka, good and right are infinitely more enduring than the Nazi war machine. The Nazis are a passing evil, a terrible social illness. You'll see, our people will endure. We will walk in beautiful parks again, roam the countryside, and contribute to the betterment of all."

"Grandpa, why does God let wars and killing happen? If I were God, all people would live in peace."

"I don't know the answer. Try to think of God as all that is good and joyful."

"There isn't much good and joyful now."

"You giggle when you are with your friends. That is good! You do that in spite of the Nazis. No? Love is the best part in us — and the love inside us is off limits even to the Nazis. It is our Godliness."

"I guess you're right. I do laugh when I am with my friends. Sometimes I laugh very hard. Sometimes I even forget about the Germans."

Ever worried about safety, Grandma cautioned, "It's great that you and your friends are laughing, Malkale. That's every child's Godly right. But you must not forget to keep your eyes open. Don't let the Nazis catch you."

"Don't worry, Granny. I'm careful. I can spot them and be out of there before they ever catch sight of me. That's why they haven't caught me yet and never will."

At Malka's insistence, Grandpa ended their nightly conversations reading aloud her favorite contraband Yiddish books by Sholem Aleichem, Sholem Asch, and Leib Peretz. From time to time, he would read passages by sage Ghetto authors — Chaim Kaplan among them — and say in a prophetic voice, "Malka, mark my words, the writings of our Ghetto writers will immortalize our suffering into an everlasting monument. Future generations will be nourished by them."

Malka could hardly imagine how their suffering could be of any value to the future, or how the suffering of a people could serve as a monument. Yet, in some intangible way, his words made her feel that some things happening at any given moment echo through eternity.

The stories her grandfather read were beautiful and brought to life remote worlds. His comments were profound and inspired hope. Malka listened and dreamed. The tiny flicker of the carbide lamp blinked, shadows danced on the walls, and Grandpa's voice flowed with comfort. At those moments, everything felt peaceful, just so.

CHAPTER SIX

Sometimes You Have to Do What Is Right

No sooner were Malka and her family constricted in the ghetto than a new decree was issued. It ordered the Judenrat to build — at the Jews' expense — a brick wall around the ghetto. Forthwith!

Malka and Hanna were horrified. "We'll be walled in! Imprisoned!"

In no time, a thick wall rose ten feet tall to block their horizon. Malka's sky shrank to a mere patch, a small closed circle. The wall had twenty-two guarded gates. Whenever the two friends passed a street with the wall in sight (which was never far) and a gate swung open for authorized traffic, they slowed their stride, peered into the forbidden world, and imagined fleeing to the freedom beyond. That fantasy was as frightening as it was enticing.

Hanna would say, "To think that we took those streets for granted only a short time ago."

"Yes," Malka would answer, "who imagined it'd be such a big deal to walk there?"

The menacing wall zigzagged at strange angles. Chłodna Street was split into three parts and divided by two walls. To increase disorientation, the Nazis ordered the Jewish Council to construct a bridge, about two stories high, with steps leading up and down the same street. Each time Malka and Mama crossed the bridge, her mother would clasp her hand tightly and caution, "Don't look at them. Don't let them notice you."

No matter how hard Malka tried to make herself invisible, she could not resist a sideways glance to inspect the faces of her tormentors. She wondered: *How could people with human faces have such beastly hearts?*

All Jewish businesses were closed, and merchandise confiscated. Only the baker in Malka's street remained officially open baking rationed bread—and selling a variety of baked goods under the table and at the risk of losing his head. With most storefronts shuttered, Malka's neighborhood looked bleak and morose.

Since it was impossible to live on the allowable 181 daily calories, a brisk black market quickly evolved. The few who managed to run underground businesses could afford to shop in secret storerooms and from street peddlers who sold food smuggled across the wall.

The high-risk street peddlers displayed on blankets and towels all kinds of staples and luxuries like butter and sugar, even chocolate. Almost at once, long lines formed to snap them up at high prices. Even the rotting foods were grabbed up quickly. Of course, being in clear sight, the street peddlers invited trouble. A policeman—or worse, a Nazi soldier—could suddenly show up and cause instant panic, sending the peddlers and shoppers running for their lives. That did not deter commerce. No sooner were the barbarians out of sight than the vendors were out again. So were the hungry shoppers. Malka's people were obstinate—and rightly so.

Once, Mama surprised Malka with a hair-raising act of valor. This is how it happened: They were shopping at a tiny open-air black market at the intersection of Nowolipki and Smocza Streets. Two Jewish policemen suddenly descended on the cluster of vendors and all hell broke loose. They swung their clubs left and right, sending everyone stampeding in panic, except Mama. Mama remained rooted, squared her shoulders, glared at the policemen, and said with disgust, "Phueee! Jews treating fellow Jews like hooligans? Your sin will follow you beyond your graves! You will never be forgiven for this shameful act!"

Malka remained standing at her mother's side, bewildered, scared stiff, sure they'd be turned over to the Nazis. Instead, the policemen defended themselves: "We do what we must. The illegal vendors are putting us all in danger!"

When the policemen left, Malka stared at Mama, not quite sure whether her mother was a hero or mad.

"Mama, you almost got us killed!"

"Sometimes you have to do what is right, not just what is safe. Besides, I knew they wouldn't kill us. They are Jews. They are in the same hell as the rest of us."

"But they are policemen for the Germans."

"Malka, as bad as they are, they are better than the Polish policemen who would have overturned the peddlers' tables and trampled on their merchandise. They certainly are better than the SS who would have shot everyone on the spot."

For the most part, Malka felt safe among her Jewish neighbors who relied heavily on mutual support. People could even count on Jewish policemen to alert them of danger. It worked like this: A policeman would whisper into the ear of a Jew on Smocza Street, "A German patrol is cruising on Pawia Street and grabbing Jews for forced labor." The news traveled with lightning speed from ear to ear, until the warning buzzed throughout the ghetto. People had to allow for a modicum of distortion. But on the whole, it kept everyone alert to danger — and perpetually jittery.

CHAPTER SEVEN

Poetry When There Was No Bread

The seasons slipped callously onward. The days were grim and gray even when the sun shone brilliantly. Beggars and homeless people roamed the streets. Peddlers spread their possessions — a musical instrument, a piece or two of elegant china, an old pair of shoes — on the sidewalks. If a passerby cast a glance in their direction, they held up their meager merchandise as if it were a pot of gold.

Although the sight of corpses in the streets was common, Malka found them repulsive and ghoulish. The fact of their irrelevance terrified her. When she walked past them, she tried not to see, but their clay faces compelled her to look and to acknowledge. A silent scream of abhorrence rose in her: *People mustn't die that way without parents and sisters and aunts, uncles, and friends shrouding them and weeping for them. God! I don't want to die that way. I don't want Mama or Tata, Grandma or Grandpa, Hanna or Ben to be discarded like that.*

The entire ghetto was infested with lice, mice, and rats. A typhus epidemic was so rife that people passing on the streets kept a distance from each other for fear lice would jump onto them. Krochmalna, Smocza, and Mila Streets were among the most crowded and most pitiful.

Mama and Grandma were on a rampage to destroy every typhus germ that might have strayed into their house. They scrubbed every corner and every surface. Even on the coldest days, they piled the bedding on the balcony and kept the windows wide open to air out the house. They punched pillows and blankets with their fists to get rid of every trace of dust and germ. When Tata came home after seeing patients, Mama checked the seams of his clothes for lice and nits. At the least suspicion, she doused them with kerosene and made the house stink. Sometimes she rubbed Malka's hair with the reeking liquid. Malka found it disgusting.

Malka's Grandma Ester would say, "Those who say that heartbreak stops you from living know nothing about life." She was right. The more hideous life grew, the more people turned to books, music, lectures, and other forms of forbidden diversions. In the midst of the ghetto horrors, there were sub-rosa theaters, cabarets, restaurants, concerts, cafés, and soup kitchens for writers and actors. The kitchens were subsidized by the ghetto-supported Jewish Self Aid Organization.

Malka and Hanna had heard people talk about the Femina Music Hall on Leszno Street featuring Jewish actors who had been acclaimed before the war. They had never seen a performance there, and they might never have seen one if Moniek hadn't sat down on the courtyard stoop next to Malka and tried to impress her.

Moniek was among the rare boys to seek Malka's attention. She knew she wasn't the prettiest girl and wasn't popular with the boys. She didn't much care. She had a best friend and people she loved. Moniek was a head shorter than Malka and dark haired. His black-brown eyes were so dark that iris and pupil were almost one when he looked at her. Like Malka, he loved books and wasn't good at sports.

Moniek said, "My Uncle Shmuel is a big *macher*. He knows everybody worth knowing. He can get tickets for me to see the 'Czardas Princess' at the Femina. Free."

Malka took her time to respond, so Moniek tried harder. "Really. He told me so. And I didn't even have to ask him for it. He said I can invite more than one friend."

"Really?"

"Yes, really. Do you want to see the show with me?"

"Of course! Who wouldn't want to see it? Thank you so much for asking me. Can Hanna and Ben join us?"

"Sure. Why not? Will your parents let you see it with me?"

"I better find out. Thanks again for asking me, and thanks to your Uncle Shmuel, the big macher." With these words she left her diminutive admirer sitting alone on the stoop.

Malka headed home, but first she had to knock on Hanna's door to tell her the news. Hanna was always first to hear her secrets, even the ones she would never tell her mother.

As soon as the door swung open, Malka crowed, "Hanna, guess what! Moniek can get tickets to see 'Czardas Princess' at the Femina! For you, Ben, and me."

"That's great, but where will we get the money to pay for these precious tickets?"

"No worries. He can get them free."

"I thought only lice and typhus are free in the ghetto."

"Hanna, I'm serious. Moniek promised me his Uncle Shmuel could get them."

"Really? I also have an Uncle Shmuel and he has nothing to give away, except woes."

"Moniek said his uncle is a bigshot, like Pan Bursztin."

Pan Bursztin was the only man in their courtyard who looked polished like a newly minted coin. Unlike most men in the ghetto, he was portly, wore well-tailored suits and starched shirts, and looked bold and self-assured — much as Malka remembered successful men looking before the war.

Hanna now asked, "Supposing Moniek gets the free tickets; will our parents let us go?"

"That will depend on our powers to convince them."

They didn't have to plead very hard to get consent. Their parents believed that art and talent touch the best in people and must be supported even (or especially) in the dark times. The girls' strongest argument was, "Femina is only a few streets away. You let us go alone to see family and friends who live just as far. And Ben will go with us. He's older and knows how to elude the SS better than anyone."

"Please, don't count just on Ben. Keep your own eyes wide open," Mama instructed.

"Yes, of course," Malka answered. "You know I always do."

Tata checked with Moniek's father, their neighbor who lived two flights above them, that everything was on the up-and-up; then they were set to go.

On a spring noon, a week after Moniek wowed Malka with the promise of show tickets, she reached for the door to prance out of the house. Tata kissed her and said, "Malka, you'll hear beautiful music today and you'll see talented artists risking their lives to perform. Enjoy it! Just be very careful and come straight home after the performance. We will be waiting for you impatiently."

Mama, Grandma, and Grandpa were equally happy for her, but they were scarcely able to separate their kisses from warnings and pleas of caution, as if Malka were setting out to climb the crest of Kilimanjaro. "Don't forget to keep your eyes open. Be careful. If you hear rumors of a patrol cruising anywhere, rush home. Immediately!"

Malka and her friends stepped into the street, their young hearts open, eager, and at the same time tense. Although the streets were crammed with desperate people, and despite the fact that not a solitary cluster of flowers or tuft of grass glorified the season, they smiled at the spring sky. Watchfully, they walked several long blocks and turned right into Leszno Street, quickly locating Number 35. The theater facade was bare and anonymous. No posters, marquee, or neon lights giving away the crime taking place behind its walls were visible. Discreetly, they strolled up to the door and slipped into the building, shutting the hostile world out. They found their seats and waited for the hall to fill and the show to begin.

In no time, music rose, resonant and gay. Curtains parted, carbide spotlights illuminated the stage, and magic was created in front of their eyes. As if by sleight of hand, the four friends were transported into a make-believe place, inside the hearts of imaginary people. For a few borrowed hours, the world was rich in colors, frivolities, songs, laughter, and fulfillment.

As wakefulness shatters a beautiful dream, just so the curtain dropped. The illusion vanished — although not completely. Some part of the magic would stay with them forever.

With the operetta still playing in their heads, Malka and her friends walked home, stopping as the talk required, pausing to laugh. They hummed favorite melodies and compared who remembered the greatest number of lines. They crossed Nowolipie Street intersection, scanned the horizon, and continued on their merry way. Halfway down Leszno Street, the cacophony of voices lost volume. As if on cue, a whisper shivered through the crowd: "*Yekies! Yekies* down the street!"

Heads swiveled to all sides. Eyes darted to all corners. Feet shuffled fast; one would think the earth was about to cave in. In one heartbeat, Malka, Hanna, and Moniek followed Ben toward an old building, pulled open a heavy gate, fell into the courtyard, and slammed the gate shut. Panic shivered in their bones.

Ben caught his breath and whispered, "Calm down. We're safe."

Safe as trapped animals, Malka murmured in her head.

"What will we do if the SS devils come here?" Hanna panted.

"Stop being so scared. They will never catch us. For now, we should stay where we are and watch what develops."

Ben had the genius and disposition of a five-star general. He never failed to find a way out of the most insurmountable situations. He leaned forward, pressed his face against the gate, peered through cracks and bullet holes, and reported, "Look, the traffic is still moving, although cautiously. They may never show up on this street."

"What if they do show up?" Hanna asked.

"Then we'll bolt to the basement." He pointed to a nearby stairway.

"How will we know when to bolt?"

"We'll know when we see the crowd run for cover."

"What if they look in the basement?" Moniek wanted to know.

"Moniek, where is your head? They won't go down into the stinking cellar. They have better hunting prospects in the crowded apartments. Think!"

Lacking a better option, they followed Ben's lead. Shielded by the inadequate gate — and petrified they might never see their parents again — they watched through cracks the drama building up in the street. For the first few minutes, they had a kaleidoscopic view of a scatter of people slinking hurriedly in all directions. Then, as if Lucifer had showed his head on the horizon, traffic picked up velocity; then, whoosh! Legs spun like bicycle spokes on a racetrack.

Before the stampede picked up full steam, Ben said, "Let's go!"

They bolted to the stairwell, flew down a flight of stairs, opened a door, and entered a spooky, dank basement. Wisps of pale sunlight filtered in through cob-webbed windows above their heads. They hunkered down and listened to the gallop of fleeing feet outside the windows fade into silence.

Then . . . a crisp beat of hobnailed boots on cobblestones rose in the distance: Clop! Clop! Clop!

"Do you hear that?" Malka asked, frightened to death.

"Yes, SS boots!" Ben said.

The clops, long and measured, drew ever closer. *It's Death walking*, Malka thought, but said nothing.

Rough voices, hoarse with power, rose in rhythm with the staccato taps, "Ja, ja!" Clop! Clop! "Verfluchte Juden! Hunde!" as though those of Malka's religion constituted an offense.

"They are only a few strides away from our window!" Moniek whispered. His voice shook.

Ben used logic to keep fear in check. "Moniek, don't pee in your pants. With 400,000 potential victims inside this wall, one

German patrol cannot do too much damage. We're safe here. It will be over soon."

Malka was near tears. "What about our parents? Are they safe? Will we ever see them again?"

Trying to match her brother's courage, Hanna said, "Malka, this is Leszno Street, blocks away from our building. There are plenty of opportunities to keep the SS busy right here."

At that very moment, a timid voice, like a weak bell, rang out a few yards from their window. "I was on my way home."

A crescendo of invectives and clearly audible thuds followed. One heavy thump after another, like the blows of a sledgehammer.

Malka and her friends knew: *They caught an unfortunate man who didn't run fast enough. Kicking him half to death.* They swallowed hard and pressed down sobs for their fellow Jew.

As Ben had predicted, that episode, too, passed. Apparently satisfied with the wake of fear they triggered, the Nazis stomped past the basement windows. The cadence of their stride echoed like pistol pops and finally faded in the distance beyond the wall. No sooner were the barbarians gone than the street filled again with the frantic tumult of ghetto life.

That evening, before Grandpa read to Malka her favorite stories, she said, "Grandpa, Ben says we should rise up and fight back."

"Darling, we are fighting back. The little kids who crawl under the wall to smuggle food to keep their families from starving to death — they are heroic fighters. No? The actors you saw today, who risked their lives to ennoble our existence with drops of beauty — weren't they fighting?"

"That's not what Ben means, Grandpa. He means fight like soldiers do."

"With what, darling?"

"I don't know. Guns, knives, frying pans, fists. That's how I fight them in my nightmares. I scratch their eyes out. I rip their faces, tear out their hearts."

"That method is scarcely enough to confront a heavily armed twentieth-century force. You have seen them in action. Why do you think Tata and I haven't raised our fists yet?"

"You're afraid they'd kill me, kill Grandma and Mama and our neighbors and half of the ghetto. And kill you first."

"You've got that right. Our only chance to survive is Hitler's eventual defeat."

Grandma added, "Malkale, when a state declares war against a civilian minority, that group is defeated before they lift a finger. Don't let Ben or any other fool tell you that people in the ghetto are not fighting. We are fighting hard to hold onto life and its best meanings. We do that despite the historic odds against us."

"I know, Grandma."

Malka then changed the subject. "I have something to tell you."

"Tell us, darling."

"Tata said I will be attending a secret school down the street. So will Hanna."

"*Shefele*, we know. Are you happy about it?"

"We are both so excited. We can't wait."

The mere thought of going to a hidden school filled Malka with hope. It implied, *Yes, yes, school is a promise that life is waiting for me. There will be more tomorrows.*

The following evening, Malka overheard her parents' whispered conversation: "David, we don't know if we will see another sunrise. Doesn't it seem a bit crazy to send the child to an underground school? Wouldn't it be more rational to let things be?"

"Sara, this may be the only taste of childhood we might be able to give her. We must do it at any cost."

Tata's wisdom in sending Malka to a secret school "at any cost" remained with her like a compass. It pointed her way even when her parents were no longer at her side.

CHAPTER EIGHT

Face to Face with Two Devils

A faded cream-colored building hidden behind a tall barrier of hedges stood on Karmelicka Street, a few blocks from the residences at No. 25. Nothing about the building invited a second glance, but to Malka and Hanna the place held a special reverence.

Each morning, they walked those few blocks, unlatched the wooden gate leading to the pale building, ran up a stone path to the door, climbed one flight of stairs, and entered a bare room where a heroic teacher, Pani Helena, met with eight brave children. Everything about Pani Helena was exceptional, including her green eyes that looked into you and understood and sparkled, and her voice that held you like an embrace and made you see things inside your head, or appreciate old things in a new way.

Not a single picture hung on the walls, not a scrap of carpet lay on the floor, and no clutter of teaching materials was in sight. Just nine chairs and a wooden table in the center around which the students and their teacher could sit in a circle. A small chalkboard was fastened to a corner wall. In Malka's mind, the chalkboard made the classroom authentic.

Back of the old building, hidden from the street, lay a small swatch of earth. A splendid chestnut tree with bowing branches stood grandly in the center. That was a big deal. Not a single park existed in the ghetto. Some ghetto children had never seen the countryside, never played among trees or chased butterflies on meadows or felt the cool touch of grass beneath their feet. Under Pani Helena's guidance, the eight students transformed the tiny patch of earth into a garden. Together, they rounded up a small treasure of black-market seeds, picked the sunniest spots, and planted: one sunflower, three cabbage heads, seven beanstalks, and a rainbow of petunias and forget-me-nots. They weeded and watered their garden and checked every day for a tendril to push through the loosened soil. All the while they were tending their garden, Pani Helena taught them the fascinating properties of plant life. On some hot summer days, Pani Helena held class under the chestnut tree. Above its boughs, the sky soared enormous and free. All fears melted in the glow of those moments.

The underground school was a fragile paradise. The students understood that. They were wizards at hearing boots a distance away and hiding, pronto, any scrap of paper, pencils, or books that would give away their crime. Malka and Hanna attended their secret school for one-and-a-half years: one full planting season, until the end of 1941 — the last year they were rooted in their homes. Blessedly, not once did their tormentors trespass into their beloved place.

You could never be sure whom you'd meet on the way to and from the secret school. If you were lucky, you met a friend or a cousin and exchanged a smile, a kiss, a few friendly words, and then continued on your way. If your luck ran out, you could bump into a Nazi uniform. Taking that fact seriously, Malka and Hanna became experts at dodging the Nazis. Before the soldiers turned their heads, the girls were out of sight. In great part, that cunning accounted for the reason they stayed alive, but that method didn't always work.

On one morning walk to class, just as they were crossing the intersection on Nowolipki and Zamenhofa Streets, they came face to face with two SS officers, shiny medals dangling from their puffed-out chests, polished revolvers poking out from their hips, skull-and-crossbones emblems on their collars, and eyes glaring with cold contempt.

Malka's mouth went dry; her body shook.

Run! was her first thought, but it was too late for that. She remained frozen to the spot, her eyes glued to the stone faces staring down at her and hoping for a hint of humanity in their hearts. Hanna stood beside her, like an anchor. On the periphery, people were silently running for cover.

After a measured silence, one brute shot a question at Malka, like a bullet, "Where are you going?!"

My gosh! I can't tell them that, no matter what. "We were just taking a walk," she lied in broken German.

"Just taking a walk," he mimicked. Small eyes behind thick lenses drilled into her, cold as a lizard's.

"And whom were you going to see? Huh? You better answer. Quick!"

"I told you the truth. We were taking a walk around the block," she lied again.

The second officer, rocking slowly on his heels, asked Hanna, "Where do you live? Take us there!"

Hanna did not answer.

He took a few strides toward her, his crop swinging menacingly in his elegantly gloved hand.

Hanna took a step toward him.

Aghast, Malka looked at the giant war-machine man. Then she looked at little Hanna, a forbidden notebook tucked into her waistband and pressing against her thin ribs, her delicate face as pale as edelweiss. She was a vision of innocence. Her eyes, although brimming with fear, held the soldier's gaze, not glancing down once.

Without taking his eyes off Hanna's face, the SS officer stepped back a pace. Then he motioned to his colleague, and both turned on their heels and left.

Malka and Hanna did not go to their class that day. They needed their parents' arms around them, to feel safe, to be together. After praising the two girls many times and uselessly speculating how they could have avoided this confrontation, Mama said, "I think Haneczka reminded the SS man of his own child."

That night in her bed, Malka couldn't shake out of her head that day's encounter. The arrogant faces of the two evil officers stubbornly stared out of the darkness like living snapshots. She felt enormously grateful that one of them had a soul, but she could not forgive him for selling it to his Nazi leader.

CHAPTER NINE

A Saintly Man

Janusz Korczak and his orphans appeared on the macabre ghetto scene about the same time Malka's grandparents settled into Malka's room. He was kicked out of 92 Krochmalna Street and forced to move his Children's Home to a much smaller building at 33 Chłodna Street. It is worthy of note that in addition to being the founder of the orphanage, Korczak was the most popular and best-loved children's author in Poland, as well as an esteemed educator and pediatrician, and Malka's hero.

Everyone in the ghetto followed Janusz's pitiful transfer because of the drama he caused over the Gestapo's theft of a cartload of potatoes belonging to his youngsters. To everyone's utter astonishment and dread, Korczak put on boots and his uniform of a major of the Polish Army and went to the Nazi administration to claim the potatoes the Gestapo had stolen. Of course, the news spread through the ghetto like a locust infestation.

Malka was horrified when she heard the story. "Grandpa, they'll kill him! Why didn't he use common sense and keep quiet?"

"It's not over yet, Malka. As far as we know, Korczak is still alive," he murmured prayerfully. Grandpa was sitting on his favorite chair, tucked in a corner close to the tile heater, a book in his lap. It pained her to see the stoop in his shoulders caused by the weight of sorrow.

Unable to contain her restlessness, she kissed Grandpa's wrinkled cheek and ran out the door to join her friends in the courtyard. Of course, they, too, were talking heatedly about the hopeless fate of their beloved author. To add to their agitation, Ben burst in from the street with an astounding announcement: "You will never believe what I just heard about Korczak's arrest!"

"Is he alive?" Hanna asked.

"So far he is. Listen to this absurdity: When the Nazis realized that the man quarreling about the potatoes destined for Jewish children is himself a Jew and not wearing an armband with a Star of David, they threw him into prison and interrogated him to give them names. They couldn't believe that his insolence did not stem from connections with the underground. You've got to admire his chutzpah!"

"Chutzpah schmutzpah, is it worth getting killed over? His children need him, and I need him, too. I really do," Malka said.

"Don't worry, he's out already."

"How did he get out alive?" they gasped.

"His former pupils appealed to the community and managed to collect enough money to buy him out of prison before he was sentenced."

That was the end of that harrowing event and the start of Grandpa's heroic and fatal involvement with Korczak and his Children's Home. Indirectly, Malka became his accomplice.

One clawing wintry day, Malka and Grandpa were carrying food to her destitute Aunt Sonia who lived on Pawia Street. When they rounded the corner of her street, Grandpa stopped and whispered, "Look ahead, Malka, do you see that gaunt man with the small cluster of children walking toward us?"

"Yes. He looks familiar . . . like a shadow of Janusz Korczak. The same goatee and intense, deep-set eyes." She was astonished.

"That's him, all right. My God, how much he's aged in the short time since I last saw him!"

"Look at the children, Grandpa. How skinny they are! How ashen their faces! It scares me to look at them."

But she looked, and identified with their fears and innocence, with their losses and helplessness, and felt humbled by Korczak's extraordinary humanity.

After a long silence, Malka said, "Grandpa, I cannot get them out of my mind."

"Neither can I, my darling."

The following morning, Grandpa was the first at the breakfast table, looking groomed and ready to leave the house. That was rare. He spent nearly every waking moment sitting on an upright chair tucked into a corner near the tile heater in the living room, as if he were hiding from the world. Always with a book in his hand. He left the apartment only when he had an urgent errand to run. He dreaded to see the plight in the streets.

"You look ready to take on the world, Dad. Are you planning something special today?" Tata asked.

"I am."

"Is it something important?"

"I think so, David."

"Oh? What is it?"

"It really has nothing to do with our family, but it is important to me. I am going to pay someone a visit. I have no idea where it will lead me. I will tell you about it when I get back."

"Okay, but be careful," Tata said without pressing for more details.

Grandma was less acquiescent. "Surely you will tell me where you are going."

"Of course. Later."

"Isaak, you make me feel very uneasy when you talk in riddles. Since when are you keeping secrets from me?"

"I will tell you everything when I get back. I won't be gone long. There is absolutely no reason for you to fret, my dear."

Grandpa gulped down his breakfast, kissed Grandma, Mama, and Malka, gently tapped Tata's back; then he draped a scarf around his scrawny neck, threw on his coat and hat, and left them standing at the door with their mouths wide open.

Grandpa was gone the entire morning and a good part of that afternoon. Mama and Grandma sat home watching the door. Malka, on the other hand, flew off with Hanna to her underground class with a strange premonition.

On ordinary days, her school hours zipped by as fast as a blink. Not that day. Such strange thoughts entered her head. Her eyes drifted toward the window. Images of her previous day's encounter with Janusz Korczak and the famished faces of his children billowed with the clouds.

After school, she rushed home without making the usual plans to meet with her friends. She opened the door gingerly and stepped into a morose silence. Her heart dropped.

"Mama? Grandma? Where is everyone?"

A tiny voice chirped, "I am here."

Malka found Grandma standing behind the curtains staring out the window.

"Hi, Grandma. Are you okay? Why is it so quiet here?"

"Your grandfather is not back yet. I don't understand what is taking him so long." She looked forlorn.

"Grandpa is okay. He is smart. He knows what he is doing."

"Being smart is not enough. Not now."

"Don't worry, Granny. We'll wait for him together. He'll be back soon. Where is Mama?"

"She went upstairs to see Pani Rotenberg."

Mama came home a few minutes later. Together, the three stood vigil at the window, praying silently for Grandpa to hurry and come home. The clock ticked, ticked, dark and heavy like the pulse in Chopin's Funeral March.

When the day began to grow as dim as their hearts, they caught sight of Grandpa stepping up to the wrought iron gate. Serenity washed over them when they finally saw him standing in the doorway, cracking a guilty smile and saying in one long breath, "I'm back, I wasn't gone too long, was I? Didn't I tell you not to worry? I hope you took my advice."

Grandma, Malka, and Mama were too dazed and perplexed to respond. He hugged them and winked a conspiratorial wink at Malka when their eyes met. She thought: *Something important is cooking in his head. I recognize that look.*

"Well," Grandma finally said, "when will you tell us where you were? I was worried sick, if you are interested to know."

"Let me take off my coat first and sit down and I'll tell you everything."

"You were gone all these hours. Did you eat?" Grandma asked. She always worried about keeping everyone well fed and fit to endure potential starvation.

"Yes, I ate. Do I look hungry?"

They gathered around the kitchen table and Grandpa began, "I went to Dr. Korczak's Children's Home on Chłodna Street. I spent the entire time with a saint and his two hundred children." He paused as though he were stepping out of a dream. Mama and Grandma looked puzzled. Not Malka.

"Why would you go there, Dad?" Mama asked.

"Yesterday, when Malka and I were on our way to Sonia's house, we saw Korczak passing with a small gaggle of his children. Their plight was so sharply etched on their faces that I couldn't separate myself from them. So, I resolved to go to the Children's Home to find out how I could help."

"Korczak's children are not the only ones who are suffering. We are all in the same hell," Grandma said, with an implicit warning not to get involved.

"You are right, as usual, but Korczak stands out sharper because what he is doing is the noblest confrontation of the human with the inhuman. Think about it: one man taking on the responsibility of looking after two hundred children. Trying to feed them, clothe them, and look after their physical and mental health."

He stabbed the air with a finger for emphasis. "Mind you, he does that in spite of repeated offers of asylum by his admirers on the Christian side. He chooses to stay here, in this hell, and take care of the children — the holiest creatures — even if it may mean his death."

"Grandpa, did you actually talk to Janusz Korczak?" Malka asked in near disbelief.

"Darling, I did. I also met his children and talked with them. They are disarmingly winsome and so well behaved. I asked one boy, 'Do you always get along with each other so well?'

"He looked at me very seriously and said, 'When we are mad at someone, we sue them. We have our own court, you know. We can even sue Pandoktor [Korczak] himself.' Pandoktor in the children's mouths is one word and has become a nickname, a term of endearment."

The family listened in utter amazement as Grandpa's voice filled the room with a magic rooted in love. "You should see how serene and nurturing that place is. When Korczak sat down, children rushed around him from all sides and didn't leave him alone. The younger ones climbed onto his lap while we carried on a calm conversation."

Malka was bewildered. *How can one man possibly have enough love to embrace so many children? How could so many children share one father? I could never share Tata with that many others. There would be too little of him left for me. Also, how in the world could such a large number of children under one roof feel at home? What if, God forbid a million times, I found myself in their place? Unthinkable! But frighteningly plausible.*

"Grandpa," Malka interjected, "you said I have to see the place for myself. Can I go there with you?"

"Yes. You will be greatly impressed."

Grandpa talked about the incredible Children's Home until dusk descended and Tata came home. Malka was first to greet him. "Tata, you're home! You'll never guess where Grandpa went this morning."

"I will not even try. I will wait 'til he tells me."

This is how Grandpa's support of the Children's Home began. It was paved with small but meaningful successes — and peril. Naturally, kindness can be as infectious as cruelty. Sharing her room with Grandpa, Malka got involved with all his machinations on behalf of Korczak's children.

"Grandpa, how do you plan to help the children?" she asked.

"I must find food for them. They are so heartbreakingly undernourished."

"Where will you find food for them? The streets are choked with famished people."

"Grandma already interrogated me about that. You know that, in fact, there are a few rich people sprinkled among our vast starving majority. Some are even elegant."

He did not need to elaborate. Malka was fully aware that a modicum of illicit commerce went on among the oppressed ghetto people. A minority eked out a living as tailors, shoemakers, doctors, black-market merchants, and smugglers. There were small-time smugglers — some no more than eight years old — who risked their lives to keep their families from starving to death, and there were big-time sharks who dealt directly with Nazi guards.

Malka responded, "Right. But how many rich people do you know?"

"At the moment, not many. I can think of one neighbor in particular."

"I think I know who you mean."

"Do you know how Korczak finds food for his children? He leaves the Children's Home in the morning and goes to the Jewish Aid Committee, he calls at the houses of the rich, and he appears even at the homes of known collaborators. He begs, threatens, and quarrels. He is ready to raise hell over a sack of flour. He doesn't care who it is who gives or whether enough is left for the donor. He is a father of two hundred children and must provide for them. I can do the same: knock on rich people's doors."

"Yes, but it will be easier to turn you away than it is Korczak. He is a famous doctor and celebrated author."

"We will see. I think it is time to pay Pan Bursztin a visit. What do you think?"

"Yes!"

Pan Bursztin's ostentatious lifestyle remained a source of suspicion to all neighbors. No one knew where he went when he left in the morning carrying a briefcase and looking like a high-powered prewar entrepreneur.

"Grandpa, do you think Pan Bursztin is a collaborator or big-time smuggler?"

"Maybe he is neither. It's not a good idea to jump to conclusions."

"Maybe. But I am sure he isn't kosher."

"That is a reasonable deduction."

"What will you say to him?"

"I will appeal to his conscience and I will reason. I will cajole and plead."

"Don't forget to flatter."

"I will flatter."

The following evening, Grandpa knocked on Pan Bursztin's door and invited himself in. He hung around and schmoozed Pan Bursztin into making a generous monetary contribution for Korczak's children.

Grandpa was jubilant when he came back. "You see, people have hearts. You just have to give them an opportunity."

Everyone in the family shared Grandpa's joy.

Mama said, "I am proud of you, Dad!"

Tata said, "What you are doing is very commendable. But please, Dad, don't venture too far. Your beard makes you a prime target."

Mama echoed Tata's concern. "Dad, you must shave your beard."

"The beard is part of me. I cannot fight them with my fists, but I can keep my neatly trimmed beard."

"That's not reasonable, Grandpa," asserted Malka. "Your beard is a provocation. What if they pick on you?"

"Don't worry, Malka. My chances of not being hunted are getting better with each miserable passing day. Lately, the

Nazis are avoiding the ghetto as much as they can. They are afraid of typhus flying in the air and the profusion of lice. The epidemic is my protection."

Grandma said, "Oy! That sword has a double edge, Isaak. They still surprise us with their bloody patrol visits. You better listen to your granddaughter. Sometimes the egg is smarter than the rooster. Or the hen."

Grandpa brushed away everyone's pleas, kept his beard, and went on with his mission. He knocked on doors of potential donors, appealing eloquently to their consciences. Some responded with suspicion, some with annoyance, and some with modest contributions. When he was done with his day's collection, he rushed to the Children's Home to deliver it.

At bedtime, in their shared room, Grandpa reported to Malka and Grandma his encounters with donors and ranted at those who turned him down. Mostly, he talked about the Children's Home. His descriptions sounded like fairy tales where the weak and innocent outshone the villains. Except, in fairy tales, you have the confidence of enjoying a happy ending.

"Malka, the place is a peaceful oasis, a children's world as simple and as near perfect as you find only in dreams or in Korczak's books you have read. But here the children-heroes are real and therefore more inspiring.

"Throughout the day, you find Korczak meeting with his children and helping them solve their problems, just as would any loving father. His love is as simple and as essential to their lives as rain. At night, exhausted from his daily efforts of finding food, medicine, and clothes, and tottering under the terrible responsibility and care for the fate of his two hundred children, he retires to the sickroom where he writes and sleeps nearby the sick children."

Grandpa's wondrous story continued, and Malka swallowed each word to nourish her soul with faith in love.

"How can one father manage so many children, Grandpa?"

"That's what is so amazing. The place is a children's republic, exactly like in the book you love, *King Matthew the Great*. It is complete with a parliament, newspaper, and court system.

Instead of hitting one another, the children holler, 'I'll sue you!' Mind you, a preponderance of the children were taken off the streets. Some have survived by petty crimes; they're not model citizens. But they are encouraged to become so through their orphanage court run by the children. They are learning to be held responsible for their actions, but the judges need to look for mitigating factors, to take into consideration the reason for the misconduct and offer an opportunity for betterment."

That is how Grandpa calmed Malka's fears with a true story of nobility and brought light into her darkness. She listened until her eyes got heavy with sleep and her heart felt appeased.

Grandpa kept his promise to take Malka to visit the Children's Home two unforgettable times. On her first visit, she and Grandpa were met at the door by a boy and a girl, both thin as reeds, neat in appearance, and near Malka's age. Their smiling eyes met hers as they introduced themselves. The girl said, "Pandoktor and we are rehearsing our play. Would you like to join us?"

"Oh, yes, thank you. I saw one of your performances at a temple. It was beautiful; everyone loved it."

Initially, the communal orphanage living overwhelmed Malka with sadness. It troubled her that the children were not as lucky as she was to live with her parents. The drab colorlessness of poverty stared down at her from the walls and surroundings. It bothered her greatly to notice that the children looked undernourished: their bellies distended, complexions sallow, hair dry and stiff like shoe-brush bristles. An oppressive aroma of cooked turnips hung in the air. She was grateful to notice that it was eased by a faint whiff of sugary dough, refreshing as a dab of cologne.

Grandpa headed in another direction and Malka followed her hosts. The Home hummed with sounds of children doing the same forbidden things she liked to do: drawing, reading, and playing with stick airplanes, rag dolls, and chess games made of cardboard and marked pebbles. Others were helping with household tasks. The presence of caring adults gave Malka a feeling of security. Gradually — and much to her amazement — the place began to feel homey.

They turned down a short corridor and entered a small rehearsal room. The children stopped what they were doing and looked at her. She felt timid and awed by the arresting presence of Janusz Korczak. He shook her hand and put her immediately at ease.

"So nice to have you here with us. Actors love an audience."

He was thin, medium height, and dressed simply in a faded sport-shirt and scuffed shoes. A neatly trimmed, graying goatee drew attention to his gaunt face. His deep-set eyes behind steel-framed glasses looked at her knowingly and kindly. Malka felt as though she were in the presence of a saint.

Korczak's children, perhaps two dozen, welcomed her cheerfully. Some appeared to be her age. They were as curious about her as she was about them. One tall boy with huge smiling dark eyes said, "We're glad you're here. Pandoktor is right, we like to perform in front of an audience." She felt grateful.

They chatted with her briefly, then the room fell silent. The performers stepped to the front of the room, their voices rose above the hush, and, as if by magic, Malka felt herself transported to remote places and into the hearts of imaginary people.

In her mind's eye, she sauntered with them in a beautiful countryside, among majestic trees, wide-open horizons speckled with gaudy flowers, and ponds to splash in. While in reality the performers' stomachs ached with hunger (she, too, was famished), in her head she feasted with them on roast goose, apples and cherries, and delicious pastry drenched in sugary icing.

Too soon, Malka heard a knock on the door. Her grandfather entered. In one heartbeat, reality returned. Grandpa thanked the hosts for the hospitality they extended to Malka, and they left.

On the way home, Malka told her grandfather about her day and the fabulous rehearsal that made her forget all sorrows.

Grandpa said, "The plays Korczak writes for his children are inspired by his fondness for Buddhism. To soothe his children's anguish, he teaches them to meditate: to think loving thoughts and do the best they can do in the present moment."

"How does he do that?"

"To calm the children's fear of death hanging over them, he flings the windows open for them to behold the circus of stars. He inspires them to pray and thank God for flowers that provide fragrance, for the glowworms that gleam, and for making the stars in the sky sparkle."

Her grandfather's voice flowed, low and warm, opening windows in her head to the mysteries of thoughts. Their synchronized stride tapped in her ears, steady as a mother's heartbeat. A wintry wind stung her cheeks, ghoulish ghetto street-scenes scrolled past them, and Grandpa's voice continued. He kept her enthralled until they reached home safely.

There was a second visit to the Children's Home. This time, Malka joined the children to hear Korczak read to them a book he was writing and changing the plot line and characters according to the children's input. When Grandpa came to take her home, she left with the expectation to be back many times, but the future is hard to predict. As it turned out, there would be no more visits. Janusz Korczak and his orphans crossed Malka's path one more time — the final and most unforgettable. That happened a bit later.

The second time Malka walked home from the orphanage with her grandfather, snow began to fall. A metallic wintry light settled over the rooftops. As they turned into Zamenhofa Street, a sharp gust of wind sent a trashcan crashing against the asphalt, making her knees rattle. She had a foreboding feeling. She looked around. The coast was clear. She thought, *A wild animal can sense the presence of a predator before he appears on the scene. Maybe I have extrasensory perception. Ben does. He always spots the Nazis before anyone else sees them.*

She perked up her ears. Obnoxious sounds of mating feral cats assaulted her eardrums and made her bristle with disgust. *Something doesn't feel right.*

She entwined her hand in Grandpa's arm. That very instant, she and her grandfather became aware of people clearing the street. They glanced into the rapidly thinning crowd and caught sight of two SS men rounding a corner, just one block from them.

The soldiers came to an abrupt stop, backs straight as rifles, chins locked, heads high, exuding an air of self-importance. Their arrogance reduced everything in the street into insignificance. They glanced in all directions, then swiveled ninety degrees to face Grandpa and Malka.

Malka and her grandfather froze in place like biblical salt pillars — but only for one heartbeat. Their survival instinct kicked in, and they motioned to run with the fleeing crowd for cover.

"Halt!" A voice hit them like Mephistopheles' fist. A shiny pistol pointed at Grandpa from less than one block away.

"Malka, run!" Grandpa ordered.

Malka clasped her grandfather's sleeve, desperately trying to drag him with her. "Grandpa, you run, too!"

He yanked his arm free and commanded, "Do as I tell you! Run!" His staying rooted to the spot was the surest way to shield his granddaughter.

Malka didn't want to run without him; that isn't what a loving granddaughter does. But she ducked into the crowd and headed toward a bombed-out building a few yards away. She climbed over a pile of rubble and jumped down into a ceiling-less basement. Above her, rooms with sloping walls hung suspended in a precarious balance. She crawled into a corner, coiled into a ball, tight as a fist, and flinched at the sound of boots drawing close.

A shot rang out. She felt herself falling into a dark abyss. *God, where are you?*

Silence.

Then Grandpa's voice, "I am not trying to run away!"

He's letting me know he's still alive. Oh, dear God.

The boot slaps drew closer and came to an abrupt halt at the very spot where she had left Grandpa standing alone. Shouts rang from the Nazi mouths, hard and sharp like steel blades. Although Malka knew who the victim was, she prayed, "Oh, God, let it be someone else. Let it not be my grandpa they are tormenting."

She heard Grandpa's controlled voice trying to appease. It was instantly silenced by diabolic screams and a volley of thuds.

In her head, Malka witnessed the two shameless Nazis kicking one old man, her beloved grandfather. The feeling that she ought to run out to make them stop lifted her to her feet. She wanted to, but when the time came to do it, she lost her nerve. She didn't move.

After the Nazis had their fill, they exchanged jovial remarks, spun on their heels, and left.

Malka thought: *A proper granddaughter would run after the soldiers and scream.*

When the brutes were out of sight, Malka came out of her hiding place and approached her grandfather. Streaks of blood trickled from cuts on his face and ears. His coat was ripped and covered with snow and dirt. He tried to talk but was barely coherent.

"Oh, Grandpa, what have they done to you?" Malka lamented.

He muttered with effort, "Malka . . . you . . . okay?"

A small circle of horrified people gathered around him. They turned their sad faces to Malka and asked, "Is this your grandfather? Do you have parents at home? Where do you live? Does your family know a doctor?"

"Yes, my dad is a doctor. Please help me take him home. I cannot leave him alone while I run home for help. What if the SS men come back?! We live a few blocks away."

"Of course," they said in chorus. Two men helped Grandpa get up onto his hands and knees and then his feet. He was tipping to all sides, unable to stand erect. The men placed a shoulder under each arm to steady him and trudged forward. Malka followed close, carefully avoiding stepping on the trail of dark red droplets her grandfather left behind.

From that day on, Grandpa was never the same. He was mostly bedridden, saying little and asking for even less.

Grandma was inconsolable. Deep lines of sorrow, where there were none before, etched her face. She looked as brittle as old lace. *The Nazis kicked the courage out of both of them,* Malka said to herself.

Malka's bed was moved into her parents' bedroom. Grandpa slept a great deal. From time to time, his eyelids would lift, and his eyes caressed the people around him. A muscle on his neck would ripple and word fragments would form on his lips, sounding vaguely like, "Don't worry about me. I am at peace. You must take care of yourselves."

Grandpa was most alert in Malka's presence. She was first to understand when he asked for water to moisten his parched lips. She heard when he pleaded wordlessly, "Go out and play, Malkale. Life must be lived joyfully." Isn't that what he always told her, wanted for her?

She would answer in her head, *Grandpa, please live. I cannot imagine life without you.*

His eyes would blink in reply, *Malkale, you must live richly, lovingly.*

Tata's medical care, love, and prudence kept the house on an even keel. Mama, too, knew just what to do and say to keep others from falling to pieces. Malka could not sleep at night, though. Whenever she closed her eyes, she saw Grandpa lying on the street. Such strange thoughts kept coming to her head.

Friends called to invite Malka to join them, but she was afraid to leave her grandfather's side. Her parents persuaded her to attend the one-room school she so loved. "It's only a short distance away," they coaxed. "You know Grandpa would want you to go."

She did as they asked, but Pani Helena's inspiring presence and her friends' laughter were barely a distraction from her preoccupation. A perpetual voice in her head prodded, *I must run home and check to see if Grandpa is alive.*

At one point, Moniek came to see her and brought a rare piece of chocolate.

"How did you find such a treasure?"

"I know people."

"Was it your Uncle Shmuel, the member of the ghetto minority who live in prewar style?"

"That's a real stretch of exaggeration. Let's say that by our standards of living, he is suffering in relative luxury."

"Anyway, thank you, Moniek. I haven't seen chocolate in ages. I'll shave off a sliver and place it on my grandfather's lips so he can savor a hint of deliciousness. I hope he'll recognize what it is."

In the depth of one night, Malka was awakened by pitiful sobs coming from her grandparents' room. Before she could lift her head from the pillow, she saw Mama stepping into the room she shared with her parents. A yellowish candlelight cast a spooky, quivering shadow of her on the wall.

"Grandpa!" Malka cried out.

Mama's tearful whisper, "Yes, Malkale."

Trembling as if an electric current were passing through her body, Malka dashed to his room, calling to him, pleading, "Grandpa! Oh, Grandpa!" as if her cries would bring him to life. He remained unreachable. Yet, a soundless aura of kindness, generosity, playfulness, and wisdom permeated the space around him. Malka felt overwhelmed with grief, guilt, and bitterness. Tata, Mama, and Grandma entwined their arms around her and held her close.

Grandpa was buried in the Gęsia Street cemetery. The place was busy with wretched people digging graves and pouring out grief in laments. A white shroud of snow covered the city. The world felt empty and hopelessly frightening.

Grandma died of heartbreak shortly afterwards. Malka felt abandoned again. Afraid. Could such emptiness ever be filled? For days, she sat at the window with her arms resting on her grandparents' favorite book by Sholem Asch. She remained silent, staring into space as if she were feeling her grandparents' essence in the air molecules. Friends called out to her, "Malka, come out and join us." She remained in her solitude, hugging the book, noticing nothing and talking to no one, except occasionally responding to her parents.

Only Hanna remained at her side like a limb. Hanna respected Malka's silence and knew just when to lift her friend's sadness with tidbits of trivia. At first, Malka offered no sign that she had heard. Then, slowly, she responded to her friend's voice with an upturned tilt of her head, a blink of her eyelids, a tiny smile curling her lips.

With Hanna at her side, Malka began to wake up from her grief. Gradually, she took note of clouds giving way to blue skies, and her heart echoed friends' laughter. In time, the people she loved, and life itself, took on a renewed splendor in contrast to her grave loss. Although she never ceased missing her beloved grandparents, she discovered that people who die don't vanish from your life. Her grandparents appeared in empty chairs and empty corners — especially when she felt overwhelmed by fear or despair. Their love and wisdom remained as her beacons, pointing her way out of darkness.

CHAPTER TEN

The Plan

S purred by a panicked awareness of time running out for the walled-in people, Malka's parents embarked on a heart-breaking search to hide her on the other side of the wall. To begin with, finding a reasonably safe place was a huge challenge. Few Christians were willing to risk their lives to save Jews. In addition, her parents would need to secure false documents to back up Malka's assumed Christian identity.

That was not all. Malka would have to beware of inform-ers roving the streets for Jews and turning them over to the Gestapo. The predators stared down passing pedestrians and pounced on them at the vaguest hint of fear in their eyes, the faintest shiver in their bodies. "Hey, you! I know you're a Żyd," they would attack. Who else but a Jew had reason to be scared? They bullied and interrogated their prey mercilessly. Some did it for money, others did it to satisfy their bigotry, and some for both reasons. To survive such a rough test, Malka would have to teach herself to stay cool and act bold, even cheeky. Of course, she would also have to be creative in masking her true identity from neighbors and acquaintances. Anyone could be a potential informer. At the same time, she would have to behave with the absolute confidence of someone who belonged and who was beyond suspicion. Frightening as this option was, what better choice did Malka's parents have to save their child from Hitler's decree to kill every Jew?

The instant they sat down to talk, Malka knew from her parents' tortured faces to expect the worst, but she never imagined hearing what followed. Tata was first to speak.

"Malka, please listen patiently to what Mama and I have to discuss with you. You know as well as everyone else that our lives in the ghetto are in peril. Sadly, we cannot protect you from that knowledge. However, there is a chance to save you from the Nazi death decree if we succeed in placing you with kind Christian people on the other side. Other parents have sent their children to convents, orphanages, or trusted friends until the war is over. Please try to understand. We want you to live."

Malka was horrified. "What? You want to give me away? I'm not going without you. Never! I'd rather die!"

The thought of separating from her parents was more terrifying than death. She continued to plead, "I don't want to leave you. I'm not afraid of dying as long as I'm with you. I don't want to be abandoned on the Christian side where I'll be alone among people who hate me and where I'll be afraid of being myself. You can't make me do it. It's my life."

Tata's caressing voice steadied her. "Malka, nothing has been arranged yet. It is an option we must look into. For now, we are asking you to permit yourself to recognize that you will be safer on the other side. We will make sure to find a secure place for you and keep you informed of every step we are taking."

Mama pleaded, "Try to remember, my darling, there are kind Polish people — albeit not many — who are willing to risk their own lives to save Jewish lives. You may be one of the lucky ones."

"I don't want to be without you. Mama, you believe in miracles. I don't!"

"We must act as though miracles could happen. Life is sacred. It is noble to fight to stay alive. You must live, Malkale."

At that moment, Malka's parents' chances of finding some-one with the extraordinary courage and compassion to risk their own lives to protect Malka from being murdered were remote. Still, one must never forget that among the worst calamities there are people willing to heal those who are harmed. Their first ray of hope to rescue their child came from Ben's heroic undertaking to save his family from starving to death.

CHAPTER ELEVEN

Two Fates Converge

J ust as pious people turn their faces to heaven in prayer for God's mercy, Malka's people prayed for American airplanes to appear. However, no wings of hope showed up. People continued to scrounge for morsels of news in hopes of salvation. They snapped up gossip smuggled across the wall and printed in underground newspapers. The ghetto was a virtual beehive of gloomy news. From June through November 1941, Germany invaded the Soviet Union, laid siege to Leningrad, drove on Moscow, and captured Kiev and Rostov on the Don River. People lamented, "Hitler is already in Africa! Where will he go next?" Although Malka knew nearly nothing about these distant places, she understood that Germany was swallowing the world.

Mama said in a prophetic tone of voice, "Wait until winter catches up with the German troops trying to cross the desolate Russian steppes. Mark my words, German soldiers are no match for the Russian winters. They will be trapped without food or cover. They will face the same humiliating defeat as Napoleon's troops did."

Malka took her mother's words seriously and conjured up images of columns of starving Nazi soldiers leaning on each other and pushing against blinding winds and icy sheets of snow. Vengefully, she imagined them looking pitiful in retreat: their noses, fingers, and toes frostbitten like those of the beggars in the ghetto streets.

As Mama had foretold, the Soviet counteroffensive drove the Germans from the Moscow suburbs in chaotic retreat in early December. A few days later, the Nazis and their Axis partners declared war on the United States. A chink of hope rose on the horizon. "Finally, America has entered the fight!" echoed throughout the ghetto.

Despite hopeful war news, life in the ghetto remained grim. Although Tata had a small income from his medical practice, Malka's family often went to bed very hungry and their apartment felt as cold as the Russian steppes in the winter.

In Hanna's home, matters were more dismal. Ben was heartsick to see his parents and sister starving and shivering with cold. One day, he said to himself, "I cannot do anything to protect them from typhus, but I can save them from starving to death. Other boys do it."

And so, he set out on a secret and dangerous mission to find food for his family. To accomplish this goal, Ben often left his home in the morning and wasn't seen most of the day. Pani Rotenberg asked, "Ben, where in the world are you spending all these hours? Why can't you stay in the courtyard like the other kids do? You know how we worry. Why are you doing this to us?"

"I'm only going to see some friends. What's the big deal?"

"Who? What friends? If you tell me, maybe I will not worry."

"Mama, stop pestering me," he would answer. "I know what I am doing. I am not a child." Then he would leave.

Ben told no one, except Hanna and Malka, where he spent the unaccounted hours. Of course, he had a reason for doing that. He knew the two girls would spot him, sooner or later, where he did not want to be seen. To protect his secret, he took them into his confidence — with the proviso they would not tell their parents.

He confided that during his daily disappearances, he walked through the overcrowded streets, past poor peddlers, past beggars, past corpses covered with newspapers, until he reached Leszno Street facing the wall. Then he stopped, found a secluded niche in a bombed-out building with a view of the wall, and watched the exciting and dangerous activities of young smugglers.

Malka was aghast. "Aren't you afraid to stay there? It's a very dangerous spot."

"Every spot in the ghetto is dangerous, Malka. You can get your head blown off in your own courtyard."

"That's a lot less likely. Anyway, go on."

"You should see the kids crawling through inconspicuous holes at the bottom of the wall where a few bricks are missing. Some are no older than eight. They pull behind them sacks of food. Once they are through, they sling the bundles over their shoulders, stooping and staggering under the burden. Some carry potatoes and onions under their clothes. They look like little hunchbacks. Carrying food on their backs and leaving their hands free is smart. This way they can run faster."

"Ben, you make it sound like a soccer game. Are you forgetting the danger they run?" Malka asked.

"Of course I'm not forgetting, Malka. I'm not an idiot. I feel their pounding hearts when they crawl through the holes, eyes darting in all directions to dodge potential bullets. I also feel their gratitude for beating the overwhelming odds against them. And I most certainly feel their pride in knowing their families will not go to bed hungry that night."

"Where else do you go to watch such dangerous scenes, Ben?" Hanna wondered.

With the unrelenting drama of a true storyteller, Ben continued to describe other scenes he observed. "You should see the kids who sneak through the cemetery wall bordering the Christian side on Gęsia Street. They step on each other's shoulders, throw a coat over the barbed wire coils and glass shards on top of the wall, and haul themselves over the barrier and down to the other side. Much of the smuggling across the wall takes place during the night."

Hanna's large eyes filled with fear. "Ben, what is going through your mind? Everyone knows that most of the gun pops we hear at night are aimed at the little Jewish smugglers. The Christian smugglers are punished, too, if they are caught, but only the Jews are shot. I hope you'll never think of doing anything that dangerous. Not even for one second."

"Of course not."

"Are you planning to be a day smuggler?" Hanna asked. "That's also deadly."

"I know, Hanna. I also know the smugglers are not the only targets. You can get a bullet in your head while walking down the street. At least the smugglers have a chance to save their families from starving to death."

With a distinct air of distain, he mentioned the big-time smuggling run by adults who lived on both sides of the wall. At agreed-upon times, bribed guards and policemen turned a blind eye while carts with all kinds of food drove through the ghetto gates right under their noses.

Ben concluded, "Of course, these operations pose little risk and are quite entertaining. People furtively watch them all the time from café windows facing the wall on Leszno Street."

"Are you also spending time studying their skills?" Hanna asked.

"Don't worry, I know I cannot aspire to be in their league."

"But you're thinking of becoming a small-time smuggler. Yes?" his sister pressed.

"As a matter of fact, I would consider it, if I knew the risk would be no more punishing than starving or freezing to death."

"Why aren't you telling your parents about these ideas? Which you should, if you ask me," Malka said.

"I want you, Hanna, and you, Malka, to promise me you won't tell my parents — or anyone else — if you happen to see me at any scene near the wall. The fact is, right now I'm a mere observer and I'm not the only one. There is no harm in that."

He straightened his shoulders; his face looked earnest, resolved. He said, "It is very important to me to protect Mom and Dad from unnecessary worries. God knows, they are suffering enough. If — and that's a big if — I ever decide to join the smugglers, I want to be the one to tell them. I'm perfectly aware I won't be able to hide it from them, anyway. Look, I trusted you and told you everything. I'm counting on you not to let me down."

One drizzly April morning, Malka and Hanna were on their way to see Josek, a school friend who lived on Leszno Street. When they turned into his street, Malka stopped, leaned into Hanna, and pointed to a figure standing tucked in a far corner of a collapsed building facing the wall. She stuttered, "L-l-look!"

"That's Ben!" Hanna gasped.

They remained riveted for a moment, then Malka asked, "What should we do? Should we continue on our way?"

"No. I want to see what he's watching."

They stepped into an abandoned store entrance and observed the dangerous activities along the wall. The scene was as mesmerizing as it was frightening. Every so often, a few bricks were shoved aside at the bottom of the wall. A head peered out of the opening, then the whole figure of a boy wriggled through, dragging behind him a heavy sack. His eyes looked to all sides, then his skinny legs took off, whoosh. He blended into the dense stream of noisy pedestrians, and the perilous scene was over. Malka and Hanna stared with wide eyes and thrashing hearts.

Malka finally caught her breath and said, "We can't hang around here forever. In fact, we shouldn't be here at all, if we want to stay alive."

"I know."

The girls left Ben standing in the obscure corner among the ruins. They took note of his eyes scanning every segment of the wall—his wide forehead furrowed with concentration as if he were trying to solve an important puzzle.

"Hanna, do you really think he'd do something that dangerous?" Malka asked.

"Who knows? He is stubborn and he wants to save us from starvation."

"Aren't you going to tell your parents?"

"I don't want to cause an unnecessary fight and make life more unbearable at home. He promised he'd tell our parents if he ever decided to take this daring risk. Maybe he won't do it. He isn't the only one captivated by this frightening scene."

The following day, Ben kissed his mother on the cheek and stepped out the door.

"Ben, please don't do anything dangerous!" she implored.

"Don't worry, Mama, I won't," he replied.

A few minutes later, Malka and Hanna got permission from their parents to visit Josek again. They had lied about their intentions. They were on their way to spy on Ben.

A bombed-out building bordered the ghetto wall on Leszno Street. It had jagged walls, door frames without doors, floors and stairs slanting precariously, and barred windows staring out of a dark basement. No one would ever think this wreckage would still have the potential to be of use.

That very day, standing in the observation niche facing the wall and ignorant of the two girls spying on him, Ben caught sight of a boy slinking out from the Leszno Street ruins bordering the wall. A stuffed rucksack dangled from his shoulders. He scanned the horizon, then blended in nonchalantly with the milling stream of pedestrians. The boy was about Ben's age, perhaps a bit older. He was slightly taller, his body thin and athletic, his hair the color of sand. As if prodded by an invisible hand, Ben followed him.

Hanna and Malka tried to shadow them from a safe distance but lost them quickly in the milling crowd. Of course, the girls missed hearing the conversation between the two boys. If they had been close enough, as they fervently wished, this is what they would have overheard and observed:

The boy was the first to speak. "Are you following me?" he asked Ben without slowing his stride or turning his head.

"Yes. I saw you coming out of the ruins near the wall."

The boy snapped back sarcastically, "You saw me? So, you want a bribe?"

"No! Of course not! I just want to talk to you. My name is Ben Rotenberg. I want to ask you some questions." Ben talked fast. "My family is starving. I must find food for them."

The boy slowed his pace to let Ben fall in beside him and responded, not unkindly, "So you think I'm a magician and can tell you an easy way to find food in the ghetto?"

"I know there is no easy way." Ben rushed his words. "I have been watching boys climbing over the wall and crawling through holes on the bottom, like rats. And I did not miss hearing gunshots mingling with the sounds of their running feet. I know I can get killed if I get caught, but if I get away my family will eat."

"I am Heniek. Where do you live?" the boy asked.

"25 Karmelicka Street. And where do you live?"

"A few corners away from you, on Zamenhofa. Come to my apartment tomorrow morning at 10 o'clock. 25 Zamenhofa Street, first stairwell on your right, second floor, apartment 3." And he took off.

Ben turned and walked toward home feeling a strange elation, as if he were about to dive off a ravine into a mysterious space. He believed that he was on the brink of something important, something he must conquer.

"What are you going to do now?" Malka asked after they lost sight of Ben.

"Go home and wait for him."

"Then what?"

"I want to know what he wants from that smuggler."

"Will he tell you?"

"He will. I'll convince him. Ben doesn't do many things without a good reason. Neither do I. He was smart to confide his secret to us. He knew, sooner or later, we'd see him watch the action at the wall. He was right. In fact, we did spot him where he has no business being. If he gets any closer to danger, I'll have to let my parents know. He knows that. He'll talk, all right."

Malka was in Hanna's apartment when Ben stepped through the door. She observed his face light up with gratitude to find that everyone he had left that morning was still there. In the ghetto, you took nothing for granted, not even finding your parents alive when you got home.

As always, Pani Rotenberg rushed to greet him, so happy he had come back in one piece.

"Ben, you are home!"

Pan Rotenberg no longer scolded him for wandering out of the courtyard. He just embraced him and held him close. For an instant, father's and son's breath rose and fell as one. "Please stay safe, son," was all he said.

With the greeting over, Ben went to his room. Hanna followed behind him and motioned for Malka to fall in step beside her.

Hanna bent her head around Ben's door and said, "Ben, we must talk to you."

"Not now. I'm not in a talking mood. I have a headache."

"Ben, it's important."

"I told you, not now."

Hanna pushed herself into the room and pressed, "We'll be only one minute. It's very, very important."

"You're a pest! What's so earthshakingly urgent that it can't wait?"

"Thank you, Ben." Hanna took another step into his room, pulled Malka in behind her, shut the door, and said, "Ben, we saw you standing on Leszno Street watching the smugglers at the wall."

"Were you following me?"

Malka jumped to their defense. "No, we weren't following you. We were on our way to see Josek. We just happened to see you standing there. We couldn't help it."

"What did you see?"

"We saw you watching the smugglers as if you were planning to do the same," Hanna said.

"So, you think you're mind readers?"

"We saw you walk away from the wall with a smuggler. Will you see him again?"

Ben's eyebrows went up. He remained silent for a second, studying the girls' morose faces and trying to figure out how to stop them from complicating his plans.

"Hanna, did you talk to Mom or Dad about seeing me near the wall? Of course, I haven't done anything except look at the wall and talk to a boy."

"He wasn't any ordinary boy, Ben. He was a smuggler and you walked away with him. Where did you go? If you tell us, we won't tell our parents about it." She quickly added, "Unless we think you might get yourself in trouble. Don't forget, we have enough problems without you adding to them."

Malka remained silent. The ground felt as if it were slipping from under her feet. Ben was among the few good and joyful things still existing in her life. She could hardly bear the thought of the potential danger he was playing with.

"You didn't exactly answer me. Did you tell our parents what you just told me?" Ben pressed.

"Not yet," Hanna said.

"Malka, did you tell your parents about your suspicions?"

"No, I didn't."

"Listen up, both of you. I will repeat what I had promised you once before: If I ever decide to be a smuggler — without taking too much risk — I will be the first to tell my parents. Besides, I won't be able to hide it from them anyway. You know that as well as I do."

Hanna nodded.

For good measure, he added, "Some smugglers even find ways to live — sub-rosa — on the other side."

"Are you thinking of abandoning us and becoming a goy?" Hanna asked.

"Don't be stupid. Maybe I'm thinking of smuggling you out and getting rid of a pest? Look, I trusted you and told you everything there is to know. You've got to promise me not to blab to Mom or Dad. They are in no condition to worry more than necessary. Leave them in peace 'til I make a decision."

"Okay, I promise I'll let you be the one to tell them the minute you make such a crazy decision. I hope you don't," Hanna said.

"Malka, can I count on you to keep a secret a while longer?"

"You can," she responded. "Good night. I hope you don't do anything stupid." And with that, she left.

The rest of the evening passed uneventfully in Malka's household. She waited patiently for Mama to put a watery soup on the dinner table and a breadbasket containing rationed bread that had the color and appeal of mud. Of course, there were napkins beside each plate. Mama insisted that a meal was civilized family time. Its importance must be maintained with respect.

As always, Malka's family went early to bed, hoping for sleep to numb their nagging hunger and clawing cold.

CHAPTER TWELVE

A Dream

M alka's head was a pot of stew that night, churning and
bubbling with images of Ben's encounter with the smuggler who crawled out of the Leszno Street ruins. These images
soon transformed into dreams, spinning with hair-raising danger and grandiose rewards, fueled by hunger and fear.

While her head was resting on a plump pillow and the house
murmured with the soft sounds of sleep, a weird dream took her
to wild places. Magically, she found herself moving across the
night and along the ghetto streets — dark, deserted, and as silent
as a morgue at midnight — to meet Ben and the boy-smuggler.
They were waiting for her under a doorframe vaguely resem-
bling that of the bombed-out building on Leszno Street.

In her sleep, the trio soared in the air between partly collapsed buildings looking for *food*. She heard gun pops, "Tat,
tat, tat," but she felt beyond fear. They hopped from doorframe
to doorframe suspended in midair. They peered into empty
spaces, searching all the while. They stood on the tallest ledge
of the ruins towering above the ghetto wall, looked boldly into
the Christian side under an infinite moonlit sky, stared into

streets aglow with lights and store windows laden with groceries, peered into streetcars carrying people free as birds as far as
they wished, and watched children on a merry-go-round laughing blissfully.

Just as the tip of the sun began to rise above the rim of
the horizon and spread a fringe of orange lights, a doorframe
appeared at their feet inviting them to cross. The boys motioned
with a bow for Malka to be first to step across the threshold.

Miracle of miracles! They found themselves floating among
stars and tables topped with mountains of food. Golden-brown
roasted geese on silver platters, trays of potato fricassee, bowls
of chocolate pudding, globs of butter, stacks of sizzling hotdogs
garnished with her favorite mustard, salami, more potatoes,
slabs of cheese, platters with herring, and heaps of bread and
bagels. Oranges and gooseberries! Cakes galore! Treats Malka
once took for granted but had nearly forgotten.

Malka put out her arms to reach for the goodies to stuff
into her mouth, to pack under her shirt — as she saw the young
smugglers at the wall do — and bring to her parents. Somehow,
she could not reach any of them. The more she tried, the more
unreachable the food became.

When the sun rose on the real world, Malka found herself
in a gloomy, cold apartment, bare cupboards staring down at
her. The stark reality of Ben's dangerous involvement with the
smuggling world loomed dark and ominous.

CHAPTER THIRTEEN

They Sat Like Wooden Figures

The day Malka woke up from her strange dream, Ben informed her and Hanna of his decision to join the smugglers' netherworld. Malka stared into his feisty face and wondered: *Is it a mere coincidence that he lives his life like the fabulous heroes in the stories he used to make up when we were little?* She was as proud of his hubris as she was angry at him for causing so much anguish.

"How will you get across the wall?" Hanna asked.

"We'll cross through the ruins on Leszno Street where I first caught sight of Heniek with his stuffed rucksack. It's much safer than burrowing through the wall or climbing over it like the smugglers at the Gęsia Street cemetery do."

"The wreckage with the barred basement windows that borders the wall?"

"Yes, that one. Oddly, the basement beneath it isn't much damaged. It leads to a labyrinth of dark, secret cellars that end on the other side of the wall. Heniek knows the subterranean route, including the sewers, like his own backyard."

"Aren't you afraid of squealing rats or SS men pouncing out of dark corners?" Malka asked.

"Aren't you afraid of rats or SS men in the ghetto?"

"It's much different than being trapped in a dark, dank cellar under the earth."

"Not that much."

"How will you get through the barred basement windows?" Hanna asked.

"Hanna, the Nazis place iron bars on all the windows over-looking the wall. They seal and reseal every hole, but smuggling continues all day and night. Look, I told you and Malka every-thing. I've trusted you, and you're old enough to do your part to keep our parents from collapsing. My job will be to stay close behind Heniek. He knows his way through the no man's land beneath the wall. He can do it with his eyes closed and is none the worse for it."

"Is this your final decision?" Malka asked.

"Yes, and we'll start the day after tomorrow, Wednesday morning, at ten o'clock. That's a good hour for small smugglers. The streets are crowded with people and the guards are dis-tracted by counting their bribes from the morning traffic across the gates."

Ben reassured them, "Don't worry, Heniek and I went over every step of crossing and reaching his trading contacts beyond the wall. The gang leader who keeps blackmailers away from the wall, for a fee, is his pal."

He paused, then looked straight at his sister and appealed, "The hardest part will be telling our parents. Can I count on your help, Hanna?"

"Absolutely not! I do not approve of this dangerous decision."

"Fair enough." A brief silence. Then, more morale boosting, "Just think, I'll trade the extra food I'll smuggle in for coal. We'll no longer freeze. I might even smuggle us out of the ghetto and find a place to hide 'til the damn war is over."

"Oh, Ben! You're a hopeless dreamer," Malka said.

"No," he responded. "I'm an optimist."

Malka was not present the evening when Ben told his parents of his daring decision. She learned what happened from Hanna the following morning.

Malka was first to start the conversation. "Did Ben really tell your parents what he is planning to do?"

"Oh yes, he did!"

"How did your parents respond? I can hardly imagine."

"If you stop talking, I'll tell you."

"Okay, I'll be quiet."

"While my mother was preparing our supper last night, Ben said, 'I have something important to tell you. Can we all sit down?'

"We found seats around the kitchen table, stared at him, and waited for him to speak. Ben said in a decisive voice, 'I cannot stand by any longer and watch us starve to death.'"

"What was your parents' response?" Malka asked.

"Their jaws dropped, and they stared at him suspiciously. My dad asked, 'What do you mean, Ben? If it were possible to keep us from starving, don't you think I would do it?'

"'That's not what I mean, Dad.'

"'Then, what do you mean?'

"My mother rushed in, begging, 'What can we do, Ben? The war will end soon. I heard rumors that Hitler is losing. We must be patient.'

"Ben swatted her words away. 'Mama, the ghetto is always rife with rumors. In one street they have Hitler dead, in another he is marching on to Moscow. We cannot count on rumors.'

"He straightened his back, lifted his chin high, looked into my parents' eyes with the confidence of a general, and said, 'Now hear me out. And, please, don't interrupt me. I made friends with some smugglers. Don't worry. They are nice boys. And their parents are nice, and very loving. The boys are my friends and they found a way to get food for their families.' He spoke firmly, but respectfully."

"What did your parents say to that?"

"My parents jumped to attention as if a clap of thunder struck the room. My mother implored, 'What are you planning to do, Ben? You must not do anything foolish or dangerous. I want you to stay safe.'

"My dad said, 'Ben, I hope you are not thinking of getting mixed up with the smugglers. That's far too dangerous. You have never given us any trouble. Don't start now. Things are bad enough without you adding to it. I am asking you to promise me not to give it a second thought.'

"Ben insisted, 'Starving to death isn't safe. I'm asking you to trust me. If the other kids can do it, so can I. No one can stop me. I promise I'll be careful. Please listen. I'll need your help to get started. I need either money or something of value to trade for food.'"

"Did he really believe your parents would do that?"

"Malka, my mom insisted, 'We have no money left. That's why we are starving.'

"Ben had a ready answer. 'I know. I gave it a lot of thought and came up with an idea. We still have a few pieces of silverware hidden. I know you treasure them, but we need food to stay alive. Silverware is replaceable.'

"No matter how hard my parents objected, Ben remained resolute. 'There's no point arguing. I'm old enough to make up my own mind. Dad, I know you do all that is possible, but only kids my age, or younger, can sneak across the wall to save their families from starvation. It's true that it is not a safe thing to do, but neither is starving to death. Don't even try to stop me. Neither you nor Mama can.'

"Malka, my parents beseeched, reasoned, and lamented, 'That's too dangerous, Ben. You must stay alive, Ben.' They wrung their hands and shed buckets of tears. But it was obvious that neither the threat of bullets nor their pleas would stop him. I know my parents wanted to run into the street and howl and scratch and bite and shriek at the Nazi barbarians for what they are doing to us. Instead, they sat like wooden figures, helplessly listening to Ben's plot to save us from starvation."

CHAPTER FOURTEEN

The Vigil

A gray mist hovered over the ghetto when the two boys met in front of Heniek's house on Zamenhofa Street. They exchanged a few words and blended in with the throng of agitated pedestrians scurrying to survive another day. Malka and Hanna observed that meeting from a guarded distance across the street and followed the boys.

When they reached Leszno Street, the boys walked past the bombed-out building, looking carefully in all directions.

"Why are they walking *past* that wreckage?" Malka asked. Her heart was hammering.

"I think they're making sure no guards are in sight."

Hanna was right. The boys turned back, slipped away from the milling crowd, jumped into a ditch beside the ruins, removed a few loose bricks they felt with their fingers, crawled through the opening — legs first — hopped down to the basement floor, and vanished.

The stalkers, Hanna and Malka, turned around and walked back home to wait for the boys' return. That wait turned out to be as long and arduous as waiting for a hanging reprieve.

Malka and her parents were in Hanna's house late that afternoon while the Rotenbergs stood vigil at the window, waiting
for Ben to come home. When darkness swallowed the ghetto,
they peered between the cracks of blackout windows. More
than on any other night, the intermittent bursts of gun salvos
made their hearts shrivel with fear. The clock ticked like the
perpetual "drip, drip, drip" of a leaking faucet.

Pani Rotenberg, unable to contain her anxiety, wrung her
hands and cursed the Nazis for the torments they forced upon
them, for the curfew forbidding her to search for her son, for
the starvation that forced Ben to risk his young life, for their
helplessness, and for all the indignities — big and small — the
Nazis poured on them. Pan Rotenberg remained silent, his face
pinched, eyes dark with worry. Hanna couldn't stop herself
from shivering. Neither could Malka.

If Hanna and Malka would have been with the two boys
on their return trip through the basement labyrinth, they
would have known that curfew beat them to the exit ditch at
the Leszno Street ruin. They would have known that the boys
removed one loose brick from the escape hole and waited: for
the streets to grow as dark and silent as caves, for the intervals
between gunfire to grow further apart and more distant. At that
point, Heniek stepped on Ben's shoulders, pulled himself up
to the level of the ditch, and climbed out. Then he took off his
jacket and lowered it to help Ben climb out. Heavy bags of food
dangled from their shoulders.

They worked their way out of the ditch to the street
level with the same caution. Then Heniek bolted as fast as
a bullet to the building across the street, ducked in a doorframe, paused, listened, and looked all around. Ben followed
like a whirlwind. They paused again to judge the distance
and direction of gunfire. "The devils aren't asleep after all,"
Ben murmured. "I wonder how many smugglers they'll kill
tonight."

Another dash across the moonlit street and back into the
shadow. They repeated this pattern from corner to corner, from
one side of the street to the other.

Of course, Malka saw none of this, but Ben would later boast to her and Hanna how he and Heniek fooled the Nazis at every step.

Just as the apprehension of the two families waiting at the window reached past endurance, they spotted a shadow of a figure with a hump on his back, creeping along the courtyard wall. The shadow grew longer as it moved closer.

"Ben!" Pani Rotenberg shrieked.

"Ben! Ben!" the others cried more mutedly in chorus, afraid of bringing the "masters of the universe" to their door.

Hardly able to contain their relief and gratitude, they smothered the young man with affection. They repeated a thousand times: "Thank God you're okay. We were so worried. Why did it take you so long to get back? What happened?"

To spare them needless additional anxiety, Ben said not a word about his dangerous crossing or walking incognito on the forbidden terrain. Instead, he showed them the small mountain of food he brought.

He reassured his parents and everyone in the room, "You see, I told you it can be done. What's more, I met a remarkable black-market speculator. He is a socialist, a partisan, and has connections that may save the lives of some of us."

"Ben, what connections are you thinking of now?" Pani Rotenberg pounced on his words as if to protect him from imminent danger.

"Never mind now, Mama. He's just a decent Pole with important contacts. I'll tell you more tomorrow."

Ben's father brought the tormenting day to a conclusion. "That's enough for today. We all need some rest. We have all day tomorrow."

CHAPTER FIFTEEN

A Mensch

Morning light barely brushed Malka's face and she was wide awake. She stepped out of bed, walked across the floor, and opened the window. The sun was rising on the horizon, a blazing orange that seemed to be climbing toward the wet roofs. A deadening curfew silence stretched as far as her ears could register; not a stir came from her parents' room or Hanna's apartment above. She went back to bed and worried about what Ben might be plotting now besides smuggling food.

Slowly, sounds began to fill the silence, rising note by note, until they reached a restless crescendo. As if on cue, blips of neighbors' conversations and clinks of eating utensils spilled out of courtyard windows. Her parents' voices eventually came to the foreground, and Malka joined them at the breakfast table. She gulped down a few bites of dark bread and said, "I'm going up to Hanna's."

"There is no hurry. Give them a little time to be alone with Ben," Tata said.

Finally, a familiar knock on the door. Hanna stepped in and

said, "My parents asked if you want to come to our house. Ben is up and he has much to tell."

They gathered in the kitchen, the warmest room in the apartment, to hear Ben's daring story. A bitter indignation welled up in Malka: *He only went a few streets from where we are sitting — an easy walking distance — and he almost paid with his life for this crime!*

Ben started his story. "The streets on the other side of the wall don't stink like they do here in the ghetto. They are sparkling clean. You see no beggars or corpses, stores are open, and people are free to go wherever they want. Of course, it doesn't mean the Nazis don't treat the people there like a subservient class, but it is no comparison to the brutality they heap on us."

"Ben, I'm sorry to interrupt, but when will you tell us about the exceptional Pole and his promising connections?" Pani Rotenberg asked, not expecting a good report.

"I was just coming to that, Mama. His name is Stefan. In addition to being a black-market operator, he is a socialist, a partisan, and a mensch."

"How do you know he's a mensch?" his mother asked.

"Mama, I entered his house expecting to meet a probable anti-Semite interested in making money off our misery. Instead, the tall, chain-smoking Pole said this: 'The shock of seeing the tragic conditions of people under sentence of death in the ghetto gives me a sense of personal humiliation and shame at being a so-called Aryan.' He even shared a political secret with important ramifications for us." Ben stopped to let his words sink in on his listeners.

"What exactly did he tell you, Son?" Pan Rotenberg asked.

"He said he heard a rumor the Germans are planning to deport all Jews from the ghetto sometime this summer."

"How reliable is the information? Where did it originate? Did he say?" Tata asked.

"He didn't vouch for the validity of the information. He heard it in his circle and was told that it came from a reliable German source. He advised us to try to hide on the Christian side."

"Brilliant! Did he tell you who would let us in?" his mother asked with bitter sarcasm.

"As a matter of fact, he did. He told Heniek and me that he has contact with Father Boduen, who hides and protects Jewish children in his orphanage. Have you heard of him?"

"I have," Tata said.

"He also has contact with a convent near Warsaw that shelters Jewish girls. His sister is the head nun there. I gave this a lot of thought. I'm thinking, in the event the deportation rumor turns out to be true, it could be a godsend to hide Hanna and Malka in the convent."

Malka panicked. So did Hanna.

"That's preposterous. I don't want to be tossed into an orphanage or a convent with total strangers whose motives we cannot be sure of. I don't want to be cut off from everyone I love and trust," Hanna protested.

"I was afraid you might come up with this idea! I don't want to hide like a hunted criminal," Malka echoed.

Ben said, "Be reasonable; your lives may depend on it. You cannot afford to ignore that fact. Besides, you wouldn't be alone. You'd have each other."

"Ben, don't be so smart. Hanna and I are fourteen already. We're perfectly capable of enduring whatever you and our parents can endure," Malka said.

"That may be true, except I'd make an odd convent candidate," Ben retorted. "Imagine the commotion I'd cause. By the way, that fact also applies to everyone else in this room, except the two of you."

To ease Malka's and Hanna's fears — and her own despair — Mama said, "It is useful to acknowledge that nuns are committed to showing compassion and mercy to all in need. My brother, Simon, suffered a head injury when he was a young man. His life was saved by nuns who nursed him to health and showed him much kindness. If going to a convent can save your lives, we must not disregard the possibility. Life is sacred." Her voice sounded tight with pain, on the verge of breaking.

Malka understood the sacrifice her parents were ready to make to save her. She excoriated herself — *A good daughter protects her parents and does as she is told* — but terror overcame her and she continued to protest.

The discussion ended with the agreement that for the time being, Ben would learn as much as he could about hiding the two girls in a convent. He promised further not to take flagrant risks to accomplish this goal.

CHAPTER SIXTEEN

Rebecca

Since the last escape discussion, Malka and Hanna hardly ever let their parents out of their sight. More than ever, they cherished and clung to the people they loved.

Ben, too, grasped morsels of love and life's meaning from each ephemeral moment. As soon as he came home from his smuggling expeditions and reassured himself that his family was intact, he stepped into another reality. He washed as if scrubbing the netherworld out of his skin, put on fresh clothes, and announced, "I'm going to Heniek's house for a bit."

"You just got home," his parents would remind him.

"I won't be long," he would say, placing a kiss on his mother's cheek and setting off with a jaunty stride and a twinkle in his eyes.

Malka and Hanna quickly guessed that it was Rebecca's giggle, irresistibly catchy, and her fetching blue eyes that sent Ben flying to Heniek's house. Rebecca was Heniek's younger sister. Their romance captured the girls' imaginations. When they saw the couple crossing the courtyard, Rebecca's graceful figure swinging like a reed in step with Ben's firm stride, they murmured, "They're the most romantic pair in the world."

"Where could they be going to find a beautiful, discreet place to be together?" Malka asked.

"I don't know. There are no parks with benches beneath acacia trees. No swans gliding on silver ponds to glance at while they hold hands. No open countryside to escape to, not even a movie theater," Hanna answered.

As Rebecca became a frequent visitor to Ben's house, Malka asked her, "Where do you and Ben go when you have a date? All the nice places are closed to us."

Rebecca answered with her pretty head held high. "We cannot stroll in the park or the countryside, but we can attend underground concerts and lectures and we can dream with friends of a homeland where we no longer will be punished for being Jews. We always have the freedom to dream, you know. Sometimes, we go dancing at underground cafés where musicians play beautiful music."

Dancing to beautiful music impressed the two girls most.

Rebecca's answer gave Malka faith that goodness always exists, even if it is squeezed out in tiny drops or savored in dreams. Ben's and Rebecca's courage became Malka's inspiration. So did their romance.

CHAPTER SEVENTEEN

A Toothache

When Pani Rotenberg heard that the British had bombed Cologne in May 1942, bringing the war home to Germany for the first time, she exulted, "Good!" Being a pacifist at heart, she felt compelled to justify her *schadenfreude*: "There is a huge difference between bombing to end a war and bombing to conquer. If it were up to the Allies, the war would be over this very minute." Despite persistent bombing of their cities, Germany continued to inflict brutalities in occupied countries.

Undeterred, Ben continued his heroic smuggling trips across the wall. With dogged determination, he made contact with the sister of Stefan, the influential Polish black marketeer. The kind nun pledged to hide Malka and Hanna and return them to their families, or nearest kin, after the war. With the help of Stefan's underground connections, arrangements were made to slip the girls out through the secret subterranean passageways and deliver them to the convent on July 25. Then, just as that decisive date was approaching, life in the ghetto abruptly changed.

Until July 1942, Malka could pretty much count on hearing voices spilling out of her neighbors' windows. She could look forward to meeting courtyard friends, Felusia, Moniek, Mata, and Zyga. Above all, Hanna remained near. In the eerie curfew silence, when she called to the room above hers, "Hanna, I forgot to tell you," she could count on hearing a reply, "Malka, are you up?"

Until then, the streets remained packed with peddlers, beggars, homeless, and all sorts of bedraggled people. As soon as the sun began to set, everyone was locked indoors. The streets stayed pitch black; wails of stray cats, clangs of toppling trash cans, and distant gunfire salvos chilled the night.

So, life limped forward until rumors about deportations reached the ghetto streets. The rumors spread even before the notices were posted. The news threw everyone into a panic and brought Ben's effort to smuggle his sister and Malka out of the ghetto to a screeching halt. The carnage that followed would have led any sane person to conclude that the girls' likelihood of being rescued was nil, but one can never presuppose fate's whimsy.

"What will happen to us?" Malka asked her parents. "Will you have the time to send me away from you and hide me in the convent?"

"Probably not," Tata said.

"Good!" Malka countered. "At least we'll be together, whatever happens."

On July 22, a shocking news item hit the ghetto: "The SS has ordered the Judenrat to begin rounding up all ghetto Jews for resettlement. Immediately!" And then, on July 23: "Adam Czerniaków [head of the Judenrat] committed suicide by taking a cyanide capsule." Everyone understood that Czerniaków's suicide foretold the demise of the entire community.

A shroud of doom entered every household and every heart. Like all the others in the ghetto, Malka's family was left with two equally perilous choices: follow orders and report to the deportation depot, thereafter to board a freight train to be carried off to a promised resettlement place; or hide and take the risk of being shot on the spot if found. The decision had to be made that day. Although her parents could not hide the terror in their faces, Malka drew courage from the way they kept their fear in check and confronted the worst that might happen.

Tata said, "Sara, I don't know what is the best thing to do: to follow orders or to hide. I doubt anyone knows. Your instinct has always guided us well. In the absence of reason, I say we follow your heart. You decide and we will abide by that choice."

Mama's gaze, stricken with grief, turned inward and looked deep into an invisible distance. She remained silent for a short eternity. Then she said, "I think we have a better chance to stay alive if we hide."

"Then that is what we will do."

"Where can we hide in our apartment so the Germans won't find us?" Malka asked.

"Good question. We will come up with something. We still have a few hours to decide," Tata said.

Her parents checked with neighbors. Many decided to follow orders and march to the Umschlagplatz to be sent to an undefined place where they were promised food and shelter. Others determined to defy orders and hide in their apartments — although it meant a sure bullet in the head if they were found. Some planned to hide under beds, behind sofas, between mattresses and box springs, in cupboards, in drawers, in closets, behind curtains. Some resolved to hide in a secret room. This was what Malka's and Hanna's parents chose to do. To deflect detection of the hidden room, everyone living in the same vertical row of apartments placed a wardrobe in front of the same door. None of these choices were ideal, but where else could one hide in the ghetto?

The deportations proceeded on schedule. They were carried out with contemporary know-how and Stone Age values. Daily, hordes of armed German and Ukrainian soldiers blocked off clusters of streets and rounded up everyone they could find, marched them to the deportation station, and loaded them onto freight trains.

When Malka's family heard the sounds of pandemonium coming from the street where people were being snatched up, they bolted to their hiding place.

After every raid, Malka and Hanna looked at each other with enormous gratitude: "Thank God they didn't find us. We're so, so lucky! I was so afraid I might never see you again."

On reconsidering, Hanna recognized the absurdity of their gratitude. She rebelled, "For God's sake, it's stupid to be thankful! We should be furious at God for being a bystander. Why isn't He putting a stop to the slaughter? Isn't He the Almighty! Aren't we His favorite children? No, Malka! We're not so, so lucky! Besides, it's not right to be happy to be alive when so many people are dashed into oblivion."

"Hanna, I'm as horrified as you are. At the same time, I'm sooo thankful we weren't deported or killed."

"You mean we haven't *yet* been deported."

"*Not yet* is the only thing real to me at the moment. When I think we could have been on one of the freight trains going to the end of the world, I'm immensely grateful they missed us."

With each raid, Malka's world shrank, leaving her feeling limp inside. No one ever heard from those who were deported, until a handful of people slipped back to the ghetto under the cover of night and told about horrific train rides to a place called Treblinka, where the people were gassed to death. The word "trains" now trembled in whispers. Desperate, heart-wrenching songs and ballads now conjured up images of parting glances, fading gasps, final heartbeats, and an unbearable longing for lost lives. And terror.

An order was issued: Janusz Korczak's orphans must be delivered to the Umschlagplatz, post haste. When Malka heard of this decree, she took shelter in her mother's embrace and lamented soundlessly, acrimoniously: *They've killed nearly everyone I loved and knew. Now it's Korczak's orphans' turn. Not even his love can protect them. After all, how powerful is love compared to Nazi evil?*

According to underground sources, as soon as Korczak's Christian friends heard about the order, they made their final, futile attempts to smuggle him out of the ghetto. Korczak responded, "When a child is sick, you don't leave him alone in the middle of the night."

He gathered his children and told them, "At last we will be able to exchange the horrible, suffocating ghetto for meadows and flowers and streams where you can bathe, and woods where berries and mushrooms grow." With a child on each side, he marched with them in rows of four through the grieving ghetto. Staff members, clutching children's hands, followed close behind.

Some part of Malka marched with Janusz Korczak and his children. Sitting near her parents, numb with grief, Malka followed, step by step, circulating reports of the macabre procession to the Umschlagplatz, where children and staff were loaded onto chlorinated freight cars. The train set out for the Treblinka extermination camp. Those who braved the witness of the saintly procession said the children did not look scared.

Janusz Korczak and his children vanished, but Korczak's humanity followed Malka to the darkest corners in her life, never ceasing to nourish her. She heard the ring of his children's laughter in the laughter of all children, forever after.

Hanna woke up one day with a toothache. Ordinarily, her parents would have taken her to the dentist, and that would be the end of the story. However, nothing was ordinary at that time — least of all finding a dentist among the remaining ghetto Jews. The Rotenbergs had to resort to home remedies. They wrapped a compress around Hanna's swollen cheek and gave her chamomile to rinse her gums. Nothing helped. Her tooth continued to throb with pain, her right cheek swelled like a melon. Her desperate parents turned to Tata for help.

Tata rushed to Hanna's side. He pointed his flashlight into her mouth; his fingers probed ever so gently. When he was done, he checked her fever, gave her a pill to swallow, held her hand, and said, "We will find a way to help you, darling. In the meantime, continue rinsing your gums with chamomile solution."

Tata took the Rotenbergs aside and whispered, "Her gum is badly infected. I doubt the aspirin I gave her will do much good.

I'm sorry, but that is all I have. We must find a dentist before the infection spreads."

"Without a doubt, David! But tell me, where will we find a living dentist among us?" Pani Rotenberg said bitterly.

"I saw Dr. Szmitberg, a dentist, early this morning. He lives a couple of buildings down the street. You must try to contact him. Hanna's condition is very serious."

A brief, agonizing pause followed, then Pani Rotenberg's resolute voice rang out, "It is late afternoon and it is reasonable to assume the Nazis are done with their day's work. I can hear people milling in the street. We are taking Hanna to Dr. Szmitberg before curfew, before the infection gets worse, and before the dentist is deported."

Pan Rotenberg, in full agreement, turned to Ben. "You'll stay here, Son, until we get back."

Tenderly, Pan and Pani Rotenberg wrapped their arms around Hanna's sagging shoulders.

"We'll be back in no time," they said as they kissed Ben and stepped out the door. Hanna looked forlorn.

Hours passed. The summer-blue sky dissolved into charcoal, and still there was no sign of the Rotenbergs. Filled with dread, Ben, Malka, and her parents stationed themselves at the window with a view of the gate and waited. The cacophony of street sounds slowly faded into ghoulish curfew silence. The night sky spread out like an endless scroll, the stars mysterious yet distinct in their message: "You may never see them again."

Malka yammered, "Where are they? What happened to them? Please, God, keep them safe."

Ben's face was a mask of agony: muscles taut; eyes wide, piercing, restless. No longer able to contain his fears, he lurched toward the door, declaring, "I'm going out to find them. I know how to dodge the Nazis; my parents don't."

Tata gently placed a hand on Ben's shoulder. "Ben, we can't afford to be rash. You cannot run out in the street now. Your parents have enough to deal with. Imagine how they will feel if they don't find you here when they return."

"What if they need my help?"

"At the moment, we don't know where to look for them. Let's not give up hope. Maybe they were delayed and are waiting in a safe place for curfew to end. We must wait until morning."

"What if they don't come back? How will we find them?" Malka asked as calmly as she could, mindful not to upset Ben. Her teeth chattered; her stomach churned.

"Ben and I will look for them first thing in the morning, as soon as curfew ends," Tata promised — as if there was a grain of hope remaining.

Ben understood the futility and reproached himself bitterly. "What was I thinking? God, where was my head? I should've gone with Dad to take my sister to Dr. Szmitberg instead of letting my mother go."

His self-recriminations stirred past demons in Malka's head: *A proper granddaughter would've never cowered behind ruins while her grandfather was kicked half to death.*

Morning came. Tata and Ben went out to look for Hanna and her parents. There was not far to go nor many friends or family left to ask.

They never saw Hanna or Pan and Pani Rotenberg again.

Malka's beloved friend, Hanna, was gone. A vital part of her was amputated. Vanished. How would she live without her best friend, with whom she practiced holding her fears in check and counting on love? Would she ever laugh as heartily, as senselessly, as she had with Hanna?

The immediacy of her latest loss made her forget how much pain and sorrow the human heart can endure. She brooded as deeply as she had when her grandparents died. Again, she thought: *People we love must be immortalized in our hearts. We must mourn them forever. If I were killed — God forbid — and my parents and Ben would cease grieving, my existence would be erased.*

As before, however, the exigencies of life began to tug at her with the passing of time. Her stomach demanded to be fed, her broken heart craved to be comforted, despair turned into prayerful hope. More than ever, she cherished her parents' and Ben's lives.

Ben bore his grief in bitter silence. There was no room for mourning. His world was in upheaval: parents without children, children without parents, husbands without wives; so many solitary as stones and in imminent danger.

The deportations started on July 22, 1942 and lasted until September 12. Then they stopped. No one trusted the cessation. In less than a mere two months, 99 percent of the children had disappeared from the ghetto. Nearly all the old people were gone. It was a world shorn of the sound of children, stripped of the presence of grandmothers and grandfathers — a universe cleansed of promise and memory.

Shortly after the deportations stopped, Ben redoubled his effort to whisk Malka out of the ghetto. As expected, he and Heniek headed to Stefan's house on their first post-deportations subversive trip. They returned with the sad news: "Stefan was arrested five weeks ago. His desperate wife told us."

Malka thought: *I know I shouldn't feel that way, but I'm glad. Maybe now they'll stop trying to send me away. With Hanna gone, I'm even more frightened of being abandoned behind the wall.* Undeterred, however, Ben found new contacts and continued his efforts.

CHAPTER EIGHTEEN

Hanna's Spirit

To keep the remaining handful of Jews locked up in an orderly bundle, Heinrich Himmler isolated them in three separate, tiny sub-ghettos. A German factory was located in each confined subdivision. The sub-ghettos were surrounded by a vast desolate area from where people had been deported. There, winds hissed through lifeless streets and curtains flapped out of broken windows and feral cats and dogs roamed. Any Jew spotted there by a Nazi patrol was shot on the spot.

Only the people who managed to get permission to work — gratis, of course — in one of the three German factories were permitted to live in the sub-ghettos. All others were declared to be "useless" and slated for "liquidation." Mama was among the fortunate few to obtain a permit to mend German soldiers' uniforms, without pay, at the Schulz Shop. That humiliating concession was a big deal; it allowed her to stay in her apartment and provided a secret shelter for Malka, Tata, Ben, Heniek, and Rebecca. Other "useless" people hid among the minuscule "useful" population.

The "useless" people existed like phantoms. They ventured out into the street mostly when the workers walked, unescorted, to and from the factory. During these brief interludes, they relished the simple joy of hearing the ring of friends' voices and seeing their own smiles mirrored in friends' faces. And yes, they even allowed themselves to crack a bitter joke and laugh at their otherworldly existence. At such moments, Mama would say, "We must be going mad. How can we laugh in this hell?"

Perhaps laughter is as essential to man's sanity as a sip of water is to life?

While the workers manned the factories, Malka, Tata, Ben, and the other "wild people" would remain locked in their apartments to hide from marauding Nazis and to prepare for armed resistance.

"It's better to die fighting the Nazis than to die in Treblinka. Besides, we have an account to settle with those bastards," Ben, Rebecca, and Heniek declared with steely determination.

Apparently, they were not the only ones to arrive at that conclusion. Armed resistance began to form as soon as people heard about Treblinka. Tata, Ben, Rebecca, and Heniek joined the ŻOB (Jewish Combat Organization). The preponderance of fighters had, like Ben, lost their entire families. Heniek and Rebecca were the only survivors of their own immediate family.

The fighters began building bunkers in basements for entrenchment and hiding. They also set out to create a maze of secret, subterranean passageways. To accomplish this subversive act of engineering, they pounded holes in the basement walls of adjacent buildings in each sub-ghetto block and beyond. That tactic allowed them to crawl from building to building and navigate the width and length of blocks unseen, like moles. They dug a network of tunnels to traverse city blocks and breach the wall to obtain weapons from the Polish underground. In addition, they made use of the network of sewers under the city.

One chilly autumn afternoon, sitting beside the warm kitchen stove, Tata looked up at Malka with great tenderness and said, "Malka, I have something important to share with you."

Malka's parents always communicated major decisions with her and never shielded her from truth. That policy was wise, because it armed her to face the inevitable with courage.

"We never know when the next round of deportations might occur," Tata continued. "We don't yet have a final word about getting you out of the ghetto, but we are working hard on it."

"I hope you never succeed. I don't want to part from you."

"At this moment, to protect ourselves from further deportations, we — along with several friends — are planning to build a bunker for hiding." Actually, the purpose was larger than just hiding. The shelter was also meant to be used for entrenchment for the freedom fighters, but Tata did not bring that up. "The bunker will be equipped with all essentials needed to keep us alive. The first step will be to move to a ground floor apartment and construct the bunker in the basement below."

Relieved to hear that she would remain with her parents — at least while the bunker was being built — Malka asked, "Which apartment will we move into, Tata? We have a wide choice, you know. We are the only remaining family in our entire building."

"Mama, Ben, and I have chosen the ground floor apartment where your friend, Felusia, used to live. It is located in an inconspicuous corner at the far end of the courtyard and has a window with a clear view of the gate."

Mama nodded her acquiescence.

"How will we survive hiding under the earth?" Malka wanted to know.

"No need for you to worry about that. The bunker will have everything necessary for us to stay alive until the war is over. We'll store food, books, bedding, and other essentials. We will even have a dynamo generator to produce electricity in case we run out of carbide for the lamp."

Being an optimist at heart, Malka read into Tata's voice a tone of awe when he mentioned the "dynamo generator." She allowed herself to imagine: *The bunker will be equipped with the cutting edge of twentieth-century technology.* She had never heard of a dynamo generator before. Beyond that, she tried not to think too much about her existence below the earth. She couldn't envision not seeing the rising sun, not being able to stick her head into the blue crispness of day, or picture her horizons reduced to the four walls enclosing the bunker. The thought, *How will we know when morning breaks and night falls?* entered her mind, but that was too frightening to dwell on. She simply trusted the wisdom and love of her parents. They were her safety.

Tata added, "You will even have a tutor in the bunker. That is, if we don't manage to send you to the Christian side before that." In Tata's mind, the prospect of a tutor was a way of denying that his child had no future.

Malka's family transferred to a ground floor flat within a couple of days. She was grateful her parents allowed her to sleep in their bedroom. Her bed was only a few steps away from her parents' bed, which leaned against the opposite wall. In case of danger, she could land in their arms with two hops. On the rare days that Ben was home, he slept on the living room ottoman. She treasured his presence. Most days he stayed at the fighters' headquarters on Miła Street. He also spent a considerable time on the Christian side cruising with Heniek and Rebecca—incognito—to obtain weapons for the ghetto fighters.

Without wasting a moment to protect their lives, Tata and his friends rounded up materials. They hammered, sawed, stacked bricks, and created a bunker-netherworld that reminded Malka of the River Styx that formed the boundary between Earth and Underworld she had read about in her Greek mythology books.

Where did Tata and his friends find all the materials to create this miracle? Malka didn't ask. She assumed much of it was pilfered from the vacant homes of her deported neighbors and that the rest was smuggled in. She was proud of the fighters' ingenuity and prayed for their invincibility.

Absolutely no stores or businesses existed in the sub-ghettos. Ben and his lionhearted cronies smuggled in from the Christian side some provisions: canned food, potatoes, and other kinds of sustenance. Malka looked on silently and wondered, *Will we have enough food stored to keep us from starving to death, enough fuel to cook and keep our toes from freezing off of our feet, and enough soap to wash our underwear?* But she did not ask. She had good reason to believe that her parents might not have an answer. She chose to have faith in their wisdom.

Keeping their place warm turned out to be no problem. Tata hauled doors from vacant apartments in their building and chopped them into firewood. Their supply of wood was virtually inexhaustible. Every neighbor in their building had been deported.

Chopping the furniture and doors was a highlight in Malka's day. Tata knew that and let her help him get the job done. He showed her how to swing the ax without lopping off her feet or destroying the floor, how to split the wood with the grain and avoid knots. She whacked the furniture with a volley of pent-up bitterness and muttered grimly, "This is how I'd love to chop the Nazis' necks."

Mama would say, "Then you will be no better than they."

"I really don't care, Mama!"

Best of all, when she chopped wood, Tata was near. Whenever he left her sight, Malka was afraid she might never see him again.

"The bunker is virtually done. We have one problem left to solve," Tata announced one late afternoon after a meeting with his friends.

"What is the problem?" Mama asked.

"We cannot think of a good place to conceal the trapdoor." He turned to his daughter and said, "See if you can come up with an answer, Malka. Young people often outstrip their elders with fresh ideas."

Wow, Tata is asking me to help solve a life-and-death problem! Malka felt flattered. She remained in his presence long enough to look into his eyes and determined to justify his trust in her. Then, she padded into the bedroom, stretched out on her bed, and set her mind toward a single-pointed quest to identify an invisible entrance to their bunker.

Initially, Malka was sidetracked by her lifelong habit of relying on Hanna's counsel. She grieved silently: *If only Hanna were alive! Without her, I row with one oar. How much easier it was to bear the bombardment with her beside me. How much less frightened I was to dodge Nazi patrols when we were together.*

Malka could hardly stop herself from talking in her head, as if Hanna's spirit were listening. *There's no one my age in the entire sub-ghetto. Children under fourteen are outlawed, forbidden to exist. "Child" is what everyone here calls me affectionately, although I stopped being a child the day the first bomb fell on Warsaw.*

There is one real child among us — just one — a little girl, three years old. Niunia is her name. She and her mother are hiding among us, the "wild people." Niunia is oblivious of the Nazis and she knows nothing about hate. Her large, dark eyes sparkle with trust and the joy of living. A mass of soft, black curls encircles her pretty face. She looks like a baby Queen Esther. Niunia is the holiest thing among us. We squeal with delight to hear her ringing laughter; at the same time, we jitter lest a Nazi might hear her. I wonder if Niunia ever saw the full majesty of the sky. Perhaps she sees a small patch of heaven from her window. Her mother never takes her out of their tiny apartment. Tata often goes to their house to check on them. I sometimes go with him and I get to play with her for just a few wonderful minutes. Hanna, how much less frightening the world was with you at my side!

Thinking about Hanna cleared Malka's head, as if she had whispered a secret into a well and expected no reply. She was back on track, searching her mind for the best spot for an invisible trapdoor. She pondered until she drifted into a deep slumber.

Mysteriously, the ultimate answer to her puzzle revealed itself when Malka was sound asleep. From beyond the boundaries of Malka's consciousness, Hanna appeared in her room, real as life. She drew close to the bed and whispered into Malka's ear, "Look at the rectangular pantry-closet floor in the kitchen."

"Hanna!" Malka called and put out her arms to embrace her. She couldn't reach her, though. The more she tried, the more remote Hanna became. As with the other people in all her dreams, Hanna vanished just as Malka felt she was about to touch her, leaving her feeling utterly bereft.

Hanna's image stayed with Malka when she woke up that morning. Dreamily, she stepped out of bed, pattered out of her room, crossed the kitchen floor, and opened the door into the pantry. She looked inside, estimated the depth, width, and height, and concluded, *Yes! The floor can be made into a trapdoor! The edges will conceal its outline. No one will ever suspect. And yes, the opening will be big enough even for a large adult to climb through and step down the ladder into the bunker. Simple and clever! I wonder what Tata will think.* She rushed to tell her parents about the notion that had come to her.

Some might say the idea was the result of her subconscious mind working in her sleep. Not Malka. She was convinced that Hanna's energy had a hand in her inspiration. She didn't believe in ghosts, but she knew that people who die don't cease to shape your thinking, even to influence your ability to love or hate, or have courage or not.

When she announced the concept to her parents, Tata said, "I knew you would come up with a good answer!"

Mama beamed, "Malka is so clever!"

Her parents' pride felt good. But more than that, she appreciated their trust in involving her. It proved to her she was capable of surmounting the seemingly insurmountable.

The bunker partners eagerly accepted Malka's suggestion.

There were always secret goings-on around the bunker. Sometimes, Malka noticed fighters discreetly meeting with Tata there. No one told her they were fighters, nor did she ask. She understood the importance of secrecy. But she could tell who they were from their thousand-mile stare into the distance. She felt both very frightened and very proud of knowing that the ghetto was preparing to fight back. She told herself: *We no longer can resist by having secret schools and theaters, but we still have will!* She detested the bitter, strangling feeling of not being able to strike back in self-defense.

One time, Malka saw a boy prowling in the basement where she sometimes went to escape boredom. The streets were not safe. He was snooping around the area of their bunker. A faint beam of light crawled down from the open door on top of the stairwell and made him barely visible. He was a skinny kid, her age, and a tad shorter than she. He moved as softly as a cat, peering into corners.

She had heard about this boy. Everyone in the sub-ghetto knew of the boy who was seen roaming the dusky basement labyrinth and reporting to the Germans the locations of bunkers. In return, they protected him from death.

Malka glared at him angrily, accusingly, thinking: *What have they done to you to make you do such a thing?*

At first, he wasn't aware she was observing him. He turned his head toward her for a split second. In the semidarkness, his face looked pale, his eyes pitch black and arresting.

"Moniek?!" she called out in horror.

Turning his back to her, he stuffed his hands into his pockets and slunk away into the darkness, leaving her forever mystified and tormented: *Could that have been Moniek?*

Another incident caught Malka by surprise. She heard metallic sounds coming from the alcove. She stuck her head in and saw Tata sitting on the edge of his bed. He looked at her for a few seconds and took his hand from the pistol he had been holding.

"Is it real?" she asked. As if she didn't know. Yet, it was hard to believe.

"Yes," he said, looking steadily at her.

"Will you use it against the Nazis if they come after us?"

"Yes, Malka," Tata said.

She winced.

"Don't worry about it," he said.

"They have tanks, and machine guns, and bomber planes. I'm afraid for your safety, Tata."

"I'll be very careful."

Underneath her fear, Malka realized that not fighting back wouldn't protect them. Waiting for the war to end had made good sense before they found out about Treblinka. Not any longer. "I understand, Tata," she stated.

Malka was now more frightened for Tata's safety than ever

before, but she had complete trust that he was doing what had to be done. Tata was her beacon.

CHAPTER NINETEEN

The Suitcase

D anger awaited Ben, Rebecca, and Heniek at every corner
when they stole out of the sub-ghetto to get sorely needed
guns from the Polish underground for the ghetto fighters.
Malka's and her parents' hearts were filled with love and fear
each time they saw them head out.

"Don't worry; everything will be all right," the young people would say. Unshakable faith in the validity of their cause,
confidence in their resourcefulness, and determination to carry
through their missions successfully resonated in their voices.

As soon as the three fighters departed, Malka moved a chair
to a corner near the window, careful not to be seen from the outside. Like an outcast, she peered at the world through the cracks.
She stared at sunbeams bouncing off rows of windowpanes and
clouds drifting in the sky, casting long shadows on the mor-
bidly vacant buildings surrounding the silent courtyard. Above
all, Malka watched the gate for Ben's, Rebecca's, and Heniek's
return. Sometimes they were gone for days. The instant she
spotted their silhouettes slinking toward her stairwell, she
bolted to the door eager to throw her arms around them — so

grateful they survived yet another perilous mission, so proud of their valor, and praying for their struggles to be over.

Time stopped when they all gathered to listen to the three heroes' tales. Their stories scared the breath out of Malka. At the same time, she felt such gratitude for their presence in the room with her and so keenly aware of the preciousness of life.

Hardly able to wrench herself from the impressions left by her perilous encounters, Rebecca said, "You face many dangers on the Christian side. For one, the Germans sometimes round up Poles in the streets and send them to Germany to work on farms. It's not a fraction as bad as Treblinka; nevertheless, you may end up where you don't want to be. Especially if you're a Jewish male. But the greatest danger by far is being recognized as a Jew."

"Even for you? All three of you look far more Aryan than Hitler, Goering, and Goebbels put together. And your command of Polish is as flawless as Jósef Piłsudski's," Malka observed.

"Yes, even for us. Mind you, if someone treats you rudely and in a moment of weakness you lower your eyes, the die is cast. Who but a Jew has anything to fear?"

Malka especially loved to hear Ben boast about Rebecca's pluck: "You'll never believe Rebecca's daring and quick wit. Now, you have to imagine the following scene. She is at a tram station carrying contraband concealed in her suitcase. Armed Nazis descend and decide to search everyone. Rebecca doesn't panic. At the last moment, she hands over her heavy suitcase to a German soldier in a Wehrmacht uniform — they have the reputation of being more decent, you know. He is so taken by her that he gallantly accompanies her to the streetcar, past the line of German guards, without the slightest suspicion of what he is carrying."

"Wow! Where were you and Heniek? Weren't you with Rebecca?" Malka asked.

"Close. We managed to slip away unnoticed from the hot spot. We hid in a building — a safe distance away — and waited for the commotion to blow over. I was carrying ammunition hidden in loaves of bread; Heniek had a grenade hidden in his underwear. Heaven forbid anyone pushed us too hard."

"Rebecca, how do you keep your wits when death has you cornered? I'd look for a hole to hide in, or else I'd run," Malka said.

Rebecca answered in her melodic voice, "Scared, yes. Lose my wits, never! The importance of my mission — and my determination not to get my head blown off — keep me in check. I convince myself I am the only one who knows who I really am. That puts me one jump ahead of those from whom I need to protect myself. When your life depends on it, you'll be every bit as cunning and bold, Malka."

Rebecca reminded Malka of heroes she encountered in legends. Who else but a true hero would tunnel her way under the ghetto wall and travel throughout the Christian side — often solo and always incognita — to obtain arms for the ghetto fighters? Malka vowed: *If I'm not killed before I'm old enough to join the fighters, I'll strive to be like Rebecca.*

CHAPTER TWENTY

The Messenger

Nineteen hundred forty-three marked big victories for the Allied forces. In February, Soviet troops broke through the Axis lines surrounding Stalingrad, trapping the German columns in the city. In spite of major defeats, however, Germany continued to torture people in occupied countries.

The Nazis were skillful in carrying out surprises. In early January, they conducted manhunts in the Christian neighborhoods of Warsaw and arrested thousands of Poles. The purpose of these raids was to fool the ghetto fighters into believing they were safe for a while. Ironically, desperate Polish underground members made their way into the ghetto to seek temporary refuge. That set of circumstances led to a strange encounter between Tata and an old friend, and it altered Malka's fate.

It started one brisk winter day when a group of fighters met in Tata's bunker. The purpose of that gathering was to take advantage of the German operation on the Christian side and plan for a response to the next round of deportations. Mama was busy sweeping the kitchen floor and Malka was staring out the window into the desolate snow-covered street and listening to the shattering silence. There was nothing else for her to do. Suddenly, Tata burst through the secret bunker trapdoor holding a folded slip of paper in front of him as if it were a gift from God. He announced, "You will never guess who is hiding from the Nazis in the ghetto!" He didn't wait for a response. "Marcel Jabkowski!" Marcel was his dear friend with whom he had attended medical school.

"Marcel? Here, in this hell? How could that be?" Mama asked.

Malka remained nailed to the spot, waiting to hear the rest of the improbable news.

"Yes, here in this hell. You will never believe why he is here. The Nazis are conducting a manhunt on the Christian side. As unlikely as it sounds, members of the Polish underground are sneaking into the ghetto to hide until the raid is over."

"The Poles come here to seek safety? Poor fools! Maybe now you'll give up trying to send me to the Polish side?" Malka said.

"How do you know he is here? Did you actually see Marcel?" Mama asked.

"No, I have not seen him yet, but I will tomorrow." Tata extended his hand with the slip of paper and said, "Look, he sent me this note!"

"He sent you a note? How?" Mama asked.

"He sent it via a friend he met yesterday at the Miła Street headquarters."

"What does he say?"

Tata unfolded the slip and read, "David, I must see you. Meet me at the Miła Street headquarters tomorrow at 11 a.m. I must talk to you about Malka."

Why does he want to talk about me? Worrying thoughts began to swirl in Malka's head.

The following day, Tata left the apartment and headed to the basement to take the secret subterranean passageway to meet Marcel. He was not gone long. Time was short and the executioners near.

When he returned, Malka and her mother met him at the door, their faces pleading to hear the news. Her father understood. They seated themselves, and Tata began. He talked slowly, deliberately, as if he were trying to sort out what to say first, careful not to stir emotions, especially mindful of Malka's feelings. He started by telling them how shattered Marcel was to hear that nearly everyone he knew in the ghetto had been deported.

Mama asked, "Is his family okay? What did he tell you about the manhunt there?"

"He told me briefly that the Germans make their lives miserable. Periodically, they arrest or shoot a few thousand Poles—mostly the intelligentsia, community leaders, and clergy. He said that as horrible as that is, it doesn't compare with the crimes they are committing against the Jewish people. Jadwiga, Piotrek, his mother, and the rest of his family are hanging on. He was quick to cut directly to the chief reason he had to see me. He started by reminding me that I know as well as he does that the next round of deportations is bound to happen any day. Unfortunately, that is a fact."

Tata paused and locked eyes with Malka. In that instant, Malka thought, *I can recognize from the seriousness in his face he's about to say something I don't want to hear.* She held her breath.

"Malka, I want you to listen thoughtfully." His voice was steady, gentle, urgent. "Marcel said—and I agree—there is a single chance left to smuggle you out of the ghetto and save your life."

Malka's heart sank.

"We agreed that we are quickly running out of time. We also agreed to proceed to set the plan into action as we speak."

Tata looked at her pleadingly, reassuring, "What better option do we have, my darling? We want you to live. Mama and I will also fight hard to survive. So will Ben. Now, Marcel and Jadwiga gave your rescue careful thought. You will live with them. Marcel vowed Jadwiga and he will love you like their own child. I believe him and so should you."

"What about Piotrek? Is he happy about his parents' decision to hide a Jew and risk their lives? He'll hate me," Malka declared.

"I asked him about that. Marcel waved that question away. He said, 'As far as Piotrek is concerned, it doesn't require a great deal of imagination to realize that children of Polish underground parents learn quickly to keep family secrets from leaking out. They know their lives hang on being discreet and vigilant.' He assured me that Piotrek understands that none of us is safe as long as Nazi boots tread on our soil. Marcel has no doubt Piotrek will strive to protect you. It may make you feel better to know that Piotrek belongs to the outlawed Polish Boy Scouts."

"So, it is decided?"

"I gave Marcel permission to proceed, immediately, to obtain — through his underground connections — a birth certificate and other essential documents for you. Marcel and I will stay in touch through mutual acquaintances. We will also count on Ben's connections. Of course, you will be informed of every step involved. Mama and I have never kept secrets from you. You have never let us down. You have risen above challenges no young person your age should be subjected to."

"What else did you talk about?"

"I told him I had a premonition he would make this offer and I had thought hard about it, as had Mama. As parents, we could hardly turn it down. Of course, I thanked him profusely. He said, 'When a fellow man is in trouble, you do what you can to help. What's the big deal?'

"Too soon it was time to part. I reminded him he was saving a life. Anyone who saves a life is as if he saved an entire world. 'That's in the Talmud. Yes?' he asked. 'Yes,' I answered. We embraced, and he was gone."

Throughout the discussion, Mama sat quietly, nodding to everything Tata said. Her face was strained, dark circles under her eyes, body tense with an effort to project an optimistic posture. Every now and then she threw in a remark to reassure Malka and bolster her faith in humanity.

Malka went to bed that night feeling as though she were about to be placed on a raft and cast out, alone, on a vast sea.

On January 18, the Nazis began a second wave of deportations in the ghetto. As they had hoped, in enacting their plans to fool the ghetto fighters into believing they were safe for a while, the deportations caught the fighters by surprise.

The instant Nazi columns entered the ghetto, Tata and Ben tucked pistols into their belts in readiness to join the band of fighters. They reminded Malka of the rebel Jewish warriors, the Maccabees.

Before dashing out the door, Tata embraced Mama and Malka and held them close. He implored, "You must be strong. Take care of yourselves. Look out for each other. I love you! I love you!" and he was gone.

Although her grandfather had taught Malka, "There comes a time when one has to submit to death — much like the sun bows to the night and flowers wilt and return to the soil," her heart screamed, threshed with defiance, *Tata must not die! Not yet! Nor am I ready to die! Neither is Mama, nor Ben!*

The instant Tata and Ben were gone, Mama and Malka lifted the secret trapdoor in the kitchen pantry floor and stepped down into the dank bunker. The dismal hideout quickly filled with terrified people. Without much delay, they pulled the trapdoor shut. Malka felt hemmed in. The ceiling pressed down on her; the damp walls marked the end of her horizon.

While Malka and Mama were in the bunker, a band of Jewish fighters — Tata, Ben, Rebecca, and Heniek among them — led by Commander Mordecai Anielewicz slipped into the files of Jews who were marched to the trains. The group waited for a signal from Mordecai, then stepped out of formation and fought the Nazis. The columns of deportees ran for their lives. After four days of repeated losses, the stunned Nazis left the ghetto.

Tata and Ben came home! Malka's gratitude was boundless. She fell into Tata's arms, buried her face in his embrace, felt his beard bristle against her cheek. She was so grateful for his and Ben's lives that it made her promise God to live a virtuous life.

Fear of the consequences for the fighters' heroic achievement, however, was on everyone's mind. Tata cautioned, "We have no illusions that this is the end of the deportations. They will be back with greater force to punish us."

In light of this miserable fact, arrangements for Malka's escape commenced with renewed urgency. The plan was to slip her out of the sub-ghetto the first week in February.

CHAPTER TWENTY-ONE

Never Say More Than What You're Asked

With Marcel's involvement and help from Ben and their underground contacts, the plan to smuggle Malka out of the doomed ghetto was making rapid progress. In her heart, Malka knew her parents' decision had merit. Nevertheless, she felt frightened and angrily obstinate. The thought of not being able to reach her parents and feel the security of their embrace terrified her.

She implored, "It's my life. I don't trust any of them. I'll feel less safe being alone on the Christian side than being here with you."

Mama said, "It's not a choice we want to make. The thought of separating is excruciating for all of us. But we must protect you. Children will be the first victims again."

Ben added, "Be reasonable, Malka. There'll be fierce fighting and bloodshed when the next round of deportations resumes.

You know as well as I that you're too young to fight and you'll only be in the way. You'll best serve the cause by doing what your parents are asking of you. Be sensible."

"How soon must I leave? And how will I get across the wall without getting killed?"

"We must act swiftly before violence erupts. You will be leaving in a little less than two weeks, darling. Ben and Heniek will lead you across. You could not wish for more capable escorts," Tata said.

Malka remained silent.

"This plan should not come as a surprise to you, *kochana*. Ever since we heard about Treblinka, you knew that we were trying to find a way to save you among non-Jews."

"Yes, but I hoped it would never happen. Who will I be, Tata, if I'm no longer myself?"

"That is well taken care of. Marcel has a niece your age. Her name is Kasia Jabkowska. Marcel says you are a dead ringer for her. She is fifteen; she is tall and has auburn hair and green eyes. She lives in a faraway village. You will be given her birth certificate. Be assured that Marcel will have a convincing reason, for anyone who asks, why you — his 'niece' — will live with them."

"What convincing reason can he have?"

"You are coming to live with your uncle, Marcel, because your father died of typhus and your mother is too poor to take care of her children. That, Malka, is very plausible. The Poles beyond the wall are not exempt from poverty, deprivations, and premature death."

Malka didn't need to ask how two different people can have identical birth certificates. It was common knowledge in her family circle that Żegota (the Polish Council to Aid Jews) was forging identity documents for the small number of Jews hiding among Poles.

"I hope I can pull off this fake as convincingly as Ben and Rebecca when they are carrying out missions on the Christian side," Malka worried.

"You will. Necessity will force you. Besides, you're feisty. That's why you're not dead," Ben said.

"I'm not dead because I'm lucky."

"That, too."

Mama's tired voice urged, "We've discussed this enough for now. We'll talk more in the days to come and answer all your questions, Malka. In the meantime, you must believe it is for the best for us all."

In the remaining days, Malka followed her parents around like a shadow, so reluctant to be parting from them.

Mama kept reassuring her, "We must be grateful we know a kind family who is willing to risk their lives to save you."

"One kind family among so many from whom I'll have to hide my true self," Malka said.

"Malkale, you might be surprised to learn that there are other people who are willing to protect their neighbors. Not everyone is a bigot."

"Not everyone, but enough to keep me in perpetual fear."

They spent time going over lists of names of churches, priests, and mysterious relatives who would soon become part of her undercover life. Mama and Tata drilled her patiently and were generous with praise.

"What if I forget or give the wrong answer?"

"You are likely to be asked general questions like what your name is, where do you live, what is the name of your church. Always know these basic answers. Respond politely, say as little as possible, or change the subject. You are clever at doing that," Tata said.

"Doing what?"

"Changing the subject when it is convenient."

Malka smiled.

"Keep in mind," said Mama, "never say more than you are asked. It is never wise to act on fear or suspicion. If you have a reason for concern, stay calm and bring it to Marcel's or Jadwiga's attention."

Tata reassured, "Malkale, you have been tested more harshly than most people many times your age. You beat rough odds against you and proved yourself to be brave and prudent. You have earned the right to trust your common sense and ability to think yourself out of a box when pressed. Above all, my darling, be patient. That is how our people have survived centuries of persecution. Who knows, maybe one day Jews will have their own homeland and will no longer have to run for their lives."

Why do I have to be Jewish? Malka asked herself, not quite sure if she meant it.

She quickly cast out that thought and complained, "I'll be betraying our faith if I pray in a church to a God that isn't mine."

"Your prayers are between your God and you, regardless of where you pray. Besides, we all pray to the same God by different names," Mama said.

The final days with her parents passed like precious gifts threatened by an impending catastrophe. With melancholy, Malka gazed out of windows and watched drifts of snow drape over her desolate world. The vacant buildings looked like unused furniture covered with white sheets. She caressed trinkets and souvenirs reminding her of people and places that no longer existed.

Sometimes, she stood in front of the mirror trying to imagine herself looking Christian. She patted her wavy hair flat to her scalp and plaited it into braids to hide her curls. A scatter of disobedient hair tendrils always got loose.

She murmured in her head: *In just a few days, I'll vanish just like the days I'm counting down. I'll become a different person, with a different name, hiding my true self in my heart.*

She prayed: *Dear God, don't separate me from Mama, Tata, and Ben for long. Above all, keep them safe. They are all I have left in this world. I'll do anything: I'll give up my arms and legs to be with them again.*

Her parents went over last-minute instructions with Malka. Tata said, "When you cross the wall with Ben and Heniek, you'll take with you only what you will be wearing. Nothing else, darling."

Aghast, Malka asked, "Only what I'll have on? You mean I'll wear the same clothes every day? I'll stink!"

"Of course not, Malkale," Mama said. "Jadwiga and Marcel will make sure you have everything you need. Although they did not expect it, we sent money to them with Ben. It is meant for your use."

"What about pictures of you, Tata, Grandma, Grandpa, Hanna, and Ben? I can hide them under the lining of my shoes or in my clothes." She confided, "Sometimes I remember Grandpa, Grandma, and Hanna's faces as clear as glass. Other times they're opaque. I'm afraid they'll fade from my memory entirely; then I'll have nothing left of them."

"You will not forget them, but we understand. We will find a way for you to take a few photos. Mind you, sweetheart, just a few," Tata said.

Malka didn't argue. She understood that too many photos might provoke questions and lead to trouble.

"You will wear your warmest wool sweater, hat, scarf, and long stockings I have knitted for you. They will serve you well for a long while," Mama said.

To get the knitting yarn for Malka, Mama unraveled her own sweaters, then spent hours knitting in front of the blinking carbide lantern.

"And you'll wear your high boots. You're lucky to own them." Laced high boots, new or secondhand, were highly valued in the ghetto. Few could afford them.

"And your warm coat. I just lengthened it for you."

Malka's warm maroon coat was not too bad. The material for it came from Mama's beautiful prewar coat. It had been recut and resewn to fit Malka. It had a wide hem so it could be made longer when she grew. Although the coat had been lengthened once — and had a permanent crease circling above the entire hem — it still looked good. She did not need to fear it would betray typical ghetto poverty.

CHAPTER TWENTY-TWO

Running out of Minutes

A blackout cloaked the sub-ghetto when Ben and Heniek came from the Miła Street headquarters to begin the process of taking Malka across the wall. They had three days to prepare her for her flight from the ghetto.

The following morning, they gathered in the kitchen to go over the perilous escape steps. Mama and Tata placed their chairs protectively close to Malka. Their faces were tight with anguish. Malka sat in silent turmoil. Part of her wanted to plead, "Let me stay with you, even if it means Treblinka." A stronger part understood that she must try to fulfill their hopes for her survival. She drew herself up, like a soldier in battle, and stayed focused.

Heniek was the first to speak.

"Malka, keep in mind that Ben and I know the underground route like our own pockets. Just follow us and pay close attention. You'll be surprised how quickly you'll be on streets where people aren't gathered up to be loaded onto trains to Treblinka.

Get everything ready over the next two days, including telling your parents all that you want to tell them. The day of departure, we'll rise early, get dressed, and have a bite of food. Then we'll slip out of the apartment, as silently as mice. I'm counting on you to do it swiftly, bravely, and without tears or drama."

"Don't worry," Malka said. "I understand. I've been in dangerous spots before. I can handle it. Go on." That bit of feedback was mostly to reassure her parents and to bolster her own courage.

"Good. Our first step will be making our way through the basement maze. I'm sure you're at least a little familiar with this netherworld. I suspect you stick your head in there to escape boredom."

That was true. The few remaining children concealed in the ghetto played in secret places hidden from the sun and the sky. God forbid they would be seen alive by a Nazi soldier.

"When we reach Zamenhofa Street," Heniek continued, "we'll step out of the basement. We'll stay low, remain calm, and move swiftly without being noticed. We'll walk less than one street block, enter the sewer, and exit on the Christian side. When we step out of the sewer, a milk delivery truck driven by a Polish underground friend will pull up. We'll hop in and be off before anyone takes note. You'll be dropped off at the Jabkowskis' house on Dobra Street. Ben and I will stay in the truck to carry out a brief mission for our fighters, then sashay back home."

Heniek winked at her and said, "Courage! At this very moment, as we speak, the Allies are coming after the Nazis from all sides of the continent and whipping their asses. I have this information from a reliable source. Soon, you'll see the Nazis running in defeat and shame."

"What will we do if your Polish underground friend isn't there to meet us?" Malka asked.

"Not to worry, he'll be there. Fighters don't fail to show up. Besides, Ben and I always have a backup plan to deal with the unexpected."

Ben's short instructions followed. His words became her commandments and shield.

"Malka, you'll teach yourself to stay cool at all times. Walk with the confidence of someone who belongs there. Always mind your own business and don't call attention to yourself. If somebody tries to pick on you, act bold, even arrogant. You're very capable of outsmarting any tough fool. I know you well."

"Ben, will you come to see me when you're on a courier mission on the other side? Please, even if only for a single second. I'll be dying to see you and to know if Mama and Tata are all right."

"I can't promise that. I don't go there for visitations, you know. I'll try to pop in. But, for God's sake, don't waste your time looking out the window or watching the door for me. It might take 'til the end of the war."

Then Mama stepped in with her parting message. Her voice and face betrayed strain.

"*Ketzeleh*, you must allow yourself to enjoy all the freedoms that will be available to you there. Know that it is what Tata and I wish for you. It will be a mitzvah. Remember to take good care of yourself and eat. You must eat to stay strong and grow. Make sure to clean up after yourself. Be polite and helpful to your new family."

As usual, Tata gave a strong and encouraging message.

"I know, darling, that you are smart beyond your years. You will use common sense and keep yourself safe. We'll do the same. Stay patient, my darling. Hold on to that which is best and kindest in you and you will always be all right. Patience to endure has helped the Jewish people survive tyrants, and continue, and renew.

"Remember our Saturday walks in Saxon Garden, Łazienki Park, and Marszałkowska Street? The places will quickly become familiar to you. Permit yourself to enjoy the freedom to walk there, but with discretion, of course, and Marcel's or Jadwiga's approval."

"Tata, you needn't worry about me. I remember our Saturday walks. Be assured that the streets are vivid in my mind. I'll find my way, even with my eyes closed. I'll use discretion — but I don't want to do it without you and Mama. I'd still rather stay with you, even if it might mean death."

Tata shuddered; his eyes glowed with love. He pleaded, "No, no! You must live!"

The final evening, they huddled around the kindling stove in the kitchen. In Malka's mind their tiny room was a capsule of paradise isolating them from the hostile world. She wished for the night to last forever.

They talked in whispers and said words intended to protect and caress:

"Don't worry about me. I'll be all right. I can take it."

"Stay strong. Take good care of yourself. Don't give up."

The world was quickly running out of minutes. The last thing Malka remembered of the parting night was placing her head in Mama's lap, holding on to Tata's hand, and resolving to stay awake the entire night and remain conscious of her parents' presence; but sleep betrayed her.

And so, the last night with her parents in the ghetto ended. Tata must have carried her to her bed, because that is where she woke up the morning of her escape.

CHAPTER TWENTY-THREE

Escape

A warm kiss on her cheek shook Malka out of her sleep. She struggled to a sitting position and stared into the fading darkness.

"I'm sorry we startled you, darling. It's only Mama and me."

Tata embraced her and held her close. He whispered, "It is time to get up, sweetheart. This is a very important day."

Malka clung to her father, her head pressed to his torso. How would she exist without him? She held on to his embrace to immortalize it in her mind. Tata made a brave effort to keep his shoulders straight, but they buckled just enough for Malka to notice him pushing back tears. She had never seen her father cry. Mama's face was pale as paste. Purple pouches under her eyes gave her the appearance of an owl.

Ben and Heniek poked their heads around the doorframe, firing commands.

"Up, up, up, Malka. We have a date. Time is not waiting. Gotta get going!"

"Okay, give me time to get dressed."

Ben blew her a kiss. If the two smugglers felt any fear of what lay ahead that day, they hid it well. Their faces were bold, their stride jaunty. Malka thought: *Their bravado is their way to pump up courage before wrangling with death.*

The rest of that morning was a blur of putting on warm clothes Mama laid out for Malka on her bed; making a futile attempt to swallow a bite of food; holding back tears and shaking as if a hurricane were sweeping through her body. Then, last hugs and whispers, beseeching, "Be brave! Endure! I love you! I love you!!!"

In one devastating instant, Malka turned to follow Ben and Heniek out of the apartment, leaving her parents standing in the doorway, their desperate eyes locked onto her, unwilling to let her out of their sight.

How tragically powerless love seemed to Malka at that moment! What was love when measured against Nazi brutality?

With all their senses focused on not getting caught, the three "criminals" walked down a dim flight of stairs, into the basement and an uneasy silence.

Malka followed her leaders through the subterranean maze created by the ghetto fighters. Like rodents, they crawled through holes in basement walls between buildings and crude tunnels underneath street crossings. She quickly lost her sense of orientation and had no notion where they were heading. Heniek and Ben, however, read each twist and turn like street signs.

No hint of human life stirred, just the sounds of groaning beams and mice darting in dark corners. In the distance, stray dogs howled and made Malka think of German Shepherds following their trail.

After a short eternity of blood-chilling progress, the boys stopped. Heniek said, "Malka, we'll leave the basement now, walk one block, then enter the sewer on Zamenhofa Street. We'll exit on Prosta Street, just outside the ghetto. We must be quick, alert, and unseen."

With Heniek in the lead and Ben behind her to provide cover, Malka walked out of the underground labyrinth, up a flight of stairs, and across a deserted ghetto courtyard. All three paused, checked the coast, and stepped into a lifeless planet crisscrossed by rows of vacant buildings under a white shroud of snow. The silence was endless and terrifying, the sky the color of ash.

Halfway to the sewer, both boys came to an abrupt stop. The concentration on their faces told Malka, *They hear danger!* She heard nothing but silence crawling all around.

In a mere minute, what initially sounded like puffing wind gusts transformed into an apocalyptic purring of a car engine drawing ever closer. Ben flung open the nearest courtyard gate and they bolted into an abandoned building.

"They'll see our footprints in the snow! No?" Malka asked.

"If they do, we'll be far from this point. We know our way under the city; they don't. Furthermore, they are too afraid to stick their heads into the jungle of empty buildings. They have safer ways of killing us," Ben said.

Malka followed the boys up a flight of stairs into an apartment as ghoulishly silent as the rest of the deported area. Careful not to be spotted, they hunched below a windowsill and peered over the ledge. A shiny black Mercedes emerged on the horizon, rolled toward them, then stopped half a block away.

That will be the end of us! Malka was sure.

Four ostentatiously decked-out SS men hopped out of the car. They took a few steps to stare in all directions of the inert horizon, like proprietors checking out their holdings. Their laughter crackled and popped like logs in a fireplace. When they had their fill of this morbid sport, they stepped back into their Mercedes and drove off, leaving behind a deafening silence.

"How much longer will our luck hold out?" Malka asked.

"A few more moves and we'll be on the Christian side," Heniek said.

"This escape is even scarier than life in the ghetto."

"The last punishment is always the worst. You saw more disturbing things in the ghetto every day, Malka," Ben reminded her. "You'll be better off on the other side."

"Okay, guys, here we go. Half a block to the manhole," Heniek said.

They slipped out of the building and crept forward like convicts breaking out of prison. When they reached the manhole,

Heniek stooped, lifted the lid, and climbed down metal rungs into the sewer. Malka followed. Ben, the sweep, pulled the cover shut.

The boys switched on their flashlights and led Malka through the pitch-black grid of passageways as if they had maps implanted in their heads. Echoes of dripping water, squeals of rats, and indecipherable muffled sounds made Malka's bones quiver. Too frightened to panic, she remained completely focused on survival.

They reached the manhole on Prosta Street. Malka braced herself for the last and scariest part: stepping into the Christian sector without getting killed in the process. Not an easy feat. Two young men climbing out of a manhole would not be unusual. But a girl following them out? Her heart sank at the thought.

She summoned Heniek's instructions to her head: "Move fast as the devil . . . half a second can make the difference between life and death . . . if you spot a Nazi, you must disappear before he collects his wits and reaches for his gun . . . do it calmly and swiftly." *Ha!*

Heniek lifted the manhole cover a crack to check if it were safe to step out. He nodded and they filed out into a bustling street in the same order as they had entered: Heniek, Malka, Ben. Two armed Nazis cruised no further than a block away. In a flash, a milk delivery truck pulled up. The three fugitives hopped in and sped away, leaving a trail of puzzled faces behind them.

Before Malka was able to absorb the rapid progression of scenes, the milk truck slowed down at the Jabkowskis' address, 25 Dobra Street. Ben and Heniek nudged Malka out of the truck and said, *"Do widzenia.* You're here, home. Jadwiga will meet you in front of her house. Go!"

The driver pushed down on the accelerator and the truck took off.

For an instant, Malka remained standing at the curb, stunned. Her first impulse was to run after the truck and shout, "Stop! Stop! I want to go with you! Ben, Heniek! I didn't even say goodbye!" Instead, she took a deep breath, tried to make herself inconspicuous, and let her eyes dart to the left and to the right to orient herself. The vitality of life came at her with jarring suddenness. The street thronged with people. Laughter and the shouts of children playing rang from all directions. How frightfully lost and unsafe she felt. How envious of the pedestrians' confident stride. *They must be walking home,* she thought longingly.

Then she heard a soft call floating toward her like a life jacket thrown to one who is drowning: "Kasia. Come here, Kasia."

It dawned on her: *I'm Kasia. That's me now.*

She turned her head to the left and recognized Jadwiga — now her Aunt Jadwiga — standing in front of a building. Her arms reached out to greet Kasia. The girl thought, *I'm no longer Malka, my true self.*

PART TWO

The Other Side of the Wall

All the ideals and principles which we profess
have only such value as we impart to them
by our personal life.

Janusz Korczak

CHAPTER TWENTY-FOUR

A World of the Living

2 5 Dobra Street stood in a row of neoclassic residential buildings with tall windows. Despite the lingering war scars of
neglect and confrontation — such as peeling paint and shrapnel gashes — an aura of elegance still veiled the street. If you
glanced at the directory posted at the side of the entrance gate,
you would observe that many tenants were professionals.

You entered through a domed area. Ahead was a rectangular courtyard surrounded by four intersecting apartment wings,
each three stories high. In the center sat a small flowerbed with
a lilac tree making the open space inviting. The Jabkowskis
lived in the front wing, on the second floor.

"So happy you are safe, Kasieńka," Jadwiga whispered and
led Kasia into the courtyard.

Kasia caught her breath. Memories of prewar visits clashed
with her macabre escape scenes and the insecurity of being in
a Christian courtyard. She was startled by the sounds spilling out of windows — clangs of dishes, a dog barking, a child

crying — pulling her into a momentary state of unreality and yearning. For an instant, Kasia heard in her head Grandpa Isaak's, Hanna's, and her neighbors' voices rise above the medley of the courtyard sounds. She thought: *It's just like it used to be on Karmelicka Street before the war and before the deportations.*

It took a bit of steel to balance the blizzard of memories and longings swirling in her head, against the uselessness of self-pity when you have only yourself to count on. Kasia quickly found a firm foothold to keep her from keeling over. Jadwiga read her face, clasped her hand, and steadied her like a banister blocking an abyss.

They walked into the lobby and up a flight of stairs. The instant Kasia stepped on the second-floor landing, she heard a door creak open. It came from the right side — as she expected. She looked over and saw Tata's old friend, Marcel, peering out of a half-open door. All her yesterdays rushed back.

Marcel ushered them in, shut the door behind them, and scooped Kasia up in his strong, reassuring arms. "I am so glad you are here."

Tears ran down Kasia's face. She was not sure if she was crying with gratitude or from despair.

He looked and looked at her. "How much you have grown since I last saw you, Mal . . ." He started to say her real name, hesitated, smiled, and corrected himself, "Kasieńka. How much suffering you have endured. You will be safe with us, darling. We will make sure."

His kindness nearly broke Kasia into a million pieces. She wasn't used to hearing it from non-Jews.

She stared at him for a long moment, thinking, *He's the same as I remember, except a little different.* There were wrinkles on his face now where there had been none. As before, his countenance inspired trust, but he seemed sadder than she remembered.

And there was Piotrek standing at his father's side waiting for his turn to welcome her. She could hardly recognize him. How tall he had grown! How handsome and athletic looking! No longer the same little boy she remembered. His once rounded cheeks were now chiseled into angles. Wide shoulders filled out his shirt. His voice was raspy. He had Jadwiga's confident clear blue eyes and her silky dark blond hair casually falling over his forehead. How different he looked from the boys in the ghetto. Although most were handsome and self-assured, none had Piotrek's prewar scrubbed and carefree appearance.

He looked at her with a measuring eye. Then he hugged her and said, "I'm glad you are here, Kasia."

Will he forgive me for the danger I am bringing to his family? she worried.

Kasia sensed Piotrek was regarding her with a mixture of fascination and dread, as if she stepped out of the past with grave ghosts. She tried hard to hide her sadness, to conceal how awkward and forlorn she felt, to look pretty and likeable.

Marcel took her coat and looked around to see if there was anything else he could take off her hands.

Does he think I would have carried a suitcase? she wondered.

"I didn't bring anything else, Uncle Marcel. Just a few photos I hid in my pocket. But they'll not reveal my religion," she said, fearful of having to give them up.

"That's okay, kochana. I am glad you snuck the photos in."

Her hosts fussed, trying to make her feel at home. After Kasia washed the dust and grime off her face and coaxed her hair into looking neater, Piotrek offered, "I'll show you your room real quick while Mama is putting food on the table. You must be hungry."

"I am."

A beam of sunlight bursting in through a tall window welcomed her when she entered "her" room. It was small and cozy. A bed with a light-green bedcover stood against a side wall. She could barely resist falling into its softness. All the furniture was a monochrome of white: the bed frame, the wardrobe standing against another wall, and the rocking chair tucked in a corner. A portrait of a *gural* (Carpathian mountaineer) in a bright regional costume looked down at her from a wall above her bed. A white nightstand with a pale-blue lamp on top stood at the side of the bed.

The kindness of her hosts and the serenity of their home were so thinly separated from her despair. She closed her eyes and prayed: *Mama, Tata, if only you were here with me. If at least I could let you know that I'm okay, that you mustn't worry about me. I miss you and worry for your lives, beyond words. Dear God, keep them alive! Please, and I'll ask for nothing else.*

Piotrek waited patiently while Kasia was lost in thought. Then he asked, "Do you like your room?"

"Oh, yes, I do! Thank you."

"I'll show you my room. It's right next to yours."

She liked his room the moment she entered. It revealed much about Piotrek. She took note of the scatter of books on the night table beside his bed, a record player standing in a corner under the window, and walls covered with sports car drawings. She glanced at every item as if she were running her togue around them. Everything in the room revealed a teenager's interests. She felt a sharp pang of envy.

"I'll play my favorite records for you after you get some rest. Feel free to listen to them whenever you like," he offered.

"Thank you. I haven't heard music for a long time. Are you allowed to have books and records?"

"No, we aren't. But everyone does it anyway. The Krauts make laws, and we break them."

"I understand. Before the deportations, we also broke their laws, regardless of cost. And still do."

Kasia's head was swimming. The whole world was wobbling. She struggled to keep her composure.

Piotrek asked, "Are you very tired?"

"Yes, very, but I can handle it."

"I imagine you worry about your parents. They'll be all right. They are very brave and smart."

"That's not enough, Piotrek. Smart and brave people don't land on top these days."

"No. But their courage is admirable."

"Thank you."

He smiled and said, "Let's go to the dining room and take the edge off your hunger."

She stepped out of Piotrek's room with a sense of gratitude that Piotrek was yielding to his kind instinct to accept her presence in his house despite the danger she posed.

A grandfather clock chimed two o'clock in a comfortingly familiar way. Five hours had passed since Kasia had left her parents. They were a stone's throw away, yet as remote as the moon. Feeling her knees buckle under her, she let herself sink into a chair. The dining room, more than the rest of the house, made Kasia feel like she was hallucinating — the past peered out at her from all corners and collided, mercilessly, with the present. Distant echoes of joyful laughter mingled with present despair.

Although much in the room remained as it had once been, the dreariness of occupation was noticeable in every corner. The paint on the walls was faded. The ornate moldings and high ceiling no longer looked as snow-white as she remembered them to be. An attractive painting was gone from one wall, leaving a faded rectangle staring down at her. More than anything, she mourned the absence of people who should have been there with them, and the lack of the very lightness of freedom she once took for granted.

She sat knotted up in memories, beholden to her hosts, self-conscious, and, above all, worried about her parents and her own safety. The fright she felt while sneaking across the wall still gnawed at her. A bowl of hot beet soup was placed in front of her. Bread sufficient for all sat in the center of the table. Meatballs and potatoes followed, and compote for dessert. Kasia was very hungry, and hunger is a powerful distractor. Her eyelids were drooping and her heart was heavy, but she polished off every crumb on her plate. Then, although night was hours away, she went to "her" room and fell into "her" bed.

She sank into a long, fitful sleep: tossing and turning, meandering in and out of the sub-ghetto, and landing in front of her apartment door. She heard Mama, Tata, and Ben carrying on an amiable conversation behind the door. She knocked and called out, "It's me, Malka. Open the door! I want to come in. I want to be with you. Please!" They paid her no heed.

She saw them clearly through the wall, sitting around the table, bent toward each other and talking. No matter how hard she pounded and pleaded, they continued to ignore her. They didn't want to have anything to do with her. Malka felt devastated by their rejection.

She may have cried out in her sleep, she couldn't remember. But at an agonizing moment, a door opened and a pale shaft of light rolled into her room. Marcel walked softly along that carpet of light and sat down at the edge of her bed. He bent over, stroked her hair, and whispered shushing sounds, just like Tata used to do when she was a little girl afraid of the dark. Marcel stayed just long enough for her to find a peaceful corner within herself. Then he tiptoed out. His kindness lingered.

CHAPTER TWENTY-FIVE

No One Guessed

A tap on the door and a soft voice shook Kasia out of her tormented sleep.

"Kasia, are you ready to join us for breakfast, kochana?"

It took Kasia a few seconds to shake off her ghoulish nightmares and remember where she was.

"Can I come in?" Jadwiga asked gently.

"Yes, please."

Aunt Jadwiga entered, placed a handful of fresh clothes on the rocking chair, and turned to her "niece."

"*Dzień dobry.* Look what I have here for you." She held up each item, one at a time, and enumerated, "Long stockings to keep you warm; underwear; and a pretty dress." She waved a dark blue, long-sleeved dress with tiny white dots before her. "You'll look lovely in it."

"Thank you, Aunt Jadwiga."

"I'll leave to let you get dressed. Marcel and Piotrek want to have breakfast with you before they leave the house."

Although Kasia was still disoriented and scared, she was nonetheless eager to confront the inevitable ogres on this side of the wall. She felt as David must have felt when he was facing Goliath. She hopped out of bed, rushed to wash up, slipped into her fresh clothes, and glanced at herself in the mirror with a critical eye. She determined that the dress was a little too big. Then she shrugged: *I'll grow into it.* She smoothed it down as straight as possible and then hurried to join her protectors at the kitchen table.

Marcel was first to greet her.

"Dzień dobry, Kasieńka. How are you this morning?"

"I'm fine, Uncle Marcel, thank you."

"I think you had a bad dream last night."

"I did. I dreamt about my parents and Ben. I saw them right through our apartment wall. They were sitting around a table carrying on a friendly conversation. I knocked on the door and pleaded with them to let me in, but they ignored me completely. They did not want to have anything to do with me."

"That must have been tough. You know, in reality, they want you to be where you are now, and stay safe."

"I know."

Piotrek was next to greet her.

"*Servus*, Kasia. I missed you at supper last night." To lighten the mood, he added, "I wanted to eat the doughnut Dad brought for you, but Mom wouldn't let me. It's waiting on the table for you."

They shared a breakfast of soft-boiled eggs, rationed bread, jam, and milk. The milk was slightly watered down, but that didn't hurt anyone. The kitchen murmured with soft conversation about the day's routine. Kasia paid close attention to every word for clues about what to expect and how to respond to the mysteries ahead. Everything was so different from the hell her parents made her escape.

Before long, Marcel and Piotrek were heading for the door. Piotrek said, "See you later, Kasia. We'll listen to my records after I get my homework done."

She looked up at the clock on the shelf and began to count the hours for him to come home. With the men gone, the home felt empty and very quiet.

A cacophony of nearly forgotten city sounds rising from the street caught Kasia's attention. She walked to the window, pressed her head against the windowpane, and watched streams of pedestrians, clip-clopping doroszkas, and cars passing by. An irresistible urge to fly out the door and into the freedom, run to places where grass and poplar trees grew and the air tingled with laughter, tugged at her. But she didn't move. She remained glued to the window until the clink of teacups broke her reveries.

"Tea," Jadwiga announced as she entered the room.

Kasia joined Jadwiga on the couch. The sun streamed in through the windows. The room felt peaceful. The warmth of Jadwiga's voice comforted her.

"I know you miss your parents, Kasia, but it is best that you are here. You will be safe with us."

"Will I have to stay out of sight, hiding in a secluded room like a leper?"

"We hope not. Your chances to pass as one of us are very good. Hiding in a closet would be a last resort."

"What makes my chances so good?"

"You must realize there are many orphans here. Like you, they live with their relatives, or in orphanages. What's more, you look like the real Kasia. If it will make you feel better, there are a number of Jewish girls who are passing as Christians. The important trick is to acquire mannerisms characteristic of Polish Christians."

"Are my manners not Polish enough?"

"Your manners are just fine, but it will be helpful for you to know what girls on this side of the wall typically talk about, how they dress, what they value and worry about, and what makes them laugh. You don't have to give up your individuality, but you need to be smart about it."

"How can I change to fit the Christian stereotype?"

"Not to worry. I have a good friend who is a pro at teaching Jewish girls to act as typical girls here do. You will enjoy meeting her."

The following morning the doorbell rang, and a new angel stepped into Kasia's life. She was tall, dark haired, and charismatic. She was also a stage actress and an active member of Żegota. Her name was Irena Wiszniowska.

Irena was a genius mimic. She didn't waste time lecturing. She simply acted out conversations between individuals and you knew, immediately, to what ethnic or social group each one belonged. She made it obvious by the choice of words, topics of conversation, and body language — especially lively hand gestures as contrasted with restrained movement. She delighted Kasia by engaging her in mock conversations.

Irena was brutal when Kasia let a word, tone, or gesture mar her Christian persona. The instant the girl's choice of a word or intonation betrayed a "wrong" cultural identity, or her body language suggested an effort to hide fear, Irena would stop and help her get a clearer image of how she should present herself. Kasia trusted her pedantic criticism. She accepted it as a gift. In a remarkably short time, Irena had drilled Kasia pitilessly to perfection. Kasia felt greatly indebted to this brave woman for reinforcing her faith in humanity at a time when she needed it as much as air itself.

After five days of intense coaching with Irena, Jadwiga announced, "Kasia, it's time to let the neighborhood meet my niece. The sooner, the better."

"How will they meet me?"

"First, we will take a short walk to the police station to register your residency with us."

"Police station!" Kasia's heart sank. "Why do we have to go there? I don't trust them, Aunt Jadwiga!"

"No need to panic. It is unavoidable. Everyone here has to register with the local police, even if you only stay overnight. Once we have this behind us, your existence as Kasia will be official. Next, we'll go to the bakery and dairy to get fresh bread and cheese for *kolacja*. This will give the storekeepers a chance to get used to seeing you around. I have no doubt you will charm them. Irena brought out the real Kasia in you."

"What will you say about me?"

"Mostly, 'Meet my niece, Kasia.' If people ask questions — which they may — I will tell them just that you are staying with us. I will share a few suitable fragments of your unfortunate story. I am sure you know it by heart."

"I do."

"Of course, if we run into a neighbor or a friend on the way, I will introduce you appropriately."

"Of course," Kasia answered and wondered: *How will I ever convince anyone that I'm the girl I'm not — nor have ever met in my life?*

With that, Jadwiga stood up, and Kasia went to her room to get ready for her first act as an imposter. Standing on the precipice of death was not new to her, but one never gets used to confronting imminent danger. She laced up her high boots, wrapped herself in the wool scarf and hat Mama had knitted for her, and slipped on her coat.

All buttoned up, Kasia returned to the living room where Jadwiga was waiting for her. She observed: *How elegant and confident Jadwiga looks in her simple black coat and wool hat pulled over her hair. She's a vision of a kind no longer existing on the other side of the wall.*

Out the door and down the stairs they went. Kasia's heart hammered in her chest. Arm in arm, they stepped into the street. Everything looked brighter than on the day she had arrived. A layer of snow still covered the city, but it was soft and turned into slush under her boots. A hint of gold was in the air. The promise of spring stirred inside her. She marveled, *My God, so many people in one place, and no one looks scared.*

Nothing escaped her notice. *How clean the streets are! In the sub-ghetto, they are littered and smelly, and the buildings are as lifeless as graves.*

The farther she walked without raising suspicion, the less afraid she felt. Much to her relief, she didn't stand out in her ghetto coat and boots. Many well-worn coats passed by her. But everyone looked neat, and so did she. Before she left the house, she made sure her hair was properly combed. Her biggest challenge, by far, was not to run for cover when she saw armed German soldiers strutting in the streets alongside pedestrians.

Suddenly, Jadwiga squeezed Kasia's arm and pointed to a building ahead. "We are almost at the police station. No worries, everything they need to know is in your documents, here in my hand. They will ask a few simple questions only. You know the answers by heart. We will be out of there, and smiling, in no time."

"Dzień dobry," Jadwiga said fearlessly as they entered. Kasia repeated the greeting, dry-mouthed, and curtsied.

A cold, official "Dzień dobry" sounded from a voice behind a window counter. Jadwiga stated, with utmost confidence, the reason for their visit and placed Kasia's documents in front of the uniform. The official glanced up. His interrogating eyes pierced into Kasia's. He flipped through the documents, then looked at her again. Kasia's gut churned with terror. *Does he know my secret?*

A few questions followed: "What's your name? Why are you staying with your aunt? Where did you live before?"

She answered without hesitation, mindful to look respectful and unafraid. Apparently, he did not detect her dread, because a few moments later he was pounding her document with an official stamp, validating it — and they were out the door. Unharmed!

They walked along with impassive faces, not uttering a word. When they felt they had walked far enough to allay suspicion, they stopped to hug. Jadwiga chirped with relief, "You were great! Not at all to be suspected! Wait until I tell Marcel and Piotrek. They will be so proud of you."

Kasia didn't know why she deserved such high praise; her heart was in her throat and ready to splatter on the sidewalk.

With a somewhat lighter stride they headed to the bakery. On the way, Kasia saw people hopping on trams and going wherever they pleased. *I can do the same!* she reminded herself with anticipation. Immediately, guilt clawed at her. *God, am I selfish to dream of tram rides when Mama, Tata, and Ben are in such danger behind the wall?*

She gawked at displays in store windows. Of course, they were far more modest than before the war. There were a few fancy items, but they were still not as expensive as things on the black market in the ghetto before the deportations. In the ghetto, all the stores had been shuttered.

Jadwiga interrupted Kasia's thoughts.

"Kasieńka, we'll enter the bakery in a moment."

A shiver of fear, then composure, and they were in the store.

"Dzień dobry," said Jadwiga.

"Dzień dobry, Pani Jabkowska," echoed the storekeeper.

"Dzień dobry," Kasia said and waited for the next prompt.

Jadwiga draped an arm around Kasia's shoulders and introduced her to the baker's wife. "This is my niece, Kasia. Do you remember her?"

"Oh, yes. Of course, I remember her well."

She turned her rosy, plump face to Kasia and said with wonder, "Dzień dobry, Kasia! You've grown so much. You used to come to the store before the war. You always asked for a slice of cream torte. Right?"

A slice of cream torte was exactly what Kasia always ordered at the patisserie after a Saturday stroll with Tata in the park. It was easy to agree. "Oh, yes! I love cream torte!"

"Unfortunately, we no longer carry it," the storekeeper mourned. "The Nazi swine confiscate most of our grain. Our assortment shrinks with every new day!"

Even here, not everything is really all right, Kasia noted.

Suddenly, a customer's voice hit Kasia like a bullet. "Did you hear? Some scoundrel was caught for hiding a Żyd! He did this with complete disregard for the consequences to his neighbors."

Another customer responded, "It's unconscionable how some people try to protect them. If you ask me, I say, good riddance."

Kasia's face remained expressionless — although a silent scream of sorrow tore at her.

Jadwiga made her purchase and they left.

"I am so sorry about what you heard in there. Unfortunately, you will witness more such bigotry. Should we go home now?"

"No. Things will be the same tomorrow. We might as well continue."

"I am afraid you are right."

Resigned to the ugly reality of that time and the cruelty human beings are capable of, they stepped into the dairy shop.

Jadwiga introduced her, "My niece, Kasia. I'm sure you remember her."

The storekeeper, another rotund, pink-cheeked woman, looked at Kasia with a welcoming smile. She said reminiscently, "Yes, of course. I remember you walking into my store in your pretty red holiday dress and a white ribbon tied in your hair. That was long ago when Poland was free and life was beautiful. You're just as lovely now, but so grown up."

Kasia smiled. Her grin was genuine and came from a feeling of reprieve. She was thinking, *I'm so lucky people can be easily fooled. At least sometimes.*

When the lady asked about her parents, Kasia provided an answer based on her cover-up script. The woman shook her head with sympathy and gave Kasia a slice of cheese.

With groceries dangling from their arms, Jadwiga and Kasia left the store, stepped onto the slushy snow, and were on their way back "home." Kasia reflected with relief, *So many interactions, and no one guessed that I'm Jewish.* Her gratitude was not free of bitter indignation. She mourned, *God, I too am your child. Why must I hide who I am? Why must I fear my neighbors like death?*

Kasia was glad to be on her way to the house with people she was quickly learning to love. As her ghetto boots squished in the melting snow, she reflected fervently: *Mama, Tata, I miss you, beyond all the good things you made possible for me on this side of the wall. If only I could let you know how kind our friends are to me, that I'm free to walk wherever I want — more or less. More than anything in the world, I want to be with you.* Then she prayed: *Please, God, keep them alive.*

CHAPTER TWENTY-SIX

The Best Part of an Afternoon

K asia entered the house, shut the door behind her, and felt like a bird gone astray returning to the safety of a nest. She sat down on the overstuffed, gold-colored living room chair and considered the absurdity of her existence. Nothing made sense: not the voile window curtains fluttering gently in the breeze; not the elegant oriental rug where her feet were resting; not the armed Nazi soldiers cruising the streets; above all, not the raging brutality existing so close to kindness.

Trapped in the incongruity of her present state, she surrendered to the peace that came over her in this gentle household. Jadwiga served bread and cheese. It tasted like heaven. Her kindness was swaddling. They talked about the morning walk and coming tomorrows.

Kasia asked, "Aren't people afraid of German soldiers marching in the streets?"

"Yes, they are."

"But they didn't hurt anyone, that I saw."

"Nevertheless, the soldiers are armed, and everyone knows they are being watched."

"Your stores are open, people walk freely wherever they wish, and no one gets killed for being Polish."

"They don't kill us en masse as they do in the ghetto, but they kill the best of us. They arrest our poets, educators, artists, priests, and leaders. They send them to concentration camps or shoot them on the spot. They are afraid of smart people and of the light of knowledge."

They talked until the sun grew pale, and Jadwiga said, "I'd better get dinner ready before the men come home."

Kasia loved helping Jadwiga in the kitchen. The bubbling sounds of pots on the stovetop and spicy aromas wafting in the air reminded her of the coziness of home. Just like Mama, Jadwiga was a master at making scrumptious meals with paltry portions and meager choices of available ingredients. Food and coal were growing scarce. Shortages were especially bad during the winter months. The Nazis confiscated most of what had been harvested in the fall.

Soon, the front door flew open and Piotrek burst into the house, filling every corner with his presence.

"Servus, Mama! Servus, Kasia!" His voice bounced off the walls and made the house smile.

A peck on Jadwiga's and Kasia's cheeks and a flood of questions: "Kasia, what did you do today? What do we have for dinner, Mama? When do we eat?" He chattered as he was raising lids off piping hot pots. Fragrant steam curls lifted up to the ceiling.

The front door opened again, and crisp foot taps on the polished parquet floor brought Marcel into the kitchen. His arrival, the mere height of his frame — like a distant whiff of Tata's presence — filled Kasia with a sense of safety.

"I can't wait to hear how your morning went, Kasieńka and Jadwiga."

"We will tell you everything after you wash your hands and we sit down at the table," Jadwiga said.

Unlike the first afternoon at the dinner table, when she nearly passed out with exhaustion, this time Kasia was wide awake. What's more, she had a successful morning experience as an impersonator to relive.

Jadwiga started the conversation. "You should have seen how clever Kasia was at the police station! She looked straight into the officer's icy face and answered every question without batting an eye." Not leaving out a single detail, Jadwiga continued to share how they fooled the storekeepers into believing she was the real Kasia. Piotrek and Marcel hung on every word. Kasia was too embarrassed to add anything, although she enjoyed the praise.

When pressed for her version of the morning's events, Kasia said, "All I did was try to stay alive. When I was afraid of being found out, I thought of how Ben, Rebecca, and Heniek would have acted if they were in my place. I repeated in my head the instructions they gave me, 'Don't let fear give you away. Act bold.'

"Mostly, I copied you, Aunt Jadwiga. I looked at you and tried to stand like you — straight and confident — and speak like you, with authority. When I saw that it worked, it became a little easier." Kasia ended with what she felt most deeply: "I don't know what I would have done without you at my side, Aunt Jadwiga. Or what I'd do without all of you. I know my parents feel the same. If only I could share all of this with them."

"They will know. There are ways," Marcel said in a clipped voice. Kasia knew not to ask questions, but she hoped that the statement implied an underground connection with Tata.

After dinner, Marcel left to see his patients, Kasia helped Aunt Jadwiga with the dishes, and Piotrek went to his room to study.

The best part of the evening came when Piotrek finished his studies and invited Kasia to his room cluttered with books, records, and papers. They sat side by side on the floor in a cozy corner near the window and made the room murmur with their conversation. They shared what had happened to them since the war kept their families apart. They discussed issues and raised questions, trying to understand the distorted world they lived in and their roles in it.

Kasia told Piotrek about her hidden one-room ghetto school. "It had a small plot of land in the back with one magnificent chestnut tree standing in a far corner. We managed to find seeds and planted a tiny bed of flowers and a few vegetables and we fussed over them lovingly. Our teacher, Pani Helena, was short and roly-poly, as if she were made of spheres. She had a contagious generosity of spirit that made us believe a peaceful universe was possible. Our secret school was the only place in the ghetto where I and my friends laughed with abandon, where we almost forgot about the Nazi hell."

"What happened to Pani Helena?" Piotrek whispered as if afraid to hear the answer.

"Rounded up during the deportations."

"Damn."

Piotrek in turn talked about his school. "It's not as horrible as what you've experienced. Nonetheless, what they are doing to us is barbaric. Believe me."

She waited expectantly while he collected his thoughts, clenched his fists, and asked in bewilderment, "Do you know what the Nazis' educational theories are for the Slavic people?"

"I don't have the slightest idea."

"It's like this: According to them, the Slavs (that includes us Poles, of course) have no need of higher education. Their plan is to turn us into uneducated serfs laboring for the German race."

He continued incredulously, "No school above the fourth grade is allowed. We don't need to know how to count higher than 500, we should learn to write no more than our names, and we must be taught to believe that God commands our obedience to the Germans. All higher education is banned and punished with death. That is the official order issued by Himmler."

"But you go to school, Piotrek. Is it secret?"

"Yes! We call our hidden schools 'flying universities.' The Polish government in exile in London supports them. Our classes float from one end of Warsaw to the other and meet in private apartments and churches. The exiled Polish government also supports underground newspapers, books, theaters, lectures, and concerts." His eyes sparkled with defiance.

"We did the same things in the ghetto, and without support from the Polish government, or anyone else," countered Kasia. "Nearly all the valiant people ended up in Treblinka."

"I'm amazed that people in the ghetto were interested in theater and books when death was on top of them."

"My grandmother said, 'Those who think suffering stops you from living know nothing about life.' Chaim Kaplan, a ghetto writer, put it more poetically. He said, 'It is strange, when we don't seem to need it at all, we need poetry more than bread.'"

"The spirit of the ghetto people is amazing!"

"True."

"Now that you're here, you'll have to see our underground theaters. They are clever and rebellious. You'll love them."

"I'd like to, but I don't know if I'll be able to."

"Of course you will. My parents support the secret theater and will take you. They support all Polish cultural activities. So do their friends. However, many of them get shot for that sin."

"So, they shoot you here, too, for being human."

"Yes, they do."

They talked briefly about the resistance on both sides of the wall.

"Many kids our age belong to scout groups and carry out minor saboteur missions for the underground," Piotrek said, rubbing his hands as if warming up for action.

Kasia wondered if he were one of the saboteur scouts, but she didn't ask. She determined to wait for him to tell her.

And so, the evening slipped by without their noticing blue dusk creeping into the room. As if waking from a gentle dream, Kasia heard dishes clanging in the kitchen, the entrance door opening and shutting, and Uncle Marcel's voice filling the house.

Piotrek and Kasia looked at each other with new appreciation, reached out and hugged. Piotrek said, "It's nice to have a sister to talk to."

"Thank you," Kasia said, both grateful and in dread of the danger her existence imposed on everyone in this kind household. She thought, *I'm a fish washed up on land.*

CHAPTER TWENTY-SEVEN

Daring

*T*ime should not be measured by hours but by the enormity of events happening therein. That sentiment became apparent to Kasia after a short while on Dobra Street. Never before had she felt as haunted by far too many events fitted into ten ordinary days. Never before did she feel as lonesome and as aware of the fact that people beyond her reach were with her in spirit. She felt her parents' presence when she crawled under the wall to get to the Christian side, when she faced the uniform at the police station, and when she walked into the stores afraid of being found out for the crime of wanting to live.

At night, when she lay awake in her bed, she felt her parents' nearness as real as her breath — and as essential as a compass in the wilderness. She called out to them when the ogres she dodged during the day stared out of the darkness. To give herself courage to endure, she talked to them in her head: *If only I could tell you not to worry about me, how kind Jadwiga and Marcel are to me. Piotrek treats me like his sister. My room is beautiful.* She scanned each item in her mind, as if mentally telegraphing the images to them. *If only you could see it.*

She assured them: *I often surprise myself with the courage I'm able to muster when I'm in a tight spot —far beyond what I thought myself capable of. I know you are proud of me for that, although you cannot see me. Mama, you told me, "People find their inner strength when circumstances force them to make tough choices." I'm learning that part of me is made of steel. And I haven't lost my faith that there are good people, even if I can count them on the fingers of one hand.*

With each new challenge, Kasia felt surer of herself. Daring, according to Ben, was what counted the most. On a walk with Jadwiga to the market square on Żelazna Brama, she wasn't as frightened as she had been the first time. While Jadwiga made her purchases, Kasia meandered among traders and gazed at baskets of carrots and beets gleaming in the sun. She looked at pretty scarves, hats, bread, and kielbasa. She even watched dealers in gold and currency calling out, "Dollars, buy dollars! Rubles! Gold!"

At some point, far down the street, a police car came into sight. The peddlers grabbed their merchandise and ran, tripping over themselves. Kasia flew to Jadwiga's side, grabbed hold of the sleeve of her coat, and they bolted. Danger continued to be the norm.

Thus far, she had taken four walks in the Christian neighborhood. Not a single person had identified her as a Jew. So, when Jadwiga asked, "Kasia, do you think you are ready to go for groceries by yourself? The sooner you do it, the better," Kasia was able to answer fairly confidently, "Yes."

Jadwiga handed her ration cards, money, and a list of five items: one kilo of flour, four eggs, ten dekagrams of butter, a loaf of bread, and honey. Kasia slipped on her coat and hat and was on her way. Her heart hammered wildly, but she felt daring.

"*Jak się masz*, Kasia?" a next-door neighbor greeted her in the courtyard.

She waved back with assumed confidence.

She stepped out into the street and strode decisively, but she didn't know what to do with her eyes. She stared with feigned interest into store windows and at people's shoes.

The grocer welcomed her when she entered the store. "Ah, Dr. Jabkowski's niece. Dzień dobry. What can I do for you?"

So far, so good. Then a lady standing near the counter gaped at her and asked, "Oh, are you the Jabkowskis' niece?"

"Yes, I am."

"You don't say."

Kasia was apprehensive about what the woman might ask next, but she didn't need to worry. Another woman entered, the two began to gossip, and they forgot about her.

Kasia handed Jadwiga's list to the grocer. The transaction went quickly, and she was out of the store. On her way back, she walked around several corners to see what lay beyond, until she heard the church bell ring.

Oh, my gosh! Jadwiga is waiting for me. How will I explain my tardiness? What have I done now? Kasia excoriated herself and rushed home.

As she was turning into Dobra Street, she saw that a few strides ahead of her two brawny teenaged boys closed in on a young man, stared him down, pinned him to the wall, and hissed, *"Skurwy syn! Żyd!"*

The trapped boy's face was as white as death. A small circle of onlookers began to form.

Is the boy really Jewish? He looks like a goy. Maybe I misheard what they said?

She did not wait to find out. Nor was she in a position to come to the boy's rescue. She hurried past the scene, thinking, *So, this is what my safety here is like?*

Although her legs trembled and her thoughts were bitter, she reminded herself: *As bad as it is here, it is much worse behind the wall.*

Kasia went to bed that night with a heavy heart. Nights were loneliest and hardest to bear. That was when fears converged in her head and she missed Mama and Tata most. Before she climbed into bed, she switched off the light, knelt in front of her window, and turned her face to the sky. She let her eyes sweep the immense freedom far above and imagined: *It is remotely possible that Mama and Tata are looking at the sky this very moment.*

Maybe they hear me with their hearts as I hear their silent cries. Maybe mental telepathy really works. No one has proved that it doesn't.

She remained in this prayerful position with her eyes skimming the indifferent infinity, silently communing with the unreachable, until her eyelids grew heavy. Then, she climbed into bed, wrapped herself in the images, and drifted into sleep.

In the days that followed, Kasia continued to wander where she had not been before, speaking to anyone who addressed her. She continued to go to stores and church and to stroll in the street — testing herself, convincing herself: *I look like everyone else. Why should I be so afraid?* Just because she was, if for no other reason. She almost rose out of her shoes one moment when a young man on a motorcycle doffed his cap to her and flashed a bright approving smile.

CHAPTER TWENTY-EIGHT

The Admirer

Thus far, the neighbors at 25 Dobra Street, as well as everyone else Kasia had come across, had accepted her as one of them, a Christian. That good fortune had its downside. Considering her a member of the clan, people had no qualms about making blistering anti-Semitic remarks in her presence. Kasia bristled internally and longed to tell them how insulting and cruel their bigotry was. Instead, she kept a straight face and cursed under her breath. What else could she do? Her mouth was muzzled. She wished leprosy, cholera, boils, and every misery on the whole lot of them. At the same time, she justified to herself: *Tata, if you heard me curse like that, you'd surely say, "You might as well wish them to rise to kindness rather than wish them boils. Both have an equal chance to be realized." But I don't care.* She continued to curse with gusto and felt better for it. Besides, it didn't really hurt anyone.

There was one neighbor family Kasia had not met, but she avoided them like the pox. They lived one level above the Jabkowskis' apartment. They were Bruno and Krystyna Blok and their son who used to be Piotrek's best friend. Kasia's surrogate family cautioned her to avoid them at any price, but to do it tactfully.

"Why must I avoid them more than any other neighbor?" Kasia asked.

Jadwiga said, "It's a complicated story. The Bloks are *Volksdeutsche*. This was completely irrelevant before the war. We were friends and saw each other's children grow from infancy to young adulthood. Their son Jan and our Piotrek were inseparable. Jan practically lived in our apartment. Now he hardly shows his face, and we are grateful for it."

That dangerous coexistence between the two neighbors kept Kasia on guard and preoccupied with the Blok family. Piotrek had a somewhat similar obsession with them. When Kasia asked him, "Why doesn't Jan show his face in your house anymore?" Piotrek replied, "First of all, he is no longer 'Jan.' He is 'Johan' now."

"How did that happen?"

"In 1939, only days after the invasion, I asked him, 'You were Jan all your life, why are your parents suddenly calling you Johan?'

"'That's my real name.'

"'If that's your real name, why didn't they call you Johan before?'

"'I'm Volksdeutsche.'

"'I know. But you're also a Pole. You were born here, and you lived here all your life. You and I were almost killed by the same bomb during the bombardment. What has changed?'

"He said, 'I don't know exactly how to explain. But my parents say that Hitler's mission will correct the unfairness Germany suffered after the Great War. They say, if Poles recognize German superiority and Hitler's plan for Europe, they will be well served.'

"'Well,' I said, 'what need does Poland have of Hitler's plan? He doesn't have to worry about us. We'll do fine without his help. He can take his army and go home.'

"I wondered where he was getting those diabolical ideas from. I soon realized that he was getting them at home. His parents talked about them; he heard them blasting on their radio; they jumped out at him from the German newspapers his father brings home. He once tried to show me front-page photos of stormtroopers beating up innocent people. I got up and left."

"How did your parents deal with Johan's parents?"

"Their friendship deteriorated just as fast. Two months into the occupation, Bruno offered my dad a neighborly opinion. He said, 'Face it, Germany is armed to the teeth. Her soldiers are highly disciplined and highly literate. They will conquer the world. They are unstoppable.'

"'It's not obvious to me. Some might call them barbarians,' Dad said.

"'You wouldn't call them that.'

"'Of course not,' Dad responded with one eyebrow raised high.

"According to Dad, Bruno did not miss the intended sarcasm, but he let it slide. After all, they were still friends and neighbors and he felt magnanimous. Another time, Bruno told my Dad, 'You should meet some of the Germans who are running the Warsaw government. You will be impressed with their administrative acumen and high level of personal culture.'

"'Have you met them?' Dad asked.

"'Yes.'

"'Already?'

"'Why are you surprised? I am a lawyer with considerable knowledge and connections. I can be an asset to them.'

"'No doubt.'

"'And I can be helpful to the Poles, as well.'

"'Hmm,' is all my Dad said. He feigned a headache and ended the conversation."

"What does Bruno look like? I saw him only once, from a distance, when Aunt Jadwiga pointed him out. I looked away to avoid being noticed."

"He looks like an elegant, well-mannered man with thinning hair. He's portly and always exceedingly polite."

"How do the other neighbors get along with him?"

"Some of our neighbors feel threatened by him and his Nazi visitors. Others cozy up to him. I guess they want to be on his good side in case they need him to intervene on their behalf. Connections count high these days, you know."

Piotrek fell silent and shook his head as if he remembered something worth telling. "Here is a good example. Before the ghetto deportations started, Bruno managed to win high favor with a few people in our building. He achieved this by using his connections to force a bunch of miserable-looking Jews to put a fresh coat of paint on 25 Dobra Street. Gratis, naturally. The people were snatched off their streets, like cattle."

"Was Bruno aware of the immorality of this act?" Kasia asked.

"Hardly. He boasted to my dad, 'Actually, Marcel, I am doing the poor chaps a favor. At least they are doing something useful, and it's not like a concentration camp.'

"'That makes it right?' Dad asked.

"'Don't try to moralize to me, Marcel. You like the way our building looks now as much as I do,' he said."

"Did he ever turn any of your neighbors in to the Nazis for any reason?"

"To his credit, he never turned anyone in for having a radio in their homes—in spite of prohibition—and he ignores anti-Nazi remarks he happens to overhear. Of course, everyone watches their tongues when he's around."

Kasia was most profoundly moved by Piotrek's story about Bruno and Ruta. Here is what he told her: "One day, Dad and Bruno stopped in front of our door and talked. The three of us inside the apartment could hear them and almost died with fear that Bruno might invite himself in. Bruno can be very insistent."

"Wait, stop. Your dad was outside the door. Who was the third person with you and your mother?"

"Ruta."

"Who's Ruta?"

"Oh, I forgot that you might not know. Ever since the ghetto was formed in 1940, our house has been a temporary clandestine stopover for a number of my parents' Jewish friends. Ruta was one of them. They stayed with us until a safer place was found for them. By the way, to get our neighbors used to seeing people enter our house, my mom often invites family and friends over. Okay, can I go on with the story now?"

"Please do."

"Bruno was especially talkative, standing with Dad outside our door that afternoon. We could hear Dad respond to his stream of jabber with an occasional 'oh, yes.' Finally, Bruno left. As soon as Dad closed the door behind him, my mother asked, 'Is everything okay? I heard you and Bruno talking.'

"'He was just bragging about his connections. I managed to keep my mouth shut. It wasn't easy. Where is Ruta?' Dad asked.

"'She's in the pantry,' Mom said. 'We were afraid Bruno might follow you into the house, like he used to do.'

"Dad stepped into the pantry. The place was lined with shelves with mostly empty jars. He called out, 'Ruta, the coast is clear. You can come out now.'

"He released the secret latch hidden in the shelves, swung the left side wall forward, and revealed the secret space — a yard and a half by twenty-seven inches. Ruta sat curled up in a corner, like a frightened squirrel — she's petite. She turned her face up to Dad, her brown soulful eyes brimming with gratitude. 'Ah, Marcel, just as I was getting to feel cozy in my little castle,' she said.

"Dad offered his hand to help her to her feet and said, 'Jadwiga sometimes worries too much. The neighbor she was trying to protect you from has not set foot in our house for over a year. Nor has his wife. His son might have popped in, once or twice. That's about all.'

"Dad was right. We no longer see them, ever. Bruno is busy with his new cronies. Johan is a student at a private school, which is sanctioned and highly rated by the 'masters of the world.' I, on the other hand, attend secret classes held at a church. Johan has no time for me. Mom says Krystyna Blok, Johan's mother, is busy with patriotic causes that war tends to provide to those who are bored with life."

The day Piotrek told her about the Ruta incident, Kasia asked at the dinner table, "Why would anyone risk hiding Jews in their house when a Nazi family lives a sneeze away from your door?"

Marcel responded, "Because not enough people do it." Jadwiga nodded.

Kasia wondered: *If they can do it, then why don't others?*

As fate would have it, one day, as Kasia and Piotrek were walking on Senatorska Street, they saw coming toward them a fit-looking teenaged boy.

"You see this tall guy who is staring at you? It's Johan Blok. Get ready to meet him. Remember to act as if you never heard about him. And relax."

"Don't worry. If I didn't know how to look calm even when I'm sinking, I'd have been dead long ago."

Johan stepped toward the two, his eyes riveted on Kasia. Normally, when he passed Piotrek on the street or in the courtyard, he called out, "Servus, Piotrek! Jak się masz?" and kept walking. This time he stopped and added to his customary hand wave, "Haven't seen you lately" (like he really cared) and placed a friendly hand on Piotrek's shoulder.

"Servus, Johan!" Piotrek answered, hoping to avoid a conversation.

"How is it going?"

"Fine."

"What have you been doing lately?"

"Nothing."

"Aren't you going to introduce me to your friend?"

"Sorry. Meet my cousin, Kasia."

"Are you heading home?"

"Yes."

"You mind if I join you?"

They walked together the fair distance to their building.

"I haven't noticed you before, Kasia. Where do you live?"

"I live at my uncle's house now."

Piotrek jumped to Kasia's aid, offering a brief version of the tale of her father's death and the circumstances that forced her to live with the Jabkowskis. Johan was captivated by her story and by her big, solemn green eyes. He felt a deep urge to touch her, or at least to engage her in a conversation.

"It must be very hard to be separated from your mother and brother and your home," he prodded.

"It is, but there are many people in similar, or much worse, situations."

Johan's attention made Kasia feel self-conscious and uneasy. He was lean, but the muscles in his arms, exposed by rolled-up sleeves, were so sharply defined, they seemed cut from rock. Although he was polite and well-mannered, his sturdy physique and his self-assured, fair-skinned, deceptively ordinary-looking face put fear in her bones.

He sauntered at her side, looking at her approvingly and peppering her with questions until they reached her door. Then, he clasped her hand, held it in his large palms, and said emphatically, "Fascinating, absolutely fascinating. I must see you again and learn everything about you." (*God forbid*, Kasia thought). And he vaulted up the stairs two at a time to his home, one level above.

For reasons as mysterious as a man's heart, Johan was attracted by the very attributes Kasia found most Jewish and threatening to her. He was drawn by the sadness in her big eyes. It didn't hurt that they were a deep emerald green. He loved the way her wavy, abundant hair bounced when she walked. Most often, Kasia bound her unruly hair in neatly plaited braids and twisted it into a bun at the back of her neck, but she hadn't done so this time.

As if out of the blue, Johan resumed his old habit of dropping into Piotrek's house like nothing had changed. He said, "I don't know what happened, but I sure miss seeing you, Piotrek."

Yes. And it snows in July.

One time, Johan showed up at the door and astonished Piotrek with a Louis Armstrong record.

"I thought you found American jazz decadent now," Piotrek said. "It's always Wagner, Schubert, or military marches for you. Although I can remember the days when you'd give your soul to hear Armstrong."

"Don't be a sarcastic snob. Marches can be beautiful and

rousing. I brought the record for old days' sake. You think your cousin would like to listen to it with us?"

"I doubt it."

The more Kasia avoided Johan, the more beautiful her big eyes loomed in his mind and the more angelic her sad face became. During his resumed visits, he would leave Piotrek's room to go the bathroom when he did not really need to or to fetch a drink of water when he wasn't thirsty. All in hopes of bumping into Kasia. He dreamed up conversation starters to dazzle her.

Contrary to his hopes, when he managed to corner Kasia, she would drop her eyes with feigned shyness and reply in mostly monosyllables, "Oh. Hm. That's nice."

Occasionally he managed to trick Kasia to meet his gaze and keep her attention for a few minutes before she fluttered out of sight. Once, he made the fatal mistake of sharing with her a "hysterical" joke with an anti-Semitic overtone that made her feel as if a rock plummeted into her gut. Her big eyes glared at him for one moment. Then she looked away and said, "I've got to go, Johan."

Johan was like a clap of thunder you couldn't anticipate. Having him hang around their home was simply unsafe, but to offend a dangerous neighbor was not a smart thing to do. The Jabkowskis hoped Kasia's pointed indifference would drive him away. But it didn't seem to matter that she declined to join in listening to the records he brought to share with Piotrek. It didn't dissuade him when she declined his invitations to a concert or a stroll in the park, nor when she refused to accept the box of bonbons he brought her. Not even when she told him categorically, "Johan, please don't try to make me join you when you come to see Piotrek. I can't accept your bonbons, even though I know how delicious they are, and I must turn down your invitations to meet your parents, even if you tell me how much they'd love to meet me."

"Why is that? Girls find me attractive."

"I'm not surprised, Johan, but I am different. I don't date any boys. I'm dedicated to Jezus Chrystus. In a couple of years, I will enter a nunnery and serve God and humanity," she lied.

Did Kasia's fake piety work? Hardly. Johan had to win her at any cost. That was the point.

CHAPTER TWENTY-NINE

Pavel

Despite grief and danger, life went on, as it must. One morning, Piotrek asked, "Kasia, would you like to come with me to my friend's house after school today?"

"Who is this friend?"

"His name is Pavel. He's my *best* friend."

"Okay, sure. Thank you for inviting me. Will anyone else be there?"

"A few others."

"I don't really know what kids talk about here. I hope I won't give myself away."

"Don't worry. Most people don't know what they're talking about anyway. Besides, silence is golden," he said and left for school.

Most days when Piotrek was at school, Kasia spent her time helping Jadwiga around the house or looking out the window and observing people. She liked to study people's faces and make up stories about their lives based on their appearances.

The day Piotrek extended the invitation was different. Nothing held her attention. She agonized: *Who knows if his friends can be trusted? What if they ask me too many questions and guess I'm Jewish?* Another voice argued: *The sooner I meet his friend, the safer I'll be.* Since Kasia was not one to surrender to fear, she resolved: *I'll say as little as possible. In a pinch, I'll change the subject and ask questions—as per Tata's advice.* Still, the ground felt slippery beneath her feet.

On the way to Pavel's house, Piotrek said, "You're very quiet. Are you worried about meeting my friends?"

"No. I've faced much tougher challenges." Her bravado was intended more to bolster her own courage than to impress Piotrek.

"Good."

"Do they know I'm coming, and do they know anything about me?"

"I thought you said you'd faced much tougher challenges."

"I did; just answer my question."

"My friends know you're my cousin, living with us because your dad died. They couldn't care less about details. You'll have no trouble keeping up with the conversations. Just roll with it, as you always do so beautifully."

"Who are they, exactly?"

"My scout friends. They are principled and egalitarian, for the most part."

"What do you mean, for the most part?"

"Nothing. Just a figure of speech."

In fact, he knew some of his friends were bigoted, but he trusted Kasia's survival instinct. He knew she was good at reading people and dealing with them diplomatically.

They walked briskly through winding streets, some bordering the wall. On Wierzbowa Street, Piotrek stopped in front of a pastel-colored building and said, "We're here." He led Kasia up two flights of stairs and rang the doorbell.

"Who is it?" a baritone voice asked.

"It's Piotrek."

A lock unclicked, a door swung open, and a tall, lean man with sad-looking blue eyes greeted them warmly.

"Piotrek, jak się masz? Come in. Who is this lovely young lady? I don't believe we have met."

"Pan Rogal, this is my cousin Kasia."

Pan Rogal bowed, kissed her hand, and said, "*Bardzo mi przyjemnie.*" He ushered them into a room filled with young people, then moved on to another room.

A good-looking, brown-haired boy rushed over to welcome them. He clasped Kasia's hand, smiled warmly, and said, "I'm Pavel. So glad to meet you finally, Kasia." He paused; his eyes were the color of the sky, and he peered at her like a curious child. Then he continued, "Piotrek told me nice things about you. I can see he didn't lie this time." He held her hand, his gaze lingering on her face, and a thrill ran through her.

She returned his smile and felt her face turn crimson. "Thank you."

Young people with wholesome faces and ringing laughter came over to greet her and separated her from Pavel and Piotrek. Suddenly she felt overwhelmed. Part of her wanted to bolt. A stronger part commanded, *Stay calm.* She felt like a spy behind enemy lines.

Throughout that afternoon, Kasia said little, observed much, smiled a lot, and listened to conversations on topics ranging from the mundane to the sublime: current gossip, an underground play, a jazz concert, and the latest scout sabotage missions.

She brooded, *I have so much in common with Piotrek's friends. I share their love for music, their pursuit of a just world, and the joy of laughter — although my laughter is not as effervescent as theirs. So much in me wants to be heard — deserves to be heard — but I'm condemned to sit like a smiling clay figure. Why is the simple understanding of good and right so distorted in practice?*

Pavel sensed Kasia's apprehension and often stepped away from his friends to sit beside her and chat. "Kasia, I hope you're not intimidated by the roomful of strangers."

"Not that intimidated; just a little," Kasia said, with a blitheness that caught her by surprise. She felt safe in Pavel's company, flattered by his caring attention, and moved by the sadness revealed in his eyes.

When dusk began to creep in, Piotrek and Kasia left to hurry home to beat the curfew.

"That wasn't too challenging, was it?" Piotrek said.

"No. But I'm glad I have it behind me."

"What do you think of my friends?"

"They are interesting." She didn't tell him that she felt like an imposter.

"They enjoyed meeting you very much."

"That's nice," she said, but thought: *Would they have enjoyed meeting me if they knew who I really am?*

"You made quite an impression on Pavel."

Kasia blushed, and her heart fluttered. She thought: *Of all the people there, Pavel was the only one who made me feel completely at ease.* She would soon find out why that was.

"Is there a reason why Pavel's mother wasn't home?"

"Yes. A very sad reason."

"Can you tell me?"

"Yes, of course. His mother was a journalist before the war. A very fine one. One night, a bunch of Nazis stormed into their building, broke into their apartment, and arrested her."

"When did that happen?"

"A while ago."

"Does his family know why she was arrested?"

"No. They never heard a word. They don't know if she is dead or alive. Of course, there is no place a Pole can turn to now for help or for an explanation."

"Do you feel comfortable telling me whether she was involved in a political movement?"

"She was active in Żegota. Do you know of that organization?"

"Yes, it's the Polish Council to Aid Jews."

"Right. Given that she was the only one arrested at that time, it could mean either that her arrest had nothing to do with Żegota or that she wouldn't talk. You know what they do with people who don't talk."

"Oh, no!" Kasia exclaimed, horrified.

After a moment's silence, Kasia asked, "How come I've never seen Pavel at your house? You said he's your best friend."

"He is. You haven't seen him because he was away for a couple of months at his uncle's country estate. His dad was afraid the Nazis might come back to arrest them."

Now that Pavel was back in Warsaw, he spent much of his time at the Jabkowskis' apartment. His own home felt too gloomy without his mother there. The odd thing about Pavel was that Kasia felt as though she had known him for ages. She was not uncomfortable with him at all. Maybe it was the sadness in his smile that bonded her to him, or perhaps because he reminded her of her favorite cousin, Lolek. He had the same light-brown hair and bright blue eyes that paid attention to what you were saying.

For Kasia, the hours the two boys were at their secret school felt endless and heavy with longing. She missed her own school friends with whom she could share common interests and laugh together at nothing at all. She even missed the sting of squabbles and the warmth of reconciliation. To combat boredom, she asked Piotrek and Pavel to bring home copies of their schoolbooks and assignments for her to study. She took great pleasure in keeping up with their work and pride in not being left completely behind. When she was stumped by an assignment, she went to Jadwiga for help.

Her world lit up when Piotrek came home from school. It was especially vibrant when Pavel accompanied him. To avoid making a nuisance of herself, Kasia trained herself not to pounce on them with questions, although she wanted to know everything about their day at school and about their friends. Instead, she listened carefully to conversation fragments between them, memorized names and connected bits of gossip, and soon stitched together coherent themes and associations. The fact that she was more interested in hearing than being heard made her a welcome companion. Kasia treasured her only two friends. She loved occasionally arguing with them over points of view and dreaming together of an ideal world. She even welcomed their good-natured teasing.

The very best part of Kasia's day was when she joined the boys at the kitchen table to do homework. They loved her company and her spunk just as much. The instant Pavel noticed she was struggling with a problem he scooted his chair close and leaned toward her. His wide shoulders gently brushed against her, his breath felt warm and caressing. He guided her, patiently, attentively, step by step, until she achieved a "eureka" moment. Then he would say, "See, you figured it out."

Kasia loved his nearness as much as she valued his help and enjoyed the attention he was paying her.

Meanwhile, did Johan, their upstairs neighbor and pursuer, leave Kasia in peace? Not at all. Although his demanding school program — which included highly competitive athletic requirements and grueling hours — left him little time for uninvited visits, his determination to win Kasia's affection remained undeterred. He would pop into the Jabkowskis' house at the oddest hours and say, "I was just on my way out and wanted to stop by to say 'hi.'" If Kasia tried to hide from him, he'd seek her out and assure her, "As soon as school is out, I'll have more time to see you." Kasia would feign a pious posture of a future nun and say, "That's okay, Johan, don't worry."

At night, when Kasia communed with her parents — as one communes with God — she prayed: *Mama and Tata, so much is happening, and darkness looms between us. Two months have passed since our last embrace, and I have had no word from you. I don't know what is going on in the sub-ghetto. We're only a few streets apart, but it seems as if you're on a different planet. I can only imagine the hardships you are forced to endure. May God protect you, and protect Ben, Rebecca, and Heniek from deportation. You are all I have left of my people. And last — may God protect me from Johan.*

CHAPTER THIRTY

Two Faces of Spring

The sun's silvery winter tint turned golden, buds decorated trees, and people on the Christian side of the wall were busy with Easter preparations. In spite of deprivations, there was joy in the air. Yet, Kasia remained alienated from the vows God makes to all his children with the arrival of spring.

While she attended, incognita, the joyful holiday preparations of other people, her mind took her into a dream-world that was there for her to relive — a surreal middle point, the journey from one life to another. With her eyes turned inward, she saw herself sitting at a festive Passover Seder table, surrounded by beloved relatives and listening to her sage Grandfather Isaak recite the Passover story of miracles and freedom. Her memories were her anchor, her cove. They were her weapons and spiritual sustenance.

April 1943 marked the first Passover Kasia spent away from her parents and her community. Then, precisely on that Passover Eve, when people bowed to the One God that unites all humanity, the most ungodly act was carried out by a nation that surrendered its conscience to Hitler. On that day, the Nazis began the slaughter of the courageous handful of people behind the wall.

Kasia had escaped that apocalypse, and she felt enormously guilty as a result. Although she was not with her people — as she felt she should have been — in her heart she was dying with them. For her, all life was coming to an end, crushed under the boots of barbarians. All lessons of nobility and sanctity of life were piled on a pyre. From these ashes she heard Mama's and Tata's plea, "You must live and remember."

Passover Slaughter

Kasia found the neatly handwritten sheet of paper accidentally. Perhaps it was providential? She was running an errand near the wall. Her eyes were riveted on the charred ghetto ruins. Suddenly, an airborne piece of paper fluttered right in front of her, like a butterfly, at shoulder level. She clasped it. The writer's name was not on it, nor was there a clue for whom it was intended. Maybe it was a page from a diary that got away from the pyre? She would never know. This is what it said:

> *The mastermind behind the slaughter is Heinrich Himmler, Reichsführer-SS and Chief of German police. The monstrous idea dawned on him on January 18, 1943, when the ghetto Jews — under the leadership of Mordecai Anielewicz — put up a fight to resist deportations.* [Kasia clearly remembered the January skirmishes. Tata, Ben, Rebecca, and Heniek were among the fighters.] *He planned to start the butchery precisely on the first day of Passover, April 19, and complete it in no more than three days, in time for Hitler's birthday.*
>
> *What was the special birthday gift that would make the little tyrant Hitler so happy that he would jump with joy and click his jackboots in mid-air? Nothing less than cleansing the sub-ghettos of all remaining Jews. What's more, it would raise Himmler's esteem in Hitler's eyes.*
>
> *Events erupted with the entrance of Nazi columns into the ghetto. Tanks, armored cars, and trucks with blaring loudspeakers rolled down the streets demanding that Jews report for "resettlement." By then, everyone knew that "resettlement" meant Treblinka. They responded with resistance. Against the well-equipped Nazi forces armed from head to toe*

stood poorly outfitted, inexperienced, starved bands of Jewish fighters. They took positions on street corners, climbed on roof-tops, stepped in front of open windows, crawled through secret underground tunnels and sewers, and lobbed Molotov cock-tails and grenades at Nazi columns.

There was no end to the Jewish fighters' valor. Clashes flared up with fierce persistence, even weeks after the ghetto had been burned to the ground and the Nazis declared "the Warsaw ghetto no longer exists." Yet the band of ghetto fight-ers battled longer than it took France or Poland to capitulate.

Kasia folded the page, pressed it to her heart, and wept silently, careful not to call attention to herself. But she could not stop herself from trembling.

With the Nazi mission accomplished, the entire ghetto — as far as the eye could see in every direction — was in ruins. Not a single building remained standing. All the people were gone. All life extinguished. Not a single flower in sight, not a flicker of a butterfly wing.

What did the people on the Christian side see while their Jewish neighbors were being slaughtered? They saw the sky turn dark with bomber planes roaring toward the ghetto. They felt the earth tremble and the air thunder with explosions behind the wall. They saw enormous tongues of flames lick the ghetto sky and turn it to otherworldly colors of iridescence. Monstrous clouds of smoke billowed.

Some people stopped to look at the cataclysm. Some watched with deep sadness; some were happy it was not happening to them; some identified with the killers and said, "Serves the Jews right." Others shrugged and did not seem to care much one way or another.

Flakes of ash drifted across the wall, landing on the shoul-ders and hair of spectators and passersby. Incongruously, a short distance from the wall, a carousel went around and around, its music playing and children laughing.

In the Jabkowskis' home, Jadwiga cried out, "Where is God?" Tears rolled down her cheeks. Jadwiga, Marcel, and Piotrek grieved with Kasia. They felt deep shame for the cruelty of which mankind is capable. Kasia appreciated their healing kindness, but it did not protect her from neighbors from whom she had to hide her sorrow — if she wanted to live.

She rose every morning and forced herself to remain Kasia, a fiction her parents had promoted to save her life. Wherever she went, people talked about the tragedy. Many remarks were cruel, some were indifferent, a few were compassionate. The world went on outside her — stark and separate.

Kasia felt pierced by the two faces of spring. One side of the wall lay in complete darkness, like the shadowy face of the moon; the other side shone in spring glory. Lilac trees burst into bloom and the grass grew in lushest shades of green — difficult to imagine it being stained with blood. Nothing seemed real to Kasia. The sky hung immense and indifferent to the upheaval.

Mercifully, one ash-gray afternoon, Marcel came home with a fragment of hope. He said, "Sixty or so fighters spirited their way out of the ghetto through the sewers. They joined the Polish partisans in a forest. I heard it from a reliable source."

"Do you know their names, Uncle Marcel?"

"I don't."

"Can you find out? Please!"

"Of course, I will try."

Kasia didn't hold her hopes high. Sixty or so survivors — out of a population of 400,000 who lived in the ghetto less than a year ago — didn't hold much promise. But Kasia grasped at straws. Voices argued in her head. One cautioned: *Impossible! Don't set yourself up for disappointment and more heartbreak.* Another voice countered: *No one knows the underground maze and network of sewers better than Ben, Rebecca, and Heniek, and Tata is so clever. What if a miracle finally happened?*

CHAPTER THIRTY-ONE
Schubert's Lieder

Several weeks had passed since the Passover slaughter. Spring gradually gave way to summer. The clouds of smoke and ash had dissipated. People crossed themselves when they passed the ghetto ruins. Treasure hunters wandered in to dig in the rubble; others tramped past the charred wall to satisfy their curiosity. After a while, no one appeared to notice the grotesque mountains of wreckage. Filigreed spires of poplar, linden, and willow trees stirred a lust for life in spite of despair. The air bustled and hummed with the music of cicadas mixed with bird calls. Kasia was pulled by two contrasting realities: mourning and renewal, each equally acute.

In her despair, she clung to the dream of falling into Tata's arms. She tried to convince herself: *There is a possibility, however remote, that Tata and Ben have made their way to join the Polish partisans.*

In May, the Axis forces in Tunisia surrendered to the Allies, ending the North African campaign. The upbeat news circulated in underground newspapers and stoked Kasia's dreams. In July, US and British troops landed in Sicily, and Benito

Mussolini was deposed. Kasia's hope buoyed. Optimists rubbed their hands with glee, convinced the war would soon end.

On the less encouraging side, with school out Johan had more time to visit Piotrek and seek Kasia's company. Sometimes, he would traipse into the kitchen and start a conversation with Jadwiga while glancing at Kasia and trying to coax a response from her. Occasionally, he'd bump into her alone — accidentally on purpose — in a room with no one else within earshot. He'd tell her with utter sincerity how interesting he found her. How much more modest and smart she was than most of the silly girls he met, and certainly more beautiful than most.

Kasia thought: *What an idiot. How can he find me interesting when I hardly open my mouth?*

She knew it wouldn't be wise to offend a neighbor who could easily blow her masquerade and end her own and her surrogate family's lives, so she remained polite but remote, revealing nothing about herself other than that she was completely committed to serving her God, Jezus Chrystus.

Johan proudly shared with her that his favorite hobby was fencing. He was also a champion marksman, he said. She listened, kept her head slightly bent, eyes directed to the floor, and said little.

He assured her, "I love Poland and the Polish people. Of course, that includes you, but my duty demands I serve my fatherland with absolute loyalty."

Perhaps to impress her with his fair-mindedness, he confided, "I don't like some of the things my country is doing against some people; they don't exactly line up with my religious teaching. But it's for the good of the nation."

Kasia blinked, looked blank, and wondered: *Does he suspect who I am, or is he showing a softer side of his soul?*

Contrary to Kasia's hope, the more she ignored Johan, the more he fell for her angelic modesty and the purity he imagined seeing in her. As his ardor grew, so did his persistence, and so did Kasia's insecurity.

One day, he arrived at the Jabkowskis' door with a new record under his arm. Piotrek said, "Let me see what you've got there."

"I know what you'll say when you see it even before — God forbid — you permit yourself to listen to it." He rolled his eyes. "It's Schubert's Lieder. Kasia will love it, I'm sure."

"Man, she's a country girl. She'll fall asleep. I get sleepy just looking at it."

"I knew you wouldn't understand. Kasia is different. Unlike you — or me, as a matter of fact — she's not a *krautkopf*."

Piotrek thought it best to humor Johan and count on Kasia to brush him off.

Johan darted in to find Kasia in the kitchen with Jadwiga and said, "Kasia, can you spare a few minutes to listen to a record I brought? Just a few minutes. I think you'll love it."

She hesitated, then said, "Okay, but only a few minutes."

All three stepped into Piotrek's room. Hopeful and excited, Johan placed the record on the player. A beautiful baritone voice and piano music spilled out of the record and caressed everyone in the room.

Kasia was captivated at first but soon came to her senses. She stood up, turned to Johan, and said, "It's very nice, but I don't speak German and I don't understand a single word. You must excuse me. Besides, I've chores I must do." She lowered her head and turned to leave the room.

Johan jumped in front of her and said, "Kasia, your face showed you liked it. No? I promise to translate some of the 'lieders' for you." And he did.

The strange thing for Johan was that he felt as if he knew Kasia before he met her. He sensed her vulnerability, and her innate pride. Underneath his machismo, vanity, and stubbornness, he, too, was vulnerable. Furthermore, he couldn't help noticing Kasia's slender figure undulating underneath her modest dresses and blouses when she walked. Nor could he keep her big, sad eyes out of his thoughts.

People in love do crazy things. One day in July, Johan showed up at the Jabkowskis' house with an announcement. He made sure Kasia was in the room to hear it.

"Our chauffeur will drive Kasia to see her mother and brother. My dad approves of the idea."

Kasia was stupefied. *Who does he think he is to make such a decision without asking me first? The idiot will blow my cover and get us all killed!*

Jadwiga said, "That is thoughtful of you, Johan. We certainly will keep your generous offer in mind when we need it. Right now, Kasia has no problem getting to see her mother and brother."

"Okay, but you don't have a car at your disposal. Kasia cannot see them whenever she wants. I will make it happen. I can't see how you could turn this down."

Jadwiga had to think fast. She said, "Please don't start making any driving arrangements for Kasia just yet. She already has plans to visit out-of-town friends. These plans were made far in advance. They cannot be changed."

"You don't understand. I haven't told you yet. I'll be joining the German army in August. Surely visiting friends can wait. I will plan to take Kasia to see her family before I leave. Piotrek can come with us, too." He winked at Piotrek as if he could count on his support. After all, he was just trying to be nice.

An image of Johan, tall and swaggering, in a spiffy SS uniform, a skeleton emblem staring down from his hat, flashed in Kasia's head. She remained stiff and as silent as a cadaver. *Merciful God, thank you for your plans to send him away. Protect me until he's gone.*

Jadwiga said, "Dear Johan, go in peace. We will pray for your safety and for the war to end soon. Surely there will be plenty of occasions to show generosity toward one another. Let's leave the travel plans alone for now."

Unfortunately, Johan was stubborn and impatient and liked to have things his way. He said, "Fine. But we'll find a way to arrange matters before I leave. You can count on that."

That wasn't all. Johan's father, Bruno, got in on the act. He ran into Marcel in the courtyard one afternoon.

"Ah, Marcel! How are things going?"

"All is well. Can't complain."

"I noticed Johan is hanging around your house a lot lately." He winked and smiled a broad smile. "I cannot say I blame him. Your niece is a pretty thing. I'd be tempted to come to your house, too, if I were a few years younger."

"Johan is a fine lad."

"Yes, thank you. He talks much about your niece. It's too bad she lost her father. Unfortunately, many people suffer in war. You know Johan will be leaving soon to join the army."

"Yes, he told us."

"He must have also told you that he has my permission to engage my chauffeur to drive Kasia to see her mother. I am sure it will mean a great deal to her."

"Yes, he made this generous offer. We might take him up on it in the future, but not right now. Kasia will be out of town much of this month. We have already made arrangements."

"Johan will be disappointed. He was counting on it."

CHAPTER THIRTY-TWO

The Meadow

hree days after Johan insisted on chauffeuring Kasia to her
mother's house, Pavel and his father, Pan Rogal, arrived at
the Jabkowskis' to take her to an uncle's estate outside Warsaw.
The plan was to leave her there until Johan departed. To be
sure, it was not the safest place, but then no place was safe for
Kasia. It was the best option available.

Kasia had never met Pavel's Aunt Ania and Uncle Jan. She
knew nothing about them. She simply accepted Marcel's and
Jadwiga's decision and their assurances, "This is the safest
thing to do. Pavel's parents are our close friends. We know their
whole family. You will be safe with his aunt and uncle."

To prepare Kasia for what to expect, Jadwiga had told her,
"Pavel's Aunt Ania and Uncle Jan's estate house — including fine
furniture, family heirlooms, sculptures, and pantries lined with
porcelain dishes, pots and pans, cutlery, and fine linen — were
confiscated by the SS. Ania and Jan now live in a small house
once occupied by their gardener's family. The house is cozy and
has windows with bucolic views. Blessedly, it stands a considerable distance from the SS-occupied estate house."

Kasia never asked whether they were aware that she was Jewish. She was afraid to pose too many questions. Nor had she ever told Pavel, "You know, I am Jewish." She had picked up sound clues, though, that it was no secret to him. Furthermore, the fact that his mother was a member of Żegota made her think: *It's entirely possible his mother procured my false Kasia documents.* However, she avoided the subject out of an abundance of caution.

Pavel and his father arrived at the Jabkowskis' early in the morning. The sun was out, the sky a deep blue; the girl's heart beat wildly with hope and fear.

"Ready, Kasia?" Pavel asked.

"Yes, I was watching the door for you."

Pavel collected Kasia's satchel; she hugged Jadwiga, Marcel, and Piotrek; and then they headed out toward the green countryside, something she had not seen since the first bomb fell on Warsaw.

Pavel opened the back door of his family's old Skoda for Kasia and sat down beside her. Pan Rogal turned on the ignition, the engine sputtered, the car lurched forward and picked up speed. City scenes slipped quickly past them. The world was fluid, both hopeful and frightening. Soon, silky white birches, isolated huts, forests, and meadows blinked into view and vanished. Kasia's eyes stayed focused on the scrolling panoramas while her mind returned to a time before she had ever heard of ghettos and Treblinka.

"You're very quiet, Kasia," Pavel observed, putting his arm around her.

"I feel nostalgic. My family used to spend summers in this area when I was a child. I miss them all the time, but most when I'm closest to the things I love best."

The car rolled over bumps in the road. It sped past forest, past slashing white oaks, past towering pine trees, past meadows shimmering with flowers. The boundless majesty of nature seemed light years away from, yet so ostentatiously close to, the raging hate and destruction.

Pan Rogal said, "Pavel, we're almost there. Tell Kasia about your aunt and uncle."

"Okay. Are you ready to listen, Kasia?"

"I'm all ears."

They turned to face each other, their eyes met, knees touched, and a feathery current fluttered through Kasia.

"Here goes. Uncle Jan, my mom's older brother, is as tall and thin as a reed. He's a botanist. He loves trees and flowers, animals and insects, and everything that's rooted, flies, crawls, or walks. And he talks to all of these inanimate and animate things as if they could understand him."

"That's true. He loves all living things with equal reverence," Pan Rogal said.

"My Aunt Ania is an incredible sculptor," Pavel continued. "She makes clay come to life in the form of ballerinas, peasants, people with ordinary and striking faces and postures. She also creates the creepiest animals and reptiles with frightening exactness. When I was little, her snakes scared the devil out of me and fascinated me at the same time.

"My aunt is also a fabulous cook. She makes the most delicious jam-filled, orange-glazed doughnuts. She knows I love them. They will be waiting for us when we arrive. You'll see. Except the orange glaze will be missing. The Nazis gobble up our best things."

Suddenly, the car swerved into a side road lined with acacia trees.

"We're almost there!" Pavel called out. He pointed to a gabled roof overlooking an extensive property enclosed by a wall of trees. "This is their house, Kasia, but they no longer live in it."

"Yes, Aunt Jadwiga told me."

The Skoda rolled past a well-groomed garden leading to the main house occupied by the SS in command. It veered into a narrow side road, continued for some distance, then stopped in front of a little house with a pitched roof. Shrubs and flowerbeds hugged the house on all sides. The garden area was small but rich in textures, shapes, and hues. The hosts stood at the edge of the garden, waving. A big black poodle stood beside them, barking up a storm. Evidently, the rattling Skoda had announced their approach. Pan Rogal found a small clearing in which to park the car. The three passengers stepped out and were greeted with open arms.

"So glad to have you with us, Kasia." Jan bowed and kissed her hand.

"Dzień dobry," Kasia responded, as she curtsied and looked up at him. He was tall and distinguished looking. His kind, sad face and gentle demeanor made him seem out of place in the brutal world.

Ania, a rotund woman with friendly blue eyes, made Kasia feel equally at ease. "So glad to have you in our house," she said pleasantly.

If life were normal, Kasia would have taken for granted the simple generosity of that July day. It would not have stood out in sharp contrast to the events that preceded or followed.

The group entered a simply furnished room. The men carried the luggage into adjacent small rooms. Kasia stood back in a corner, perusing the place like one studies a stranger's face to form an impression. A vase with artfully arranged fresh flowers was the first object to catch her attention. It stood on an oblong wooden table to her left. A number of straight-backed chairs with colorful cushions surrounded the table.

Next to lure her attention was sunlight bursting in through a center window and the shadow of a bird in flight across the opposite wall. At the far right stood a tile stove. Next to it, dishes and cooking utensils were neatly stacked on open shelves. Curious sculptures peered out at her from many angles in the room—Aunt Ania's work, no doubt. The room reflected a love of beauty and man's genius for making the most of simple things. And there were scents of cinnamon and spice drifting in the air. Kasia's stomach grumbled. She felt comfortable and immensely indebted. *They don't even know me, and they are putting themselves in such danger by letting me stay until Johan leaves. How will I ever repay them?*

The group soon gathered around the table. A pastoral view was framed in the window like an enormous still life. An engulfing craving to run into the pine forest a short distance away took hold of Kasia: run and hide among the dense trees and shadows; stay there until the war ends. These forests were once her paradise.

Pavel moved his chair close to Kasia. His nearness and affectionate smile reassured her.

Ania served doughnuts and tea. The room echoed with conversation. At first the chatter was light and safe, referring to family and friends Kasia had never met, but it quickly turned to the occupation and resistance. Clearly, war does not invite trivial talk. Nor does the presence of foreign soldiers on one's property stop courageous hearts from standing up for what is right. Kasia listened with utter concentration. She stopped breathing when Ania deplored the tragic fate of the ghetto people during the uprising three months before. Their willingness to discuss dangerous topics in front of her confirmed in her mind: *They know my secret and it is okay; I no longer need to hide from them. But I mustn't ask indiscreet questions until I get to know them better. I cannot afford to assume anything.*

The weightier conversation had barely started rolling when Jan said, "It's a glorious day. Let's go for a walk. I will show you my garden. We can talk later."

They sauntered around the small garden. Jan talked about his plants affectionately, touching them gently as if he were patting children on their heads. A few chickens, ducks, and geese clucked, quacked, and honked about their feet. The serenity felt boundless. Although Kasia knew the Nazis were never far, she could taste the momentary tranquility, run her tongue over it.

She whispered in her head: *Mama and Tata, I squint my eyes and I think I see you in the shadow beyond the trees, but you're never there. I know the gift of this moment would make you happy for me, but it makes me miss you so much more.*

In the distance, peasants with stooped backs toiled among neat rows of plants. The earth looked blessed, but not the people on it. Much of the land belonged to Jan and Ania, although the Nazis confiscated most of the harvest. Jan and Ania were allowed to keep some poultry, a little milk from the cows, meat when the cattle were slaughtered, and a tiny fraction of the crops. Of course, these conditions were deplorable. Yet, Kasia knew that, under the occupation, her hosts were lucky to have a corner in which to live. Above all, they still had hope and the ability to resist, albeit in secret.

"Is it safe for Pavel and me to take a short walk in the forest or meadow?" Kasia asked pleadingly. Having been confined to the dreary ghetto, she had not seen trees or open spaces for years.

Jan said, "You'll be safe going with Pavel. But I must remind both of you, always keep your eyes and ears open. Don't go far. And use sound judgment, always. Any time you hear or sense something suspicious, turn around immediately and head home."

Kasia understood Jan's warning. In the ghetto, you had to keep your eyes and ears open from the moment the sun lit up the sky until it sank on the horizon. Yet fear didn't stop people from living, even if it meant committing capital crimes like reading books, smuggling food, or going to the theater. Fear inhibited them no more than the abyss below a cliff stops mountain climbers from reaching for the next foothold above them. She understood perfectly why the proximity of Nazi guns failed to keep people from going into the woods and from hoping that probability would work in their favor. That is what happens in time of war: Eternity is lived in a fragile moment. Paradoxically, living on the edge of death had taught Kasia things most young people her age had not learned, such as appreciating the splendor of each new sunrise. Above all, she learned to feel the depths of sadness without letting it destroy her.

Pavel and Kasia stepped out of Jan's garden.

"You decide where we should walk, Kasieńka," Pavel said.

Without hesitation, she pointed, "There! The pine forest."

"This would be my first choice, too, but we need an earlier start for that. How about the forest tomorrow, the meadow today? We can gorge ourselves on wild berries, chase butterflies, and stretch out on a carpet of wildflowers."

They struck out across the meadow. Life stirred everywhere the girl looked. The summer air bustled and hummed. Flies, bees, gnats, grasshoppers, butterflies, and beetles appeared all over. They crawled, flew, and hopped from leaf to leaf.

My God, there is so much life in every bit of space here, while the ghetto is as silent as death. She shivered and turn her head to shake off the image. Pavel's eyes met hers. He clasped her hand.

They walked far into the horizon, picked gooseberries and currants from thorny bushes, and stuffed themselves like poor relatives at a rich uncle's feast. Kasia plucked wildflowers and held them like a precious heirloom. She braided them into a wreath and put it on Pavel's head. Then she made one for herself and smiled at Pavel and at the glory of the moment.

Pavel said, "You look as beautiful as a summer goddess." She blushed and reached for the brightest flowers to make a bouquet to bring to Ania and Jan.

When they grew tired, they stretched out on the grass. Their hearts brimmed with youthful love. They didn't move too close to each other, although they yearned to. Behavior that would be considered prudish even a generation later was felt to be proper then. They held hands and talked about things nearest to their hearts. Kasia told Pavel about her beloved friend, Hanna, and what had happened to her and to nearly everyone she loved and knew. Pavel mentioned his own family.

"Did you hear about what happened to my mother?" he asked.

"Yes, I did. Piotrek told me. And I know that you have no idea what the Nazis did with her. She was very brave and noble to work for an organization dedicated to saving Jews."

"She didn't think she was brave or noble. She just felt she was doing what was right."

"Do you believe she did what was right even though she is paying such a high price for it?"

"Yes, I do."

"If your mother and my surrogate family can do it, then why don't others?"

"Yes, that is the question. Why?"

CHAPTER THIRTY-THREE

The Window

Borrowed moments of contentment are easily marred under the yoke of occupation. This was true that summer afternoon when Kasia and Pavel rested on a bed of wildflowers. Suddenly, a rifle shot rang out and shattered the serenity. A momentary silence followed. Then, three more blasts, "tat-tat-tat."

The two young people sat up and looked guardedly in all directions. Not a soul was in sight, but they heard men's boisterous voices and sporadic rifle pops drawing towards them from an invisible distance. It was no mystery who the intruders were. Who but Nazis carried weapons in broad daylight?

Pavel whispered, "The shots aren't far off. We don't have time to make a run to the house. You must hide in the berry bushes, there." He pointed at a thick cluster of shrubs. "Stay there until I come to get you. You know my special whistle. When you hear it, you'll know it's me."

"What about your safety? I want us to stay together!"

He talked fast, "Do as I tell you. It's a gang of Nazis hunting for rabbits or whatever. Girls are not safe in the presence of soldiers who've probably had too much beer to drink." *He didn't say, "Especially girls with false identities,"* Kasia thought. "I speak enough German to be able to point them to the best hunting spots. Of course, away from where you are."

Then he hissed, "Run, Kasia, before it's too late! Now!"

And he then stepped jauntily away, whistling as if all were perfect with the world.

Kasia hunched her shoulders and ran so fast her skirt billowed out behind her. It seemed as if she were no longer touching the ground. She reached the edge of the meadow and ducked under a cluster of thorny bushes. She tracked the sound of Pavel's whistle fading slowly in the distance even as the German voices grew louder and closer. Fear shivered through her arms and legs and every part of her. The world grew stark and ominous, although the sky remained as clear as glass. Swarms of bees buzzed rapaciously. Even the mosquitoes sucked blood out of her with greater ferocity. Curled up in her vulnerable hiding place, Kasia felt one with a frightened little rabbit tucked among blades of grass, an arm's length from her. The rabbit looked up at her, his eyes big and brown and rimmed with black, then darted away.

After a brief eternity, Pavel's whistling stopped abruptly. So did the shooting. The entire world stopped breathing. Then, the rowdy noise resumed, but it changed direction, away from Kasia's hideout.

Kasia prayed, *God, I hope that means that Pavel lured the brutes to hunt somewhere else. Please, God, keep him safe and send him back to me quickly.*

Thirty minutes passed. The rifle pops continued to stun the countryside, and there was no sign of Pavel. Thirty minutes is a very long time when bullets explode in the air and you fear for the safety of someone you love. *What if Pavel is in danger? I must run to the house and tell them what happened. Maybe Jan can look for him?*

That wasn't the first time Kasia had to think and act fast. She pondered and calculated: *Passing strangers on the way will be no problem. For all they know, I'm one of them. If I see a Nazi soldier, I'll hide if I can; or I'll do what every Pole does, look past him and keep walking. If Pavel comes back for me, as he said he would, he is smart enough to check at the house before he panics.*

She crawled out of her hiding place, rose to her feet, and looked around. No other human was in sight. She scanned the landscape and realized she didn't remember the way back. She excoriated herself: *I didn't count on having to return by myself. How idiotic not to have paid attention to where we were going. Now what?*

She could have walked to the nearest hut and asked for directions. Everyone in the area knew Jan and Ania. In reality, she had nothing to fear from the neighbors. There was nothing about her that would betray her at that moment. But she decided to avoid being asked questions. To give herself heart she reasoned, *Jan's estate isn't far, and it dominates the landscape. How hard could it be to find?*

She walked a fair distance and eventually spied the gabled roof peering above a fence of tall trees. She was amazed how far she and Pavel had strayed from the estate; she picked up her stride toward the road. A couple of women in colorful babushkas passed her. Kasia bid them good day and traipsed on nonchalantly. They turned their heads and whispered, probably wondering who she was.

When she got closer to the property, she saw that the dirt road branched off from the main road in two opposite sides of the estate, one to the left and one to the right. The intersection was a beehive of activity, with officers and soldiers in Mercedes sedans and on motorcycles zooming past.

Now, which dirt road leads to Jan and Ania's house? she asked herself. She had no clue. She stood at a safe distance, studying both roads for a familiar landmark. Nothing stood out. It might have been happenstance — or providence, if you believe in it — but her eyes riveted on a row of acacia trees on the left side of the estate, triggering a recognition. *Aha! I remember seeing the acacias as we swerved into the dirt road when we had arrived!*

When no one had been near the entrance for about three minutes, she approached the road on the left, walking rapidly, trying to look sure of herself. Her heart hammered. But so far so good.

She was two steps away from the dirt road when a motorcycle thundered out of the estate. She looked away and quickened her stride to almost a run, but it was too late. The two SS officers astride the noisy vehicle spotted her and immediately called out, in a mixture of German and broken Polish, "*Panienko, halt, bitte. Hab kein Angst. Prosze bardzo. Bitte.*" She knew what they were after. She could hear it in their lewd voices.

Don't panic, don't panic, she told herself as she searched for an escape. She caught sight of the thicket of tall grass and brambles behind the row of the acacia trees. *The motorcycle cannot get through this. Bolt!* a voice in her head commanded. And she did.

Kasia plunged into the thicket and could already feel her heart pounding hard, even before she started to run. They continued to call after her, "Pretty girl, stop. We won't hurt you. We just want to speak to you. Take you for a fun spin. Ha ha!"

The roar of the motorcycle, their crude voices and coarse laughter, made the sky shake. Kasia took a single deep breath and ran on. She heard rustling in the grass behind her but was too scared to turn her head to check the source.

She ran, ignoring the scratchy weeds and swarms of mosquitoes. Her breathing was shallow and panicky. She ran even after the two SS men stopped calling out to her. She didn't feel she could stop or even slow down until she was inside Jan and Ania's house and the door closed behind her. Her breathing was so labored that each time she inhaled she wheezed like a little animal chased by a pack of wolves.

Ania took one look at Kasia and dropped the dish she was holding into the sink. "What is it, Kasia?" she asked, alarmed. Jan and Pavel's father stopped their conversation and jumped up from their chairs, apprehension stark on their faces.

"What's happened? Did anyone hurt you?" they asked. "Where is Pavel?"

Still panting hard, Kasia told them why Pavel was not with her.

When she finished her story, Pavel's father said, "They are out there yet. I can hear the gunshots coming a short distance east of us. I am going out to look for Pavel."

"Wait," Jan said. "I know the top SS commander who lives like a king in my house. Ironically, the bastard is a renowned botanist. I will go there and ask him to send a couple of his men to find Pavel."

"Why would he do that for you?" Pan Rogal asked.

"Because I have a professional relationship with him dating to before the war. He wants Ania and me to think he is a civilized man. Can you believe that?"

Thirty minutes later, Jan returned and reported, "The bastard Schultz sent a couple of soldiers to find Pavel and deliver him home."

Now, the familiar vigil began again. Once more, Kasia stepped to the window, feeling like a caged sparrow looking between bars to catch a glimpse of freedom. She stared into the road beyond Jan's garden for a hint of Pavel's return. The clock ticked, dark clouds bruised the sky, and still no sign of him. Thunder shook the earth, windows rattled, and she remained glued to the window, waiting.

Jan, Ania, and Pavel's father had good reason to be hopeful that Pavel would be okay. Most people in their lives, although not all, didn't disappear forever. For Kasia, on the other hand, waiting for Pavel felt no different than waiting for her beloved friend, Hanna, to return from an emergency trip to the dentist. Hanna had never come back; neither had her parents who left with her. It felt no different than the hours she stood at her ghetto window hoping to see a friend or neighbor walk by. No matter how long she waited, or how hard she wished, the street below her window remained scrubbed clean of people.

It might have been luck. How else could one explain Pavel's arrival right before lightning split the sky and sheets of rain began to pour down, making the world look like glass? He was escorted by two strapping Nazi soldiers.

Everyone was happy beyond words to see Pavel. At the same time, they hoped with all their hearts that the soldiers would throw rain gear over their heads, turn around, and be off. Jan even offered them umbrellas. Instead, the soldiers wiped their boots on the doormat and entered the room, politely. Kasia looked for a quick getaway, but it was too late for that.

The unwelcome guests clicked their heels and doffed their caps. "*Guten Tag*," they said graciously. They bowed extra low to Ania and Kasia. "*Guten Tag, gnädige Frau, Fräulein.*" The skull-and-crossbones insignia above their visors flashed in front of Kasia's eyes. Her heart was in her throat. She was prepared for the worst to happen, for death to assault the room.

Jan tried to take control of the situation. He thanked the men for bringing Pavel home and remained standing at the open door.

"*Bitte sehr*," they replied. "Do you mind if we invite ourselves in and wait for the rain to pass?" they asked and perched themselves on chairs on either side of Kasia. They glanced at her and smiled as if they recognized their own humanity in her. She couldn't get over how ordinary the two Nazis looked. Both were blue eyed. One's hair was dark, and his cheeks were speckled with tiny zit scars. He looked as Aryan as Goebbels or Hitler. They smiled affably.

Kasia was taken aback. Never before had she witnessed such civility from Nazi barbarians. She trusted their courtesy as much as she trusted March weather, though — one moment the sun is out, the next it hails. She knew that under their amiable Dr. Jekyll facades, the evil impulse of Mr. Hyde was lurking. She shrank into herself, struggled valiantly to keep her composure, and feigned the demeanor of a normal, shy girl.

To keep the soldiers' attention away from Kasia, Jan and Ania showered them with questions about their homes and their families. They answered civilly, then turned back to Kasia and chattered away. She understood nearly every word they said but responded with a shrug, a blank face, and a single sentence in Polish, "*Ja nie rozumiem.*"

One soldier pointed at himself and said, "Ich, Kurt." Then he jabbed a finger toward his colleague and said — slow and loud as if she were deaf — "Heinrich." He tipped his face and hand toward her, expectantly, "*Du?*"

She looked puzzled, shrugged, and repeated, "Nie rozumiem."

Heinrich tried flattery. "Your eyes are beautiful," he said with a predatory grin.

She shook her head and stuck to her response, "Nie rozumiem."

The summer storm continued to rattle the windows. Rain poured down the rooftop and rainspouts for a short while longer. Then, it stopped just as suddenly as it started. A pale afternoon sun lit up the countryside; the air smelled sweet and pungent. The two Nazis stood up, promised to come back to take Kasia for a walk or a motorcycle ride, bowed courteously, and left. Kasia didn't miss noting their haughty stride, ramrod backs, domineering glances — as if they were the proprietors of the planet. The metallic clicks of their hobnailed boots made her skin prickle.

The display of civility by the SS men left Kasia with many unanswered questions about humans.

CHAPTER THIRTY-FOUR

The Forest

P avel and his father returned to Warsaw the following morning. Kasia stayed two weeks longer. She fervently wished
she could repay Ania and Jan for their enormous and rare kindness, although there was no need for her to feel indebted at
all — not from their point of view.

Every little crumb of benevolence felt huge to Kasia. She
rose early every morning and helped Jan turn the soil in his little garden and look after plants. She toiled cheerfully at his side
and listened to him talk about the uniqueness of each plant and
the amazing universality of all living things. She hung on to his
words until she forgot the dark side of life. Jan's compassion and
humility reminded her of her grandfather and Janusz Korczak
and touched her very core. She shuddered to think how sad the
world would be without the presence of the humble people who
do what is good and right, in spite of raging brutality. Indeed,
they are the healers of the world.

At a "safe" distance from Jan and Ania's little hut stood the
main estate-house occupied by the local SS authorities. The
Nazis were seldom seen near Jan's house. That was good. But

they were not far enough for Kasia to avoid hearing their boisterous voices and the general unchecked ruckus they created.
To tune out the barbaric clamor, she turned her attention to
the glory of the vast countryside. She listened to the chirps and
whistles stirring in the bushes; she let her eyes wander over the
ever-changing ribbons of color draping the abundant land; she
breathed in the freedom soaring in the vast sky, trusting: *There
is a good chance that Tata and Ben are looking at the same sky at
the very same moment I am.*

That method worked fine during the day. When night fell
and darkness spread over the Earth, Jan's hut seemed to grow
more vulnerable, at least as far as Kasia was concerned. Precisely
when she and all the villagers were trying to catch some sleep,
the rulers at the estate — full of drink and hilarity — made the
night perch on edge.

One particular night, their frolicking ended with a crescendo
of gunfire that went on clear past morning hours. Apparently,
Herr Schultz, the eminent botanist who ruled over Jan's property, as well as all other area properties, had thrown a hunting
party to ingratiate himself with his powerful SS friends. The
volleys of gunfire prompted for Kasia an image of purgatory.

One might ask, wasn't the proximity of the SS headquarters
to Uncle Jan's hut more threatening to Kasia's safety than staying in Warsaw would have been? The answer is, hardly — especially while Johan was on the scene. Moreover, in Warsaw, Kasia
could not trust her neighbors, and the Nazis were on everyone's
heels. They roamed streets, parks, and trams. Sometimes they
descended with planned suddenness and conducted *łapanki*
(roundups) in the most unexpected places: churches, train sta-
tions, and ration lines. Those who the bad fortune of being in
the wrong place or who did not run fast enough were sent to
Germany to perform indentured labor, but no one was gassed.
The Poles' right to live was not denied them, as long as they
submitted to German authority. Kasia knew herself lucky to
have been brought to the Christian side of the wall, but brutality in any degree is still brutality.

Pavel and his father returned to Jan's house two weeks later to take Kasia back to Warsaw. The instant they hopped out of the old Skoda, Kasia noticed a heightened agitation in their faces, an edgy energy in their strides. Before she could pluck up enough courage to ask what had happened, Pavel put his arms around her and said, "Dad has something to tell you that will make you very happy, Kasieńka."

"That's right, Kasia," Pan Rogal confirmed. "But let's sit down first." He gave her a radiant smile.

As they took their seats, Pan Rogal cleared his throat, turned his face to Kasia, and said, "Kasieńka, Marcel and Jadwiga want you to know that your father and Ben Rotenberg are among the handful of ghetto heroes who managed to escape through the sewers. They made their way to the forest in Michalin, where they joined the Polish partisans."

A thousand suns rose in her heart. "How do you know?" she asked eagerly.

"We cannot tell you that, but rest assured the information is reliable."

"Where is my mother? Do you know what happened to her?"

Pan Rogal said regretfully, "I don't know, Kasia. I'm sorry."

It was not hard to guess Mama's fate. *What will I do without her?* she asked herself. To subdue grief, she placed the palms of her hands on her cheeks and imagined her fingers tracing the contours of Mama's face, touching the curly strands of her hair. Kasia quickly pushed feelings of loss into a far corner inside herself and suppressed her sobs.

She thanked Pan Rogal. His eyes embraced her. She didn't feel deserving of being comforted, however. She knew how much more fortunate she was than nearly all the people she had left behind. Everyone she knew and loved was dead — every single one, except for Tata and Ben. They were the whole world to her now.

The news dwarfed all else she saw, heard, or felt. Even Pavel and her kind hosts slipped into the background like outlines of themselves. The image of falling into Tata's arms superimposed itself on her consciousness, on the walls, on people's faces, and nearly crushed her. The euphoria of a reunion and the sorrows she kept corked inside for so long welled up in her.

Tata and Ben are alive! I might be reunited with them one wonderful day, soon, she repeated in her head over and over again as one would touch a talisman. At the same time, she was fully aware that there were rivers of blood to cross before that awaited moment; but there was hope.

It might seem odd that even in places teetering on the edge of an abyss, young people attend schools (albeit secret ones) and go to theaters and on dates — but that is the way of things, and with life. Our imminent ending does not preclude our fleeting beginnings and middles. And that is how it was with Kasia and Pavel that day, when Kasia heard the news about Tata and Ben.

After a mid-morning meal, Pavel led Kasia into the garden and said, "It's still early. Let's go for a walk to celebrate the news about your dad and Ben."

Kasia wiped a tear from her eye. She couldn't keep her mind off the miracle.

"Pavel, I can hardly believe *my dad* and *Ben* are among the sixty fighters who escaped alive. Sixty out of 400,000 deported and killed."

The young man cradled Kasia's hand in his. He felt enormous compassion and love.

"Pavel, do you suppose they will come to see me? They're on the other side of the wall now. Can you imagine that? I think my heart will crack. They're so close! So, so close!"

"I know. But they're hiding with the partisans. Their leaving the forest to see you is far too risky to everyone. You'll have to wait a bit longer. At least until after we take a walk in the woods. But the war will end soon." He embraced her tenderly.

He tried to lift her melancholy. "The day we took our stroll in the meadow, you looked disappointed when I talked you out of going to the forest. Do you really like forests that much?"

"Oh, yes! They remind me of my childhood paradise."

"Should we head for the forest then?"

"Yes!" Then she added lightly, "What if this trip turns out as horribly as our meadow walk did?"

"It might. At least we'll be able to hide behind trees. Tell me, did fear of the Nazis keep you behind closed doors in the ghetto all the time?"

"Hell, no. Actually, the spunky people who took greater risks had a better chance of survival. My best friend Hanna and I went to a secret school and other forbidden places. Ben and his friends were absolute daredevils. They cruised the Christian side to smuggle in food so their families wouldn't starve to death. Later, they smuggled in arms for the Jewish fighters and acted as couriers. Staying home didn't save anyone from getting killed."

"No Pole I hang out with lives by Nazi prohibitions, either. Who knows, maybe my mother would have been free today if she had taken a long stroll the morning the Nazis barged into our house and dragged her away."

They struck out across the field. Life stirred everywhere they looked. As soon as Kasia entered the forest, memories erased the present.

"Pavel, when I was little, before the war, I used to spend summers in the countryside with my aunts, uncles, and beloved cousins."

Gradually, she told him about the people she loved who were gone.

"Hanna and I spent hours playing in the pine forests near Warsaw. Some of our friends thought forests were dark, gloomy, and scary. We found them mythical, majestic, and beautiful, though. We imagined fairy creatures hidden behind moss-covered stones, under trees, and within thick clumps of needle leaves."

"Weren't you a little scared of the darkness and silence?"

"We were both frightened and captivated by the giant shadows, the swishing sound of trees, and the winds stirring in dark corners sounding like old witches whispering behind walls."

Kasia and Pavel moved as softly as forest animals, their voices muted by the giant trees.

Pavel stopped to stare into a thicket.

"Are we lost?" Kasia asked.

"Lost? Never. I'm just looking for a stick."

"I will find you one right away. I will find you millions of them." They laughed.

"I know there are millions of them here. But I'm looking for the just the right one."

"Oh."

He picked through the branches until he found one that made him nod with approval. He said, "I'll carve a hiking stick for you as a token of my affection."

They sat down on a moss-covered rock. Their faces almost touched. She could see gray flecks swimming around his irises. They leaned into each other. Every cell in her body tingled. At the same time, she could hardly silence the thought: *Tata and Ben are alive. I'm so grateful and so afraid for their safety.*

Pavel sensed her longing. He understood. He, too, knew loss. Not as grave as Kasia's, but you don't have to be hit with a sledgehammer to suffer pain.

He gazed into her eyes, remaining silent for a few seconds, then said, "Kasia, I hope you know that I love you."

His face glowed with sincerity, and he looked so handsome against the backdrop of giant trees.

Kasia's heart thudded louder in her ears than all the audible sounds in the forest. From the time they first met, Pavel had made it apparent that he found her special. Yet, his declaration disarmed her completely.

"Why would you choose to love me when there are so many beautiful, lighthearted Polish girls?"

"Because none have your grace, your sharp wit, and your courage."

"I'm not sure it's courage you see. It is my stubborn will to live."

"I love you for your stubborn will. When we both get a little older and I'm able to assume the responsibility, I will ask you to marry me. I vow my love to you forever."

He looked dashing — his wide shoulders expanded with inspiration, face tender with emotion. Millions of prisms flickered around them.

"I love you, too," she whispered. "Very much."

Pavel drew her close. They kissed.

She wanted to melt into him, trust where love would guide her. But shyness and prevailing social rules drew a firm line.

Their hearts overflowed with love, hope, and sadness. Briskly, Pavel pulled out his pocketknife and said, "I better keep my promise to carve that hiking stick for you."

Pavel carved expertly, pausing only to look up at Kasia as if she were the most important presence in the forest. She watched the blade cut into the silky bark, creating intricate designs.

"Do you like it so far?"

"It's beautiful. It looks more like a royal scepter than a hiking stick."

"Then that's what it will be."

When he finished, he handed it to her. "There, especially for you."

"It is the most beautiful hiking stick ever. With this at my side, I can hike in the forest until the war is over."

"Can I join you?"

"Of course."

"What will we do for food?"

"I don't know. You are the hunter. I just talk with fairy creatures."

"I think you can do better than that."

"True. I'll borrow Jan's book about edible forest plants."

"I will make a treehouse for us to sleep in."

"I will weave a blanket of moss to keep us warm."

"I will hunt for fur to keep us clothed. I am almost as good with my slingshot as William Tell was with his bow. He shot an apple off his son's head with a single arrow. I will shoot down birds from the sky and rabbits scampering on the ground. We will not go hungry."

"And I will collect dew from leaves, and raindrops. We will not go thirsty."

"It is decided. We will stay in the forest 'til the war is over, even if we are not yet married. But first we have to go back to the house to announce our plan to my dad, aunt, and uncle."

They stepped forward. Their feet tapped in rhythm, like joined heartbeats. In Kasia's head played a refrain, *Tata and Ben are alive. I might live to see them. There is a flicker of hope.*

"You know these woods well, Pavel," she said with admiration.

"I do. I come here with my scout group for training."

"How do you know your way without getting lost?"

"Well, for one, I carry a compass in my pocket. Besides, when I was little, I loved the forest as much as you did. I still do. I stroll here often. I'm a wolf in disguise."

He told her about his boyhood forest adventures, armed with a slingshot.

"Did you ever kill an animal?"

"Only giants and threatening trolls."

Their voices murmured, so as not to disturb the forest silence.

To give their hearts wings, Pavel said, "Everyone believes the Nazis have essentially lost the war. The occupation will end soon. They will run in defeat and shame and we'll be happy ever after." He held her hand tightly, warmly.

"I am crossing my fingers to make it happen."

"I am sure that'll do it."

They walked slowly across the meadow, unwilling to let the day end. A cool breeze fluttered around them. Nestled in the hedges, birds trilled warbling songs.

As the two young people were halfway home, a pair of soldiers on a motorcycle came to a stop alongside them, revving their engine to impress Kasia with the power under their thumbs, and tried to strike up a conversation with her. Pavel and Kasia quickened their stride and looked away. The two soldiers roared with laughter at the controlled panic on Kasia's and Pavel's faces. Giving the bike full throttle, they took off with a thundering roar and a whirl of dust.

In her dreams that night, Kasia flew across acres of green countryside, like Hermes, the Greek god. Skimming the ground — as if she had wings on her heels — she vaulted into a forest: dark, misty, and rustling with partisans' voices.

Tata's baritone voice stood out above all forest sounds, like a bell. It lured her on until she found him in a circle of proud fighters. Shafts of sun skidded through the dense needle trees and lit up his presence. Tata looked heroic, his hair darker than she remembered, his shirt white as snow, sleeves rolled up. She was so close to him she could feel his breath. Like in all her recurring dreams about people she missed, the harder she tried to touch him, the more unreachable he was.

Kasia returned to Warsaw in August. The city was crowded, noisy, and hot. As soon as she stepped into the Jabkowskis' home and shut the door behind her, she flooded Marcel with questions about Tata and Ben. "Did you talk to my father? Did you see him, Uncle Marcel? Do you know what happened to my mother?"

"Kasia, I did not see your father, nor did I speak with him, but I talked to a friend who saw your dad and Ben in the forest with the Polish underground. And darling, I wished I had news about your mother. But as long as we do not know for sure, there is hope."

"Will I be able to see my father and Ben, even if only for a single second? Is it possible? They are now on the same side of the wall as I am. So close."

"Kasieńka, the message your father sent to you is that you must be patient just a little longer. Although he can hardly wait to embrace you, any attempt to see you before the Nazis are gone would greatly endanger your life. That would be unbearable. You understand, don't you?"

"I do."

They talked late into the night. Piotrek took the lead to fill her in on the latest Johan front.

"You'll be pleased to know that Johan is packed and ready to take off. He is anxious to see you before he joins the Nazi ranks.

I guess he needs your admiration. Be prepared for a little drama. You know how nutty he's become, although he used to be the neatest guy."

"When is he leaving?"

"Next week."

Johan showed up the following morning, looking bright and full of vim. He asked Jadwiga, "Is Kasia here? I'd like to say goodbye to her before I leave. Could I see her?"

"Sure," Jadwiga answered and called out, "Kasia, come here. Johan wants to say goodbye to you."

Kasia stepped out of her room. "Hi, Johan."

"Hi, Kasia. I would ask you to take a walk in the park, but I know what your answer will be. So, can I see you alone, just for a minute? Don't say no this time, please."

Kasia hesitated a moment and thought: *He'll be gone in a few days. One minute; how bad could that be?*

"Okay, Johan."

They stepped into the living room. No one else was there.

"I missed seeing you while you were gone. I won't bother to ask where you were. I hope you had a good time."

"I did, thank you," she said and thought with relief, *Thank God it won't turn into an interrogation.*

"I was waiting for you to return. I'm leaving in a few days. I didn't want to leave without saying goodbye to you."

Kasia cast her eyes modestly to the floor and said, "Goodbye then, Johan. May Jezus keep you safe."

"Is that all you have to say? I'm going to war and I might get killed."

"Then, don't go, and you won't get killed or kill others. Killing is a sin. Killing innocent people and babies is the greatest sin of all."

"I don't agree with all the things Hitler is doing. But I cannot abandon my family's values and my country's call."

Words flew out of her mouth before she could call them back. "Even if you think they are wrong? Your ability to think for yourself is your godliness. At least that is what my church teaches."

Her heart was pounding in her throat. She lowered her gaze and crossed herself, hoping the pious gesture would protect her from him.

Johan remained unmoved by what this God-fearing girl thought. He saw the world as being either good and obedient or bad and disobedient, with no gray area in between. He struck a romantic Romeo pose—chest expanded, eyes brimming with emotion, fists clenched determinedly.

"Kasia, I know many girls, but you're the only one that matters to me. I may be sent to the front, maybe even to the Russian front. It's cold as hell there in the winter. I'll be very lonely." His voice dropped to a murmur. "Kasia, I will write to you. Will you answer my letters?"

Kasia looked at him and blinked. *Gosh, he is sensitive and capable of love. How long will it take his leaders to teach him to kill and maim without feeling a thing?*

She said, "I'm sorry, Johan. I'll pray for your safety, but I cannot promise to write back. To correspond with a boy is a transgression, completely against my religious vow. You know that."

Being a macho man, young and optimistic, he interpreted her answer as: *She's really in love with me, but she's afraid to admit it.* And so, letters from Johan to Kasia began to arrive soon after he departed. They continued to come until bitter winter settled in the Russian steppes. Then the letters suddenly stopped.

CHAPTER THIRTY-FIVE

Sabotage

The gusty fall reminded people of arriving winter and food and fuel shortages. To lift their spirits, they snapped up morsels of encouraging news circulating in the city. In September, they cheered the landing of the Allied troops on the beaches near Naples. In November, Soviet forces liberated Kiev and optimism spiked.

Kasia followed the rapid progress but took nothing for granted. She told herself: *Everyone must do his or her part to defeat the Nazi tyrants.* It troubled her greatly that she contributed nothing to the cause, while her surrogate family, including Piotrek, as well as Pavel and their scout friends, were actively fighting for Poland's freedom. *Why can't I do the same?* she wondered.

She appealed to Jadwiga, "Auntie, I would like to join Piotrek's scout group and do my part for liberty, just as you and Uncle Marcel and Piotrek, Pavel, and their scout friends do — and everyone I knew and loved in the ghetto did."

"Kasia, I am not surprised you feel that way. I know you have tremendous courage and smarts that would be an asset to the scouts. But I think it is safest for everyone involved if you do not join."

Kasia did not insist. After all, Jadwiga and Marcel were not her parents. She accepted Jadwiga's decision without uttering a word of protest. However, Kasia being Kasia, she appointed herself as a silent, standby member of Piotrek's scout group. Much to her credit (and theirs), she was well accepted by all of them. They treated her as one of their tribe — as Polish as the red-and-white flag. When they met in Piotrek's house, she joined in their banter and listened to their gossip. She contributed nothing tangible but took vicarious pride in their spirit and their subversive activities.

The scouts operated under the shield of the Home Army and served as couriers, bicycling around the city without raising suspicion. They also painted anti-Nazi slogans on walls — a shootable offense — distributed anti-German propaganda, and served as minor saboteurs. The older ones even helped free people from German prisons and blow up bridges. One may ask, why did parents permit their sons and daughters to take such risks? But then, doesn't every country offer their young — the bloom of their generation — to serve in the armed forces? Sometimes even for a malevolent cause.

On one assignment, Piotrek, Pavel, and two other scouts, Staś and Wladek, were assigned to place a mine on a railroad track at the outskirts of Warsaw. While Kasia sat listening silently to the plan, she noticed that no girl was appointed to go with them. She thought: *That's not smart. Sometimes a girl can get away with things boys ordinarily can't. Girls are less likely to be suspected of wrongdoing and can be useful as decoys. Everyone knows that soldiers are easily distracted by girls.* She remembered how Rebecca had saved Ben's and Heniek's lives by flirting with a German soldier and distracting his attention from the young men, who were smuggling hand grenades from the Christian side of the wall. Kasia was tempted to advise the scouts to include a girl and support her suggestion with facts, but she clearly could not tell them about the Rebecca incident. She said nothing. Her better sense warned: *If I open my mouth, they're sure to challenge me and ask how I know what I'm talking about.*

She decided: *I cannot tell them that one never knows when a fighter's life may depend on a girl's guile. But I could follow them — at a discreet distance, of course — as a secret backup. That is the least I can do for the cause.*

Pavel slept at the Jabkowskis' house the night before the assignment. The following morning, when the streets began to fill with traffic, the young men hugged Jadwiga, Marcel, and Kasia and headed for the door.

"Please, boys, be very careful. Don't do anything foolish," Jadwiga and Marcel implored.

"We're always careful. Don't worry," Piotrek replied.

The two boys skipped down the flight of stairs, straddled their bikes, and were off. Five minutes later, Kasia asked Jadwiga if she could borrow her bike.

Jadwiga answered, "Sure. It's a nice day for a ride." She did not ask where the girl was going, and Kasia didn't volunteer to tell her. Neither did she lie.

While Jadwiga and Marcel were waiting for the boys' return, four scouts (Piotrek and Pavel having been joined by Staś and Wladek) bicycled to their assigned spot without difficulty. Kasia kept behind them and out of their range of vision. The sky was blue, the air calm, and no one took note of them. The scouts looked around to be sure no Nazis were in sight and got down to work. Pavel stood guard while the other three boys began to place the explosives. The boys had no inkling that Kasia had parked her bike in the woods and found an unobtrusive position from which she could watch both sides of the road without being noticed.

All went as planned, until Pavel spied three armed Nazis rounding a corner and heading toward them. He stuck the tips of two fingers into his mouth and sounded a short, sharp whistle. The other scouts stopped working and looked up.

"Three Krauts are coming this way!" Pavel informed them.

They had to think fast: They couldn't run away and leave the job unfinished, nor could they stay.

In a split second, Kasia emerged from her strategic hiding spot, straightened her back, smoothed out her skirt, tucked in a stray strand of hair behind her ear, and walked demurely toward the Uniforms.

Surprised and aghast at seeing her, Pavel turned paper white. "No, Kasia! No!" he breathed. "Don't go over there!"

She continued in a steady stride, hips swaying rhythmically to her gait. She commanded her face to stay calm and forced a placid smile on her lips. Of course, the soldiers focused their complete attention on the pretty girl walking toward them. They straightened their lapels and adjusted their facial expressions and body postures to "polite." When she neared them, they doffed their hats like gentlemen. She smiled graciously. They stammered in broken Polish, "Dzień dobry . . ." and finished in German, "gnädiges Fraulein."

Kasia paused, broadened her smile, and returned their greeting. All courtesy and charm, they invited her for a stroll in the park. She didn't respond to that offer, but instead asked them for a cigarette. All the while, she clung fast to the image of Rebecca coquettishly luring a Nazi soldier to carry her suitcase filled with arms and escort her past a Nazi raid.

The three soldiers were only too happy to reach into their pockets and offer their cigarettes. With a dashing flick of his wrist, one Uniform clicked on a lighter for her. A brief glimmer lit up Kasia's green eyes.

She engaged them in a friendly chat. Each jabbered in his or her own tongue. The universal meaning driving the conversation was not lost in translation. She kept them gabbing, "Jawohl! Ach, ja, gnädiges Fraulein . . . " and tried to be as charming and distracting as possible. When she felt enough time had passed to allow the scouts to finish their work, she asked the Germans for a pen and a slip of paper. With a wink and a smile, she wrote down an address and date that clearly implied a rendezvous for the coming Sunday. She let them know two other girls would accompany her. They'd have fun, she promised. The soldiers perused the slip, grinning and winking to each other. They parted, Kasia walking one way and the Germans another. Kasia maintained her casual stride until the soldiers were a safe distance away, although she couldn't prevent her body from trembling.

The fact that she had stood eye to eye with death during ghetto selections to Treblinka did not diminish her fear now. Neither did it weaken her resolve to keep her fear in check. She remained totally focused on the existential moment — just like a soldier under a barrage of fire.

When her scout friends later heard about her audacious act, they showered her with attention and admiration and pressed her to join them.

The boys fawned over her. "Kasia, we need a girl like you in our group. What you did is really something. You saved our lives!"

The girls took pride. "Good for you, Kasia. You showed them what girls are capable of."

Kasia's heart swelled with gratification in her accomplishment, and she relished the attention. How she wanted to tell them: *I'd love to join you and bomb the Nazis out of this world, but I'm outlawed, a Jewish girl. My anonymity is paramount to my safety and the safety of the good people who are protecting me.*

So, she demurred, "Thank you. I didn't do anything special. I was just very lucky the soldiers were big fools. I'll join soon, but not right now. I'm too busy at the moment."

In private, Pavel and Piotrek took turns admonishing her. "What you did was crazy! You put yourself in incredible danger. You better not pull that kind of stunt again."

"What you and Staś and Wladek did was not exactly safe."

"Yes, but we knew what we were doing. It was our mission."

After they were through berating her, Pavel said, "You had me completely fooled. I knew you were gutsy, but I would've never guessed that underneath the shy girl I know you to be, a seductive flirt is hiding. Your act was as good as, or better than, Marlene Dietrich's best performance."

Piotrek nodded in agreement, then asked, "Where did you get the idea to do what you did? Did you ever hear of anyone acting that quick and that bold?"

"As a matter of fact, I did. Many times."

She told them about Rebecca and other ghetto girls she knew who traveled incognita on the Christian side hiding hand grenades in their clothes and in loaves of bread. She explained, "Danger awaited them at every turn. I promised myself that when I was old enough, I'd try faithfully to measure up to their courage. Never in a million years did I imagine I could lie and fake so convincingly to be someone I'm not. But I am learning that if you have a just cause, and you have role models to inspire you, the seemingly impossible is possible."

CHAPTER THIRTY-SIX

Changing Tides

The year 1944 started with the hopeful news of Germany suffering defeat after defeat and retreating on all fronts. Despite their losses, the terror they spread within the countries they still occupied increased. Public executions in the streets of Warsaw took place almost every day. The winter was brutal. Food and coal were scarce and expensive. Most mornings, Jadwiga rose at the break of dawn to get in line at the food shops. Often, the meager supplies disappeared from the shelves before she reached the counter. Meat was especially scarce. The little that was available was horsemeat, most often. The squeamish simply did not ask. A fresh egg made you tingle with greater pleasure than caviar had yielded before the war. Kasia's surrogate family had to be content to keep only the kitchen stove fueled. The rest of the house was as cold as Siberia. Kasia slept bundled in flannel beneath several blankets and a down comforter. In the morning she jumped out of bed and dressed quickly in multiple layers. All windowpanes were covered with a lattice of frost.

On Sundays and special holidays, when the world was bedecked with white snow, the tile heater in the living room was fired, family and friends were invited, and the room echoed with kind voices. The conversations were of hope and peril, the banal and the sublime, and mouthwatering aromas of holiday dishes wafted in the air.

Just like Mama, Jadwiga knew how to make a paltry meal look like a banquet. In the ghetto, when Kasia watched Mama prepare for the Sabbath dinner, Mama would tell her, "On holidays, we must spruce up the appearance of our poverty so that we don't forget the existence of beauty. You save the best ingredients and cook the most fragrant dishes to be reminded of the sweetness of life, and you show kindness to everyone around the table to acknowledge reverence for life — all life."

All the while Mama was talking, she was indeed sprucing up the drab poverty in their apartment. She spread a white cloth on the table and smoothed it out to make the best presentation. She placed the dishes and napkins with the care with which one puts a gold necklace around one's neck. She stepped from one chore to the next with the lightness of a dancer. One moment she fussed over a dab of sugar, a teaspoon of butter, a small mound of flour, a rare slice of meat she had tucked away for a Sabbath meal. The next instant she was stirring a pot on the stove, then glancing into the oven to rescue a small babka or cookies from overbaking.

That is exactly how Jadwiga prepared the house for the Sunday and holiday gatherings. She, too, spruced up the poverty with the best table setting. Like Mama, she saved the best morsels she was able to squirrel away during the week and created holiday dishes that were as pleasing to the eye as they were to the stomach. The results reminded one of the goodness of life. Best of all, Kasia appreciated the security she felt among the people around the table. Sometimes, though, her mind slipped out of the room, crossed the divide of time and reality, and placed her once more in the embrace of her beloved family and friends. Love and pain pinched closely together.

Grandma Elżbieta, Marcel's mother — tall, slender, and regal looking — was a frequent holiday guest at the Jabkowskis' house. She lived on a small countryside estate a short distance from Warsaw. Kasia loved her company. Her intelligent eyes and strong opinions reminded her of Marcel. Kasia had no doubt that Grandma Elźbieta worried about the risks Marcel and his family were taking to protect Jewish friends, as well as their participating in other underground activities. It was equally clear to Kasia that Elźbieta never questioned the righteousness of their acts. Kasia loved her for that.

In addition, Elźbieta was almost as good a storyteller as Grandpa Isaak had been. Not quite as good; no one was. But her stories, like his, were inspiring. In Kasia's mind, Grandma Elźbieta belonged with Grandfather Isaak and all the ghetto heroes who kept her soul from dying. Of course, that group included the extraordinary Christian people she had the good fortune to know.

As soon as the first hint of smoky dusk peeked into their windows, an alarm went off in the guests' minds. They checked their watches, grabbed their hats and coats, and flew out the door heading home. People were scared to death to be caught in the street after dark. Curfew wasn't just a security measure. It was a psychological control far more powerful than brute force.

Spring arrived. Birds fussed and sang in the lilac trees. The new current of war events continued to rip like a river rapidly flowing. Kasia followed the news with breathless hope and fear. In June, Allied forces liberated Rome and American and British troops landed on the Normandy beaches of France. That same month, the Soviets launched a massive offensive, destroying the German forces and driving westward to the Vistula River across from Warsaw. In July, Soviet forces began advancing on Warsaw. Bewildered by the gravity of the moment, Kasia listened to the distant thunder of detonations rolling toward her like an otherworldly drumroll.

She asked Marcel, "Could it really be happening? After all these years?"

"Darling, it is happening as we speak, but the people in Warsaw will have to step into the final battle to prevent the

Russians from stealing our sovereignty. Nevertheless, you will be hugging your dad very soon!"

Poles step into the battle against their liberators? More wars?! That thought blew her mind. She simply was too naive to understand why Marcel, rightly, feared the Red Army. In Kasia's mind, Messiah was about to arrive on the banks of the Vistula River.

Then, a miracle! At the end of July, the people in Warsaw were awakened by giant explosions and roars of armored cars and trucks rolling down their streets. *God, what could that mean?* In an instant, everyone in Kasia's household was out of bed, standing bent over Marcel's shortwave radio, and hearing a most rousing announcement: "Columns of German soldiers are streaming out of Warsaw, blowing up buildings and carrying away truckloads of plunder as they flee! Poland is at the dawn of freedom!"

With dizzying hope and fear, Kasia's Polish family watched the drama of the Nazi flight. The air was light with jubilation. For the first time in years, everyone moved and talked freely in the streets. Neighbors donned red-and-white armbands and sang patriotic songs, and Polish flags flapped from rooftops. Some Jewish people even emerged from hiding, but not Tata and Ben.

"Where are my father and Ben? Will they be here soon?" Kasia appealed.

"Kasieńka, I am afraid you will have to wait a bit longer for that," Marcel replied gently. "They are still in the forest with the ghetto fighters ready to join the Polish underground to drive all Nazi garrisons out of Warsaw. We have to be patient. It won't be long now."

What could Kasia do but wait and listen to the sustained blasts of Russian artillery and thunders of mortar roar toward the city? At first, the detonations were muted, like giant boulders rolling toward them and making the earth quake. Soon, explosions lit up the sky like gigantic fireworks. Kasia and all of Warsaw fizzed with hope and anticipation for what the next moment might yield. Marcel reported, "According to the underground newspapers, only one German garrison remains."

The detonations continued until the Red Army entered the Warsaw district of Praga on the east bank of the Vistula River. Then, bombardment stopped. Everyone was mystified by the abrupt cessation. At that point, no one suspected that this was the first step of Stalin's treacherous plan to betray Poland.

Kasia tried to imagine: *What will liberation be like? For one thing, I will be Malka again. I'll be with Tata and Ben!* She trembled as she prayed: *God, don't let them die. Not now. Not ever. We, your chosen people, have been punished enough.* She wondered: *Where will we find a home? How will my countrymen treat the few remaining Jews? How will we live with nearly everyone we knew and loved, dead?* To protect herself from disappointment, she resolved to ask for little. She prayed for a tiny apartment for Tata, Ben, and her, food bubbling on a sizzling stovetop, and finally freedom from fear or hate. She understood that freedom implies limitlessness, but she was reluctant to dream for anything beyond a safe corner with the two people she loved above all.

Big events continued to evolve. With the Russians' encouragement, 50,000 Poles, between the ages of 17 and 65, joined the Home Army to drive out the remaining Germans from Warsaw. The streets and trolleys were crowded with women moving briskly, transporting arms hidden in bundles and bags. Boys, including Kasia's scout friends, pedaled on bicycles as fast as they could to join the fighters.

Afraid that Marcel, Piotrek, Pavel, Pan Rogal, and Uncle Jan — the only Polish men she trusted — might join the fighters and get killed (God forbid), Kasia asked, "Uncle Marcel, why do Poles need to enter the fight? The Allies are doing well without Poland's help." Of course, she agonized about Tata's and Ben's fate, as well.

"There is a profound reason, Kasia. You see, a short while ago, the Soviets liberated eastern Poland. However, the Russians forced the people there to form a pro-Communist civil authority. We are determined to establish a free, non-Soviet-Communist post-war government in Poland. Therefore, the Polish Home Army resolved to attack the Germans and liberate Warsaw ourselves in advance of the Red Army. We have a clear understanding that Russian reinforcements will be available to us if needed." He predicted, "The uprising will begin any day now. It will take only a couple of days for the Home Army to overwhelm the remaining Nazi soldiers. Polish battalions will capture the bridge and join forces with the Russian brigades sitting across the Vistula. Together we will create a single army and liberate the capital. The fighting will last only a few days."

Understandably, Marcel, Pavel's father, and Uncle Jan were among the first to join the uprising. So were Piotrek and Pavel. Piotrek, the warrior, appeared to have matured overnight. A revved-up defiance shown on his face, and his swagger was appreciably bolder.

One late July morning, the two men in Kasia's household slipped into sturdy boots and windbreakers, ready to join the impending battle. When Kasia looked at them, her first thought was: *What will I do without their protection?* Then, fear for their safety began to rattle in her limbs. Numbed with emotions, she watched time move in accelerated speed. In the blink of an eye, Marcel had embraced Jadwiga and pleaded, "Take good care of yourselves. We'll be back in a few days. We must go; I know you understand. Don't worry about us. We will be flanked by the Russians and the other Allies. The Nazis will drop their rifles and run."

If only! Kasia thought.

Jadwiga tried to keep her composure. She implored, "Look out for each other. Keep safe. Come back to us."

Then Marcel turned to Kasia and said, "Kasieńka, your suffering will end soon. I will help make it happen. Please continue to stay brave."

Kasia sensed a current of excitement underneath his suppressed fear. *Is this what courage looks like?* she thought.

Piotrek raised his chin, widened his stance, and assured his mother, "Mama, don't worry. I'll use all the smarts you taught me to keep my ass out of danger." Then he kissed her. His bravado made Kasia smile through her tears.

Kasia was next. "My onliest sister, be brave and keep safe. We'll be back soon."

Also off to battle were Pavel and his father, who came to the Jabkowskis' home to take leave of the women before departing to join the fighters. Kasia didn't realize how deeply she loved Pavel until the moment they were saying goodbye to each other.

He gathered her into his arms and held her. She felt his heart beating next to hers. He kissed her. She melted against him.

"I love you," he whispered. "I'll carry my love for you wherever I go."

Piotrek's parting words, as he was stepping out the door, were: "Mama and Kasia, be sure to find cover from bombs."

Kasia wanted to ask: *Where might we find that? The basement where the ruins would bury us?* But she nodded her head in agreement. She knew that he was as worried about Jadwiga and her as they were worried about the men.

Jadwiga and Kasia stood at the door waving, unwilling to let them out of sight. Then they rushed to the window, leaned their heads out, and watched the men merge into the stream of agitated people.

Suddenly, the silence in the house was unbearable.

PART THREE

Uprising and Liberation

I don't believe that the big men, the politicians and capitalists alone, are guilty of the war. Oh no, the little man is just as guilty, otherwise the peoples of the world would have risen in revolt long ago!

Anne Frank

CHAPTER THIRTY-SEVEN

Betrayal

The uprising erupted on August 1, 1944, at 5 p.m. As if on cue, the whole of Warsaw began to echo with the sounds of rifle fire. The explosions mingled more and more with artillery and continued to thunder past the setting sun, past midnight darkness and breaking dawn—never letting up.

As soon as the news reached Hitler, the little tyrant issued a command: "Kill every Pole, pulverize the whole city block by block—bomb, torch, bulldoze as a warning to the rest of occupied Europe."

Initially, Poles took control of most of the city. Nearly every able person in Warsaw participated in the struggle—including Jadwiga and Kasia. The third day of fighting, the two women were pedaling their bicycles to volunteer at a makeshift hospital in a nearby church. They sped through side streets and alleys to avoid embattled areas. Reddish smoke covered the sky.

A hundred feet from their destination, something—a stray bullet or shrapnel—hit Kasia's arm, knocking her off her bike. She didn't so much fall as sink from her seat and ended up on the asphalt, coiled in a semi-circle. A liver-colored bloodstain was forming below her shoulder.

"Kasieńka!" Jadwiga's shriek rose above the sounds of explosions. She jumped off her bike, kneeled beside the girl, and called out, "Help! Help! Somebody!"

Dazed, Kasia slowly lifted her head, saw blood trickling off her left sleeve, and argued with destiny. *Now? After I've climbed past all the pitfalls to the top of the mountain?* She blinked and tried to sit up. The world spun. She blinked again until she got Jadwiga's terrified face into focus.

"Aunt Jadwiga, don't be frightened. I'm still alive."

Two young Polish fighters who heard Jadwiga's call stepped out of a doorframe and offered help. They moved Kasia to a nearby courtyard and tied a tourniquet around the bleeding area. With that done, they interlocked hands to form a seat and carried her, gingerly, into the church, turning her over to a matron with a Red Cross armband. She glanced over Kasia's wound and said, "It's not alarming. We'll get to you very soon, kochana," and left the girl sitting propped up on a folding chair with Jadwiga's arm around her.

Rows of cots containing maimed and bandaged fighters lined the church floor. Some of the wounded looked grotesque. The scene made Kasia realize that only luck had separated her from those who lost their limbs. *Thank God that didn't happen to me*, she thought with a twinge of guilt at her selfishness. Sitting beside her, Jadwiga perused the faces of the wounded, checking to see whether Marcel or Piotrek were among them. The air smelled of rubbing alcohol, the tang of blood, and fear — Kasia was sure that fear had an odor. Outside the windows, bombs shrieked and then exploded, making the walls, floor, and beds shake. In spite of the commotion, Kasia felt herself drifting into a dark, luminous fog.

As if pulled out from a nightmare, she heard footsteps coming to a stop in front of her. A soothing female voice asked, "Are you Kasia? I'm a medic. I came to take care of your wound." Kasia opened her eyes and listened to Jadwiga summarize the unfortunate incident.

The medic walked Kasia, gently, to an adjacent hall lined with more cots, where other medics bent over wounded fighters. Jadwiga was allowed to accompany her. After a swift examination the medic said, "You have a piece of shrapnel in your arm. I will remove it, then sew up your wound and bandage it. It will heal quickly. Please try not to be nervous; I will be as gentle as possible. I'm sorry, but we have no medicine to numb the pain. It will hurt, but there are much more serious cases here. Believe me, you are very lucky."

The medic kept up her talk, as if to distract Kasia while she was digging into her flesh. Jadwiga held her hand. Kasia bore the pain as silently as she bore all her griefs, fears, and longings. Inwardly, she screamed furious, earth-shattering screams.

They could have gone home the same day, but curfew overtook them. Jadwiga was an angel of mercy as she tended to the injured fighters throughout the night. Kasia spent the hours curled up on a hard church bench, listening to the moans of the wounded. Evening rolled into night and dawn arose. The seconds tick, tick, ticked: persistent, ominous, endless. Memories unraveled in her head, from childhood bliss on Karmelicka Street to the tribulations that brought her to this moment: her beloved parents, Grandfather, Grandma, Hanna, and all the ogres of hate in the same universe.

Black Saturday

Initially, Poles took control of most of the city. On Saturday, the fifth day of fighting, renewed numbers of SS soldiers stormed into the center of town and slaughtered 30,000 men, women, and children. Then, for good measure, Stukas dived from the sky and bombed the city. That day was remembered as "Black Saturday."

At the crucial moment when the poorly armed Polish insurgents were counting on the Red Army to join ranks with them, the Russian artillery — so powerful a few nights earlier — remained silent and allowed the slaughter. Hopeless days went by and not a single shot came from the direction of the Vistula. The Soviet authorities, who earlier had called upon Warsaw's inhabitants to fight the Germans, suddenly condemned the uprising. In addition, they refused permission to the Americans and British to use their airfields to drop ammunition and relief supplies. The Nazis took advantage of the Russian deliberate inaction and sent reinforcements to cut off the Polish fighters. Despite everything, spirits were high.

After the infamous Black Saturday, Jadwiga said, "Kasia, it is hard to imagine how much more diabolical Hitler's plans for Warsaw can get, but we must never underestimate his evil intentions and the zeal of his followers. We now know we cannot count on the Russians' help. I think we should join the flood of people fleeing the burning city and go to Grandma Elźbieta's house in the countryside. Our presence here is not helping the cause. I know that is what Marcel would want us to do."

"Aunt Jadwiga, that is a great idea! Grandma Elźbieta will be happy to see us. I can imagine how worried she is about us and frightened to be alone."

"I have to figure out the best way for us to get there. It's far and it's hot as hell."

"Why can't we do what most people are doing? Stuff a few changes of clothes into a couple of sacks or pillowcases, fling them over our backs, and join the mass of people running for their lives. Many even drag children with them. If they can do it, so can we."

"If I cannot find someone who owns a horse and wagon by tomorrow, we just might start walking."

CHAPTER THIRTY-EIGHT

Warsaw's Last Breath

The following dawn, Kasia and Jadwiga were startled by an urgent knock on their door. Kasia ran to Jadwiga's room and asked her, "Who could that be? Nazis don't knock. They break the doors down."

Jadwiga replied, "The only person who pounds on the door as if the earth was caving in is Jacek the milkman."

Another loud rap, this time followed by an urgent call: "It's me, Jacek the milkman."

Jadwiga threw on a robe and went to open the door.

"Jacek, what are you doing here? You'll get your head blown off running around the city."

Jacek, a big burly man with a ruddy complexion, shut the door behind him, removed his faded cap from his blond head, bowed humbly and said, "Dr. Jabkowski saved my wife and my sons from death more than once. There was nothing a poor milkman like me could do to pay him back for his kindness. Maybe I can pay him back now."

"Come to the point, Jacek. Bombs are raining on our heads."

"Yes, yes. I'm getting to it. I know Pan Doktor and his son are fighting the Nazi sons of bitches — excuse my language. I think he would want you to leave the city and save your lives, so he'll have a wife to come back to. If you ask me, you should leave right away."

"You are right, Jacek, but you didn't come running through the burning city to tell me the obvious. Why are you really here?"

"Pani Doktorowa, I came to tell you that I and my wife and children are planning to join the fleeing mob of people. If you and your niece can be ready in two hours, you can ride with us in my milk wagon. It will be a bit tight, but it will be Poles only in the wagon. No Nazis and no Jews. Do you have any family or friends who live in the countryside? If not, you can stay with my wife's parents. It's a very modest hut, but you'll be safe."

"Jacek, you are a godsend! We can be ready almost immediately. Marcel's mother lives in the neighborhood of Łowiec, southeast of Warsaw. If you can take us near there, we would be forever grateful. And I will pay you for the journey."

"I wouldn't hear of it. The wife and I owe Pan Doktor for saving our children's lives."

Jadwiga gave him Grandma Elżbieta's address and asked, "Will this be much out of the way from your destination?"

"Not at all, Pani Doktorowa, not at all."

Two hours later, on a sweltering August day, Jadwiga and Kasia tossed a few bundles of essentials onto Jacek's wagon. They climbed in and sat on the wooden planks of the wagon bed, squeezed in between Jacek's rotund wife, Rysia, and the couple's twin sons, eleven-year-old Wojtek and Antek. They sat with goods piled on their laps, behind their backs, and underneath them. Jacek climbed into the driver's seat, flicked the reins, and yelled a command, "*Vio!*" They were off, heading toward Łowiec and Marywil, a region dotted with manor houses, poor farms, and hamlets.

Around them flowed the throngs of people fleeing from the besieged capital. Streams of fugitives from side streets and roads merged into a river of bedraggled, frightened folk: mothers clutching a baby in one arm while the other hand dragged a toddler behind them; children, separated from their parents, wailing; older men carrying packs on their backs looking like a swarm of turtles. Some people were limping, barely able to keep up with the flow. There were no young men among them; these remained in the city, fighting against enormous odds. In the background, colossal flames devoured buildings, silvery ashes swirled in the sunlight, the air thundered with heavy artillery and the high-pitched shrieks of bombs cutting through the air. The scene resembled Dante's Inferno.

Frightened, hungry, and weak with exhaustion, the flood of humanity trudged onward. Above them, the summer sky was a resplendent blue and the sun scorched the earth with heartless indifference. The only water available was what they carried with them. Their lips were parched with thirst, their feet blistered. People tried to find shelter in churches, inns, and private homes. It was simply impossible to meet a fraction of the needs. The further they drew away from the city, the more agonizing their helplessness, discomfort, and despair grew.

Totally numbed with worry, grief, and gratitude, Jadwiga and Kasia reached Grandma Elżbieta's house just as the setting sun inflamed the earth with one final touch. Grandma Elżbieta, perched at the window monitoring the road, caught sight of them and flew out the door even before the wagon came to a full stop, her arms reaching to enfold them. So happy to see them!

"I've been standing at the window every day hoping to spy you coming down the road. I had no way of reaching you. I was so worried about your safety. I didn't know what to think. Thank God you are safe!" She didn't yet ask where Marcel and Piotrek were, but her eyes were desperately searching their faces for answers.

"My God, how hot and tired you must be," she fussed, not knowing what to do first to make them comfortable. She thanked Jacek, "*Dziękuję, dziękuję*" over and over for bringing them to safety.

"I must fetch a drink of water for you all, Jacek. Please come in and wash up, freshen yourselves a bit. You and your family can stay here. I will make room."

Jacek, his wife, and their two sons who endured the trip without complaining gratefully made use of the bathroom, gulped down water, and set off to take advantage of the lingering dusk.

"We don't have far to go to reach the in-laws' hamlet. We better move on before darkness settles in," Jacek said.

With the others gone, the coziness of Grandma Elżbieta's house and the countryside serenity felt like heaven. The hospitable lady bustled around trying to hydrate, feed, and make Jadwiga and Kasia feel comfortable. At the same time, she peppered them with questions.

"Have you had word from Marcel and Piotrek?"

"We had news from them from the battlefield two days ago. They were both fine."

"Two days ago?"

"Yes."

"Hmm." She fell silent a moment and hung her head down like a wounded bird. Then she continued, "Just tell me quickly, is anyone I know missing?"

Jadwiga briefly summarized the losses. Elżbieta sat listening at the edge of her seat, dabbing tears from her cheeks. Darkness fell and the three woman surrendered to their exhaustion, squelched their thoughts, listened to the surrounding serenity, and sipped tea in silence.

They went to bed early that night. Kasia had a cozy room with a pitched ceiling and a window with a view of vast fields and meadows fringed by a forest blacker than the black of night. Above, the sky hung in its incredible glory of myriad stars blinking the fact that the universe just is. Kasia shuddered, thinking: *How can the Earth remain so sanguine when people are being slaughtered a short distance away?*

CHAPTER THIRTY-NINE

Watching the Road

O n October 5, after 63 days of ferocious street fighting and with much of the city in rubble, news reached the hamlet that the uprising had collapsed. That was not the end of Warsaw's punishment, however. The worst came after the final surrender. It was then that the Nazis took to the methodical destruction of the city. To crown their victory and teach a lesson, they invited a group of Hitler Youth to gun down Polish fighters in a lineup and systematically leveled thirty-five percent of the city, block by block. The terrible news of slaughter and destruction spread through the countryside by shortwave radio and by word of mouth.

Teary-eyed and grief-stricken, Grandma Elźbieta declared, "The Nazis will be shamed forever for their barbarism. Mark my words, the world has a conscience."

Kasia responded dubiously, "This is a strange time to arrive at such a hopeful conclusion. You sound just like my mother, though. She also counted on the world's conscience when our people were sent to Treblinka."

"Kasieńka, your mother was right. You will see."

A dark cloud of mystery hung over the world while Kasia, Jadwiga, and Grandma Elźbieta waited for the men to return from battle. Although they had received a few messages from Marcel and Piotrek during the fighting, they had heard nothing since the defeat. They doubted their house in Warsaw remained standing. They trusted that Marcel and Piotrek would know where to find them — provided they were okay.

One morning, Kasia woke up with an overpowering sensation of Uncle Marcel and Piotrek's drawing close to her. The mirage stayed with her the entire day. Dreamily, she pulled a chair to the window, sat down, stared into the road, and felt their images tugging at her. Jadwiga and Grandma Elźbieta noticed her preoccupation. Periodically they would address her with an affectionate remark or question, but mostly they let her be.

At dusk, she spotted two men in the distance where the sky touched the road. She knew, immediately, who they were, although they were too far away for her to see their features. She stared without letting them out of her sight; when there could be no mistake she ran to the door and threw it open, calling out, "Uncle Marcel! Piotrek! You're here!"

Aunt Jadwiga and Grandma Elźbieta were there in an instant. The family hugged; tears of joy streamed down their cheeks.

Marcel directed his first words at Kasia: "Kasieńka, your dad and Ben are alive. You'll see them soon."

Kasia stood silently, waiting to hear more. Piotrek read her mind. He said, "I'd heard much about Ben's valor, but now I saw it up close. Your dad and Ben were equal to ten ordinary fighters. But then, none of the Jewish fighters were ordinary men."

"You saw Tata and Ben?! Please tell me everything about it."

"They fought at our side. They were amazing. They knew every turn in the sewers."

"Are they safe now?"

"As far as Dad and I know, they are fine."

Kasia stood expectantly, hungering for more news. Piotrek winked at her and said, "Pavel is okay, too. He sends his love. He is now staying with his Aunt Ania at the estate property."

She did not want to monopolize the moment, but she had to say, "You didn't mention his father and his Uncle Jan."

Piotrek looked at his father, deferring the answer to him.

Marcel responded, his voice dark. "Pan Rogal will be okay. He lost an arm. That is unfortunate, but we must be grateful he is alive. Jan was killed fighting."

"When will this savagery end?" Grandma Elźbieta cried out in despair.

And so, the uprising ended and liberation remained a dream. The Jabkowskis and Kasia continued to stay at Grandma Elźbieta's house. Pavel and his father lodged with Ania in the gardener's house on the estate where Kasia hid from Johan more than a year before. Their house in the city was a pile of rubble. Warsaw was charred, but some people remained in the city and lived in buildings that had escaped destruction.

With Marcel, Piotrek, and Pavel out of Warsaw, Kasia felt safer. Sometimes, Pavel bicycled the twelve kilometers from Ania's house to see her. Other times, Piotrek gave her a ride on his bike to visit Pavel. The place felt much different with Jan gone. Even the plants in his garden seemed to mourn him. They looked as wilted and neglected as the rest of Poland. Ania was forlorn without Jan.

The instant Pavel caught sight of Piotrek's bike with Kasia perched on the passenger seat behind, he dashed out to greet them.

"Servus, Piotrek! So happy you're here, Kasia!" He scooped her into his arms and lifted her off her feet; a thrill ran through her.

Pan Rogal welcomed them warmly. "Ah, Kasia and Piotrek. Servus!" An empty sleeve dangled from his right shoulder, but his left arm reached out to hug her. She relished his fatherly embrace even as her heart lamented the injury he had suffered.

Piotrek would stay a short while and then bicycle back to Elżbieta's house. Kasia remained, often for a day or two. During her visits, Pavel and Kasia took long walks. The countryside spread around them, vast, desolate, but glorious in the late autumn colors. Waves of golden wheat swayed under a pale sun. Although their hearts belonged to Warsaw, the young couple found in the countryside serenity to mourn and to find hope and renewal.

Unburdening his heart, Pavel recounted bloody battle scenes that kept him awake some nights. He confided, "Three forces kept my fighting spirit strong: thinking of holding you in my arms, love of freedom, and love of my comrades."

He kissed her tenderly and vowed, "Kasieńka, my greatest wish is to marry you when we are able to assume that responsibility—that is, if you don't turn me down and break my heart. Until that awaited day, I'll cherish each moment we're together. When you're near me, the things I love seem more lovable, the music more beautiful, and I'm more inclined to show love to others."

Kasia nestled in his strong arms and said softly, "I love you, too, Pavel. You are in my thoughts when we are apart and you're the hero of my dreams, but our love scares me. What will happen after liberation when our friends find out I'm a Jew? People like to gang up against Jews. I doubt I'll be willing to remain in a country where I can never feel secure."

"I know, Kasia. I understand. We'll surmount it."

"I hope so."

November brought cold weather. Kasia helped Piotrek and Pavel chop firewood. The boys were surprised how good she was at it.

Piotrek teased, "Where did you, a city girl, learn to swing an ax so well?"

"I learned by chopping the furniture and doors of deported neighbors' homes to heat our rooms in the sub-ghetto. My dad taught me how to prop up the planks and aim the ax parallel to the grain."

"You make a terrific lumberjack. But it infuriates me to think of what the Nazis made you endure," Pavel said.

Anxious days passed. Kasia's world remained frightening and uncertain. Liberation was near, yet so painfully out of reach. She could hear periodic Russian artillery fire coming from the direction of the Vistula. Then days passed and not a single shot broke the silence. She knew the Germans were retreating from all fronts, but that did not stop them from persecuting civilians. Her greatest fear was for Tata's and Ben's lives. They were still with the Polish partisans in the forest in Michalin.

The first snow fell in mid-November. The countryside looked bleak and mirrored the near-empty cupboards in people's homes and in their parched hearts. To escape gloom, Kasia, Pavel, and Piotrek bundled up in their heavy coats and boots. They dashed outside and stomped in the fresh snow. Their hearts beat in rhythm to their feet. The cold wind pinched their cheeks and they reveled in the simple goodness of being. They scooped up handfuls of snow, pitched them at one another, and laughed with complete abandon. Every now and then they remembered to look up at the sky in hopes of sighting Allied airplanes.

There were other isolated moments for Kasia and Pavel when the present felt eternal, moments when grief and apprehensions for the future were put aside. Kasia and Pavel took long sled rides in the countryside, where the immense sky merged with a sea of snow, austere huts stood separated by miles of nothingness, winds wailed above the loud silence, and the universe took on a stark beauty. At those moments, time stopped. They walked in awe of life and love, in spite of deep sorrow and uncertainty.

CHAPTER FORTY

Liberation

In mid-January 1945, Kasia was startled by news blasting from the shortwave radio Marcel kept hidden under his bed: "Germans are frantically evacuating Warsaw. They are emptying buildings, loading plunder onto trucks, and fleeing the city." The family was cautiously gleeful. They had not forgotten the Nazi flight before the uprising and the devastating turn of events generated by the Russian betrayal.

A couple of mornings later, a heavy barrage of detonations coming from the city startled them out of sleep. Marcel turned on his radio to this announcement: "Soviet artillery fire is echoing throughout Warsaw. The city shudders from the constant dull thunders of Katyusha rockets."

After several hours, the detonations died down. The silence was palpable.

Then, fifteen minutes later, this unbelievable broadcast: "The remaining Germans are leaving Warsaw! They are running away!"

Kasia sat motionless in bewilderment. *Could it be? After all these punishing years?*

The rest of that day and the following night passed in silent suspense. Marcel fell asleep hanging onto his radio. The others dozed in their chairs. No one wanted to miss a thing.

At sunrise, January 17, 1945, the little group was shaken out of their stupor by an announcement, "Warsaw, a dead city for the last three months, hasn't known such uncertainty in a long time. People cannot understand what is happening."

Several hours later, the long silence was shattered by the radio blasting in Polish the liberation of Warsaw: "Poles are walking arm in arm with the Soviet army. People are hoisting red-and-white flags to welcome the liberators. Jewish people are coming out of hiding."

Patriotic songs, roars of jubilation, and the grinding sounds of Soviet tanks poured from the radio.

Kasia was jubilant, but asked anxiously, "How will I find Tata and Ben now?"

"Kasieńka, we know exactly where to find them," Jadwiga assured her.

Marcel declared, "It is time to return to Warsaw!"

Kasia felt an indescribable gratitude, mingled with trepidation. She was aching to dart into freedom, swim in it. *Oh, Tata! Tata!* her heart cried with hope and anticipation.

The following day, Marcel managed to locate a horse and wagon and they prepared for departure. Another restless night passed.

The next morning, they rose before the roosters began to crow, dressed in their warmest clothes, clutched heavy blankets to keep their feet warm, and kissed and hugged Grandma Elżbieta goodbye. Kasia parted with enormous gratitude, knowing that Grandma Elżbieta's kindness and wisdom would stay with her forever.

Without losing another moment, they rolled down the snow-covered road to Warsaw to find Tata and Ben. The icy road remained unchanged from three days ago. The same harsh poverty clawed the countryside. Yet, everything looked different. The world glowed with freedom!

They soon encountered lines of Russian armored trucks and tanks rolling down the road. Ruddy-faced soldiers waved and called out greetings. Kasia waved back with unreserved gratitude. Marcel responded with much less enthusiasm. He said, "Thank God — a thousand times — we are liberated from the Germans, but with friends like Russia, who needs enemies. I pray for the day when only Polish soldiers protect our soil. God knows we've had enough of the Russians."

Kasia thought: *Who can blame Marcel for not trusting the Red Army? Still, in my mind, I see Messiah in the Russian uniforms. I'm free to be Malka again! I'm free, free to see Tata and Ben! My people are free to come out of their hiding places and the concentration camps.*

The boisterous Russian voices, the clamor of tanks, and the steady clip clop of the horse's hooves gradually faded into the background. Images of falling into Tata's arms and seeing Ben again crowded out the sights and sounds around her. At the same time, she agonized: *What happened to Mama? How will I live without her? Where will we find a home? Where will we belong?* She knew better than to ignore the existing anti-Semitism.

Despite Kasia's impatience, the miles melted and the scorched ruins of Warsaw slipped into view. The landscape grew larger and more grotesque as they drew closer. A pale winter sun oozed into crevices of the skeletal remains of buildings. Jagged walls, broken wooden beams, and half-attached staircases pierced through the snow and stabbed the sky. On the Vistula, the ice was a white stretch between two charred shores. The enormity of the damage took their breath away.

Marcel guided the horse and wagon into the city. Passing down their familiar street, they confirmed that their house was a heap of rubble.

They meandered through mountains of ruins, searching for traces of survival. Eventually, and very much to their relief, they came upon segments of streets that had escaped destruction. There were people everywhere. One could feel sparks of euphoria mixed with silent sobs. Blips of chatter, laughter, and phonograph music seeped out of doorways and window cracks.

Despite the horrors, life continued. A distinct aura of freedom drifted above the tragic city — with one devastating void. When Kasia looked beyond the crumbled ghetto wall, not a trace of life stirred, not a single voice crackled in the air, not one house remained standing. An all-encompassing specter of death veiled the ruins. Kasia shook her head, trying to align the past superimposing itself over the present, to be replaced again by . . . what?

CHAPTER FORTY-ONE

The House on Chmielna Street

U ncle Marcel brought the wagon to a stop in front of a house
on Chmielna Street. It was not an intact house; a third of
it was a heap of wreckage. The standing part, pockmarked with
bullet holes, had an undamaged door leading into the interior. It
looked as though people lived there.

"Here we are, Kasia. That is the place," Marcel said.

She looked over and caught sight of a face peering through
a frosted windowpane on the ground floor. Her heart stopped
dead for a moment.

Benio's face? My gosh! Could they be here?

Faster than a thought, she heard a muffled shout, "She's
here!"

The whole world receded into the periphery when she saw
Tata stepping into the doorframe and moving toward her. His
eyes held her. They were as reassuring as when she last looked
into them to find comfort, steadiness, trust.

Then she saw Ben — soft brown hair blowing in the wind,

face strong and confident, frame upright like a timber — following close behind Tata.

For an eternal moment she remained nailed to the spot. She was staring at them as at a miracle. Gratitude, joy, and sorrow overwhelmed her. Tears ran down her face. She whispered, "Tata, oh, Tata."

"Malkale. My Malkale." His arms reached out lovingly. She fell into his embrace and felt sheltered. She buried her face in his chest and inhaled a familiar cigarette-tinged scent. She was restored. She was Malka again.

"Everything will be all right now," his voice caressed. "We're together, my darling, and free."

"Oh, Tata. I worried so about you and Ben. So afraid I might never see you again."

She was scared to ask, but she had to know. "What happened to Mama?"

Tata held her close, his hand stroking her hair. "She was dragged out during the Ghetto Uprising, along with all the others in our bunker. I was not with her. I was fighting in the streets."

Malka had expected to hear that. She dredged Mama out of the ruins of her mind, felt the warmth of her embrace, the ring in her voice. The largest presence was Mama's absence.

Ben placed his hand on her back. She felt cuddled.

"Rebecca and Heniek, what happened to them?" she whispered.

"My plucky bride-to-be was betrayed by a rightwing Polish partisan. She was on a mission to get arms for our fighters."

He paused, kicked the ground with one foot, then said, "Heniek died fighting like a Maccabee for our right to live."

They remained silent, lamenting without a sound.

Tata recovered his composure and turned to Marcel, Jadwiga, and Piotrek. His voice was overflowing with emotion. "You saved my child at grave risk to yourselves. My gratitude has no bounds."

They embraced, and tears rolled down everyone's cheeks.

"We have been repaid a thousandfold, David," Marcel said. Jadwiga and Piotrek nodded in agreement.

Tata ushered everyone out of the cold, past the door of the half-standing house, and into a warm apartment. Tata kept his gaze on Malka.

"Have I changed that much, Tata?"

"Yes, you have." He blinked back tears. "When I last hugged you, you were a little girl. You are a young lady now. You have surpassed my prayers."

Malka could not get over how weathered and crumpled her once elegant dad appeared. The new wrinkles lacing his face made her sad. His hair was much grayer. Grief peered out of his dignified eyes.

She looked at Ben and took quick note: *The same Ben, yet different: taller, shoulders wider. A dense stubble on his cheeks makes him look so manly, eyes intelligent and proud — as they had always been — only more self-assured. So handsome!*

"Ben, you look like a storybook hero reincarnated as a smuggler, sewer navigator, and ghetto warrior of legendary fame. Only more so, although it seems scarcely possible . . . " the last words trailed into silence *Hanna would have been so, so proud of you!*

He contemplated her lovingly, admiringly, and said, "Look at you, Malka! Not only have you grown into an attractive young lady, but you don't appear destroyed by your overwhelming challenges. I can hardly imagine how brave you had to be to stay alive, yet you are so composed."

Tata gathered himself together and turned to Jadwiga, Marcel, and Piotrek. They were standing at a discreet distance, teary-eyed, clearly treasuring the reunion scene. Tata said, "We owe the miracle of this moment entirely to you. I'm eternally in your debt."

"Not at all, not at all. The gratitude is mutual," Marcel said.

"You must be starving. We have food waiting for you."

"Tata, how do you expect me to eat? I have so much to tell you. And I want to know everything that happened to you. You're such unbelievable heroes, and I'm so incredibly grateful for your lives."

"Later, Malkale, later. There will be time for everything now."

They took seats on a well-worn sofa and faded upholstered chairs. Tata said, "Friends got this apartment for us. We can stay here as long as we need to."

He asked his guests, "Do you have a place to stay? We have room for you here, of course."

"Thank you, David. We are staying with Marcel's aunt Rysia. Remember her? Her house escaped destruction," Jadwiga said.

Piotrek followed Ben to the kitchen to help him put food on the table. Suddenly Malka felt ravenous.

They gathered around a kitchen table decked with bright dinnerplates and newspaper strips substituting for napkins. They shared cold cuts, dark bread, boiled potatoes and herring, and tea. The men washed the meal down with gulps of vodka and raised a toast to liberty. Wood embers glowed in the stove. Malka was enormously thankful for the miracle and so painfully lonesome for Mama. The ghosts of Hanna and other people she loved so much tore at her heart.

Tata said, "We owe the food, drink, and crackling fire to Ben's organizing and entrepreneurial genius."

They voiced their admiration and appreciation.

Ben bowed and said, "Feel free to place your orders."

"How about penicillin?" Piotrek asked.

"It merits a try."

Intoxicated by the miraculous events, they disregarded their exhaustion and talked tumultuously about their losses and the latest political developments. They reminisced, mourned, and rejoiced, without failing to glance out the window and keep an eye on the sun's progress toward the west. War was still raging, and curfew was strictly enforced. Detonations coming from the retreating front line thundered in the background. This time, the explosions were sublime music, the grand finale of the driving out of evil.

As dusk approached, Tata, Ben, and Malka hugged their dear friends goodbye and made arrangements to stay in close touch. Tata thanked them again for saving Malka's life. Again, Marcel and Jadwiga waved it away as if it were the most natural thing to do.

That day was like no other, but so much was missing.

Tata, Ben, and Malka stayed up late into the night. They huddled close together, so grateful for the precious crumb of good fortune of being spared and reunited. Like a little child, Malka resisted going to bed for fear that the darkness of night might swallow up the two people who had returned to her. A single candle blinked on a table. There was no electricity. Malka's eyes stayed glued to the flickering wick with the same inner warmth she had felt as a little girl staring at Sabbath candles at home. Each flicker a nod: *The world is still there.*

When exhaustion defeated them, Tata and Ben showed her to a room with the only bed. Two cots were placed in the alcove that would be their sleeping area. Malka's bed was topped with a plump pillow and a thick down comforter. Tata tucked her in. She felt grateful beyond words, yet afraid to fully trust the next moment. She drifted off to sleep listening to the roar of bomber planes and explosions coming from the battlefront. The war was not yet over. They had no idea when it would end, but she felt almost safe. The Germans were on the run, Tata and Ben were with her, and they were free.

CHAPTER FORTY-TWO

Being Malka Again

The war in Europe ended on May 8, 1945. The Allies were victorious, Germany was disgraced, and Poland was nominally free. With the Home Army wiped out during the uprising, the Soviets easily established a pro-Moscow Polish government. Malka, Tata, and Ben continued to live in the crippled building on Chmielna Street. Considering that most of the city was in ruins, they felt lucky to have a roof over their heads. There was a shortage of food and fuel, but they managed to get by. Tata spent a fair amount of time seeing patients at the clinic where Marcel worked. Ben stayed busy finding food for them. Malka kept their flat tidy and tried hard to make their modest meals taste like Mama's cooking.

One sparkling summer day, strolling down Królewska Street, Malka caught sight of a band of jeering kids picking up shards of brick from a bombed-out building and throwing them at a gaunt young man. The man walked quickly, desperately trying to get away from them. Aghast, Malka turned to passing adults and called out, "Help! Help! Someone is in trouble!"

No one stopped, but when the hooligans heard her call for help, they disbanded.

She approached the young man, hesitated, then said, "Excuse me, may I ask you something?" He looked at her, his face pale under dark hair, eyes wide, tawny, luminous.

"Yes?"

"Are you . . . Jewish? You don't need to be afraid; I'm Jewish myself."

"What made you ask me such a question?"

"I don't know. I just thought you looked forlorn, if you don't mind my saying that."

He laughed, and his shoulders relaxed. Extending his hand, he said, "Yes, I'm a Jew. My name is Yurek. It's nice to meet you."

"I'm Malka. I'm pleased to meet you. I'm so sorry about those little hoodlums."

"They are only kids. They are learning it at home. Thank you for coming to my rescue. You're very brave." His voice was strong, melodious.

She kept on staring at him, unwilling to let him go. She knew so few Jewish people who survived the unbearable. "May I ask you, where were you during the occupation? You look a bit tired."

"I look a lot tired. I was in the Warsaw Ghetto, Majdanek, and a few other places."

Malka gasped. "My God! I think . . . maybe my mother was sent to Majdanek. She was rounded up during the Ghetto Uprising."

"Could be. I wouldn't have known her. Women lived in a separate camp."

"How did you survive?"

"That's a long story." He looked at her inquisitively. "How did you survive, yourself? I'm sure you had your share of horrors, although your appearance does not show it."

"I had false Christian papers. I was taken in by a very kind Polish family."

"That could not have been easy, either."

"It wasn't, but I had a chance. I was still on the run, in a sense, but you were caught."

Many questions dashed through her head: *Does he have a home? Does he have enough food? Is he alone?* She remained silent, weighing what to say next.

Although Yurek saw no reason to be concerned for Malka's wellbeing, he was no less curious about this spunky Jewish girl who had survived hell and yet looked as fresh as the blooms on the lone tree standing beside her. He resolved not to let her slip away as if they'd never met.

"Do you still live with the kind Polish family?" he asked.

"No. I live now with my dad and my adopted brother, Ben. He's about your age. They both fought in the Ghetto Uprising. They'd love to meet you, I'm sure. You must come to our apartment. It's not hard to find."

"Thank you. I'd love to meet them. Where do you live?"

"48 Chmielna Street. It's the only habitable building on the block. Come for dinner tomorrow, at two. Come hungry. I'm a good cook; I learned from my mother. One last question, if you don't mind: Is there any other member of your family with you?"

"No. I'm all alone."

Yurek arrived the following afternoon at two sharp, clutching a bouquet of lilac wrapped in newspaper. His hair was neatly slicked back, eyes striking, wide and skinny shoulders barely filling out a faded shirt. He smiled brightly, shook hands, and presented the bouquet.

"This is for you, Malka."

"Thank you, it's beautiful." She glanced at the bouquet, then at him, smiled, and said, "I'm glad you weren't caught."

He chuckled. "I was careful. The flowers come from the only surviving tree standing behind the building where I live."

Tata and Ben welcomed him warmly.

"We are happy to meet you, Yurek. There are so few of us left," Tata said.

"Thank you for your hospitality. It brings back memories of home, family, and friends."

Ben shook his hand firmly. "Servus, Yurek. Glad Malka ran into you. I'm curious to hear who your ghetto friends were. Our paths might have intersected at some point."

"That's entirely possible."

Malka ushered the men into the living room. The afternoon sun streamed in through the front window and lit up homey-looking corners she had created: doilies on a tabletop displaying photos of Mama, Hanna, Grandpa, and Grandma, and a graceful vase — a gift from Jadwiga — standing prominently under a window. Even the wall with the peeling paint and missing plaster chips looked like a still life. They took seats and the room began to murmur with friendly voices.

The conversation started with Ben and Yurek asking each other, "Where did you live in the ghetto and who were your friends?" It was not surprising they knew some of the same people, attended the same underground concerts and lectures, and were involved in the same prohibited activities. The ghetto was tiny, and they were the same age. They were moved to near tears each time one mentioned a name the other recognized — as if the mere mention resurrected them.

"What did your parents do? Maybe my dad knew them," Malka interrupted.

"My father was a member of the Warsaw Symphony before the war. He played the cello magnificently. My mother was a botanist. She taught at a gymnasium."

"It's very likely I heard your dad perform," Tata said. "My wife loved string instruments; cello was her favorite. What a small world."

"Do you play an instrument, Yurek?" Ben asked.

"Well, I played the flute."

"Why do you say 'played,' past tense?" Malka asked.

"I no longer play, because I have no instrument."

"I will talk to my friends and we will find a flute for you," Tata said. "You must continue to play."

Without much delay, Malka invited them to the kitchen table set with the nicest tablecloth and dishes Ben was able to procure. The topic quickly switched to current challenges.

Tata asked, "Yurek, do you have family left in Warsaw?"

"My entire family who were living in Poland is gone, but I am getting by and I have hope for the future. I have family in America."

"It is obvious you are resilient. Do you have friends here?"

"I have a few new friends, not many. I was lucky to run into a Jewish fellow, my age. He introduced me to his friends, all Jews, most of whom are the sole survivors of their families. They are clever and fun to be with. We help each other out."

Malka's eyes opened wide. "You have Jewish friends? Do you know Jewish girls?"

"Of course."

"I have two close friends, both boys, Piotrek and Pavel, but they are not Jewish. I love them. You must meet them. I think you'll love them too. I haven't had a single good friend who is a girl since I left the ghetto."

"You mean you didn't know any Polish girls?"

"I know all Piotrek's friends who came to his house, including girls, but I had to stay aloof for fear of giving myself away. Piotrek is the son of the family that saved my life."

"In that case, you have to meet my friends."

"I'd love to meet them."

"Can I pick you up on Tuesday, at twelve? I'll arrange for you to meet some of my friends and make sure a girl is among them."

"Yes! Thank you."

The stars were long out when Malka's family walked Yurek to the door. Malka's heart skipped a beat when he clasped her hand, cradling it in his large knobby palms, his face—a living portrait of tenderness and hope—so close to hers. "Goodnight. See you Tuesday, Malka." Then, he turned to Tata and Ben, bowed slightly, and said, "My thanks to all of you for this unforgettable evening."

That Tuesday, Malka rose earlier than usual. She slipped out of bed, tiptoed across the room, put her head into a massive camphor-scented wardrobe, and pondered: *What am I going to wear when Yurek picks me up?* Her options were few, considering what hung there: five well-worn dresses, three skirts, a few blouses and sweaters, a winter coat and boots. This paltry collection had to serve all four seasons.

Still, I want to make a good first impression. She decided on a green cotton dress with a narrow belt around the waist. *That will work, with a sweater. Just in case — as Mama would've advised.*

Yurek arrived a few minutes before noon. He stayed long enough to exchange a few pleasantries with Tata and Ben and then walked out the door with Malka. They negotiated a rickety stairwell precariously balanced between two leaning walls and out the gate. The mostly demolished block was largely deserted. From a window of a crumbling building, a young woman put out her head. Her eyes followed Malka and Yurek.

They jumped over a ditch and turned into a street with more surviving buildings and more life. Malka asked, "Where are we going?"

"To Lilka's apartment. She lives with her father on Sienna Street. They were separated during the occupation and found each other recently. My friends Sol, Josek, Mania, and Zyga promised to meet us there."

"Where were they during the war?"

"They'll tell you. Their stories are heartbreaking; also heroic." Switching gears, Yurek asked, "How old are you, Malka?"

"Seventeen. And you?"

"Twenty-two."

They continued to meander through bombed-out streets, noticing life asserting itself over destruction. Patches of green tendrils and bright-yellow weeds sprouted between ruins; sparrows, like new proprietors, trilled furiously in nests perched atop protruding beams. A lone squirrel sat up on his hind legs a few feet away from them, then scampered away.

"Did you see?" Malka pointed.

"Oh, yes."

"Where does a squirrel find food around here?"

"I suppose where there are people, there is food to be found."

"Except in concentration camps."

"Yes."

"How did you endure?"

"I'm not sure. I daydreamed a lot. My thoughts were my ultimate freedom."

"What did you dream of?"

"I dreamed mostly of the sanctity of simple moments with people I love: of sharing food with them, playing the flute and seeing the pride in my dad's eyes, walking into the open horizons, watching a butterfly or a squirrel. I don't remember noticing a blade of grass or a bird there. There was no food to lure them."

They continued to walk, side by side in even stride, bemused by each other's stories, occasionally falling into reflective silence but always very awake.

Lilka's small living room, abuzz with young voices, fell silent when Malka and Yurek entered. Everyone's attention turned to Malka. Lilka was first to greet her.

"Dzień dobry, Malka. I'm Lilka. Yurek told us how you met. We're all eager to know you."

Malka was struck by Lilka's spontaneous giggle and easy manner. She had an oval face, full cheeks, heather-colored eyes brimming with curiosity, and dark hair combed softly back. She was of average height and chunky, yet graceful. Malka was pleased to notice that all the young people in the room looked as though they had recovered from food deprivation. *They probably gorged on bread and butter and potatoes and herring, as well as an occasional luxury*, she thought.

Their voices were ebullient, but she heard deep sadness in their stories. One by one, Yurek's friends welcomed Malka and shared a sentence or two about their own torturous journeys. All of them, excluding Lilka and Malka, were lone survivors. The majority were from Warsaw. Zyga was an exception. Before the war, his home was in Otwock — a small town with a vibrant Jewish community, twenty-three kilometers southeast of Warsaw.

"Did you have a house there?" Malka asked.

"Yes, and a brick factory."

"Is it still standing?"

"Yes."

"Then why didn't you stay in your own house?" she asked.

"That's a long story. I'll tell you about it another time, if you're really interested. The gist is, my life was threatened. I feel safer in Warsaw, where I'm less visible."

Malka thus formed a bond with the tiny community of young Jewish post-war survivors in Warsaw. She met with them at their homes or in the park. In their company, she was no longer afraid of being herself, nor was she worried about being on her best behavior. They flirted and talked late into the evening (curfew was still enforced) about books they read, shared their goals and hopes, and laughed. They also spoke of their anger and struggle to forgive.

Tata and Marcel rented a large enough room for them to schedule regular weekly dances. Pavel and Piotrek provided a gramophone and dance records. They were the only Christian boys Malka knew who seemed as comfortable with their Jewish friends as they were with their Christian buddies. The dances were immensely popular. Everyone responded to the liberating language of the dance music with complete joy.

Most wonderful of all, Malka had a best friend again: Lilka. Lilka had endured Majdanek — and other camps — alone. Her father, her only other surviving family member, managed to find her after the camps were liberated. Together they returned to Warsaw, their hometown. Lilka possessed a remarkable lightness of heart and was capable of great heights of joy, despite the sad memories she carried within her. Her attentive gray eyes quickly earned Malka's trust.

Malka often walked to her best friend's house. They stepped into a quiet room and let hours pass by unnoticed as they shared their stories and hopes with one another. "How will we ever find each other after we leave Poland?" they both wondered. They knew they would have to leave their native land but had no inkling as to which country or even continent their destinies would lead them. They tried to imagine themselves in the future, but such ideas baffled them. Even so, vague pictures spawned in their minds of friendly towns rising above hilltops. There would be lots of good food, they envisioned, and every neighbor would greet them with a smile.

Sometimes they tossed away all serious thoughts, turned on the radio to the popular song station, and practiced the latest dance steps. Having a friend to share the pains of loss, the magic of hope, and the power of imagination helped Malka navigate her own path into the unknown.

CHAPTER FORTY-THREE

Exodus

The war was over, but history did not wait long to repeat itself. The young hooligans who had pelted Yurek with rubble from a bombed-out building were but one example of blatant acts of anti-Semitism committed by ordinary people and tolerated by the government. *What will happen to us?* Malka despaired.

The hottest discussion topic among Malka's Gentile family and friends was whether Poland would ever be able to form a government free of Soviet control. The most pressing issue for Jews was the urgency to flee anti-Semitism and find a country where the dignity and rights of Jewish citizens were honored. Malka listened, desperately, to friends weigh this question in the light of history. Some resolved to attempt to emigrate to the United States, Canada, or South America where they had families. Others argued strongly, "Unless we have a country of our own, we will always be treated like strangers — welcomed one day, kicked out the next." They listed examples of their forefathers who were invited by czars and kings to settle in different countries. They were loyal citizens and made significant contributions. Some were valued advisers to kings and nobility. What was their fate? One year they celebrated weddings and the births of their children, the next year they were sent running, misery pouring on their heads. "We were even held responsible for the bubonic plague, for God's sake," someone remembered.

Ben was resolute. "Since the country of my fathers doesn't want us, I will return to the country of my forefathers."

Malka took heed, but the more she heard, the more confused and uncertain she felt. Trying to enter a country where you had family made a lot of sense, especially if that country were a democracy. On the other hand, there were valid reasons to fear that a welcoming country might decide to turn against Jews, as had happened throughout history. One thing was crystal clear to her: Emigration from Poland was not simple, not even for Jews who were not wanted.

The first hurdle was finding a way to sneak out of Poland — an "Iron Curtain" country — and head for West Germany where US forces were stationed. From there, one was free to write to relatives all over the world (if one had any), apply for immigration, and hope not to have to wait too long. Another option was to head for Palestine at any risk. That was Ben's resolve. It was equally apparent that there was no point in delaying the inevitable. Once again, the earth was sliding from under Malka's feet.

The departures of friends were swift. They were running away from harrowing memories and from a threatening future, fleeing from fear toward hope. Yurek was among the first to leave. He chose his destination to fulfill his mother's plea: "Yureczku, you must live. After the war, you must go to your aunt and uncle and cousins in America. They will love you and will be kind to you." His mother had been gassed in Majdanek.

One balmy July day, Malka's family joined a group of mutual friends and escorted Yurek to the train station. They kissed and hugged; tears streamed down their faces. They promised faithfully to write to each other, although they had no permanent forwarding address. Yurek remembered his relatives' names and the city where they lived, but Malka's family had no notion where they would end up.

Too soon, they heard the chugging, heaving, and clanging of the approaching train. They looked down along the track and watched the engine approach, the passenger cars trailing behind. The train stopped, doors opened, people descended, and a voice called out, "All aboard!" Yurek stepped into the train and, before they knew it, he was gone.

Yurek's departure left a vast emptiness in Malka's, Ben's, and Tata's lives. They had grown so attached to the warmth of his presence and always looked forward to seeing him. They admired his romantic nature and resilience and missed his sharp sense of humor. There was one significant consolation: He was heading toward America, toward family and promise.

Lilka and her father were next to leave, to an address unknown. *Yet another loss of a best friend, although not as dark and final as Hanna's disappearance*, Malka thought.

The two friends hugged and cried, but they had reason to believe, in their heart of hearts, they would find each other again one day. They would write to each other copious letters. They parted with hopes and dreams for each other and for themselves. A last word of advice from Lilka: "We must promise ourselves not to expect too much and appreciate every morsel of good we find. This way we won't be disappointed."

Malka's family felt pressed to join the exodus before approaching winter. Their decision was to go to Palestine. Ben immersed himself in this plan with the passion of an idealist. Tata's commitment stemmed from deep reflection. Malka's determination was based on her grave losses, a review of history, and pride.

What could she expect from their resolve? She quickly learned that immigration to Palestine was restricted to Jews by the British protectorate and dangerous to attempt illegally. Some of the survivors of the Nazi-occupied countries who dared to enter were imprisoned and sent to Cyprus.

Ben tried to impart courage. "What's new about this situation, Malka? Tell me, where are Jews safe in this bloody

Europe? We must have a homeland where we will be able to sleep peacefully in our beds."

Pavel was the first person she told about their decision to go to Palestine. He fell silent and solemn. She tried to justify their decision. He stopped her. "You don't need to explain. I've been witnessing what is happening in this country. I understand . . . and I'm ashamed of the brutal intolerance of so many Poles." His voice cracked. He fell silent, breathed deeply to steady himself. Then he continued, "I saw it coming. I feared it. But . . . I don't know . . . I can't wrap my mind around the notion of your being driven out of this country by bigotry. And after all the suffering."

Malka thought, *I love you.*

He continued, "You know . . . I've been dreaming of following you. I realize it will be a challenge, yet I cannot imagine life without you. Thinking of seeing you is the highlight of my day. When the two of us are alone together, we can talk for hours, or sit listening to music, and I feel completely fulfilled."

He took her in his arms. She felt warm tears on his cheek. She melted.

"I feel the same, Pavel. Yet, I must leave and go on an unknown road in hopes of finding a home where I no longer will be afraid to be a Jew. In some very real way, you're coming with me. I will carry you in my heart as I carry idyllic memories of when my world was whole, before the war. You will stay within me just as do the people who saved me and who never let me forget that goodness exists even in the darkest places."

He embraced her passionately, solemnly.

Many obstacles had to be overcome and many unknowns to be faced before they would reach "home." *What will await us if we ever reach Palestine?* Malka wondered. Bible stories flashed into her head. The images were exotic and hardly resembled Poland, the only world she knew. She pieced together fragments of information from knowledgeable people, from letters sent by friends, and from what Tata had told her. All warned of enormous challenges: "You will have to roll up your sleeves to plow fly-infested fields, raise cattle, build roofs over your heads, construct roads, and fight for your land." The words "fight for your land" frightened her most.

"We'll do what must be done and find reward in that," Tata said.

Ben declared, "I'll be happy to be a farmer, or policeman, or street-sweeper, whatever, as long as my neighbors will see me as their equal. I've had enough of Poland. I'm done with trying to be liked but never fitting in."

Their first barrier to overcome was going around the prohibition of leaving a Soviet-controlled country. Only people with foreign birth certificates were allowed to emigrate to their native land.

"How will we ever get out of here?" Malka wondered, forgetting Ben's grasp of the post-war underground enterprise.

"Leave that to me," Ben said.

He burst into the house, four weeks later, waving three passports and emigration permits (fake, of course), and announced, "We are Austrian citizens, born in Salzburg." His voice was tense with suspense and pride.

Malka's heart throbbed at the thought of the danger ahead. And hope.

"Ben, how did you get these?"

"Malka, the black market is as vigorous under the Soviets as it was during the war. You should know that by now."

"I do, but I'm still impressed by your accomplishment."

They didn't delay getting ready for their journey. They had little to carry (one small suitcase each), no property left to liquidate, and a small circle of friends to say goodbye to. Malka was heartsick to part with Marcel, Jadwiga, and Piotrek, who had saved her life. Like her Grandfather Isaak and Janusz Korczak, they never let her forget the healing power of kindness and love. No more could she bear separating from Pavel, who made her feel beautiful, and loveable, and whole.

On October 12, 1947, their dearest friends walked Malka, Tata, and Ben to the train station and to the passenger car that was to whisk them away to the unknown. They hugged, kissed, and shed volumes of tears. Pavel enfolded Malka in his arms. He held her tenderly, longingly, unwilling to let her go. She clung to his embrace; their tears mingled.

The last words he uttered to her with firm conviction were, "I'll see you in Jerusalem, Malkale."

"That is a beautiful dream."

"Most realities begin with a dream!"

She boarded the train and sat down next to Tata and Ben. They had no clear plans beyond their first step: crossing into Czechoslovakia — the most secure way southwest out of Poland. They had no inkling where they would stay, or how they would reach the American sector in West Germany, or how they would make the rest of their way to Palestine. Malka was excited and very, very scared.

The locomotive blasted a shrill whistle and started to chug forward. From the window, Malka watched the station pull away. She waved furiously to her beloved friends. They waved back, blew kisses, and wiped tears from their cheeks. Pavel walked along the moving train, his eyes unwilling to let her out of his sight. The train picked up speed. The wheezing of the locomotive grew louder and stronger. Pavel started to run. His arms reached toward Malka as if to snatch her back.

Malka leaned out the window and watched Warsaw take wings and fly far behind the train into a vanishing point. With it pulled out the roots of all the experiences that had shaped who she was. She drew farther and farther away from the land of her origin. Locked in her were memories both tragic and sublime. She remained convinced that a fairer city than Warsaw before the war had never existed. Nor was there ever a happier place than Karmelicka Street, with its wrought iron balconies and noisy people. Never, ever would she tire of dreaming of her best friend sleeping in the room above and calling to her, "Hanna, I forgot to tell you . . ."

In spite of grave losses and deep sadness, Malka did not feel empty. She would never again take a sunrise for granted, nor would she forget that the meaning of life is life itself and must be revered. Above all, Mama, Grandpa Isaak, Grandma Ester, Hanna, her Polish surrogate family, and Pavel were still teaching her to love more deeply than ever before. And Tata and Ben were alive.

Malka turned her face toward the front, toward the future, and looked with intense curiosity into the unknown. New scenes of country and city framed themselves in the window and slipped swiftly out of sight. The world was fluid and unpredictable, frightening and hopeful. Malka stared straight ahead, thinking: *Somewhere beyond the horizon is home.*

Author's Note

To be able to endure the horrors of Nazi ghettos and death camps, one had to grasp at meaning. In the midst of the deepest despair, I fully realized the meaning of life is life itself: the splendor of a sunrise, the sanctity of simple moments with family and friends, above all the value of love.

Seventy-four years have passed since my liberation from a concentration camp. Yet, I remember, clear as day, the good people who kept my soul from dying. I cast them as proof that there were and always will be, at any time, righteous people on whom the healing of the world depends. Marcel, Jadwiga, and Piotrek and Pavel and his family are fictitious and represent the righteous people. Although I personally had never met one outside my isolated ghetto community, I still believed.

Malka, too, is a figment of my imagination — a reincarnation of my very, very best friend, Janka, who lived one floor below me. She was at my side when I was taking my first steps in learning to love and forgive and be a "mensch." She was rounded up during the deportations. I am an old woman now, a great-grandmother. Yet, to this very day, I feel Janka's presence on a chair next to me; or when I hike in the woods across the street from my condominium; or when I hear my great-grandchildren laugh. She appears light as air. I reach out to embrace her, and she vanishes like an apparition — but not without touching that which is best in me.

Ben, too, is a monument to the countless loving, charismatic, famished young smuggler-heroes who risked their lives to keep their families from starving to death. I did not know any of them personally, but I admired them and feared for their lives. It is no wonder that Ben stole my heart in the process of writing, to the point that I had to remind myself, from time to time, *the story is about Malka.* Furthermore, I never stepped into the Leszno Street ruins adjacent to the wall from where Ben and Heniek tunneled their way across, but I was familiar with its existence. That blood-stained segment of the wall was a common smuggling scene in the ghetto.

Although Malka and other characters in this story (with a few exceptions) are fictitious, they are true to life and based on my firsthand experiences, stories I had heard my neighbors tell, and everyday gossip circulating in the ghetto. I never lived on the "Aryan side" of the wall, but I was well aware of the living conditions on both sides of the divide. All historic events referred to herein are factual.

A few real people appear in the story. Janusz Korczak, a much-loved author of Polish children's books, is one of them. The heroes in his books were as real to me as my best friends and as inspiring as faith in God. The examples he set in the ghetto were as noble as the Nazis' conduct was evil.

A description of my brief, profoundly moving firsthand encounter with Korczak can be found in my memoir, *Transcending Darkness*, published by Texas Tech University Press. While Malka's interactions with Korczak are imaginary, references to his documented accomplishments as a writer, educator, and founder of the Children's Home are accurate. So is the depiction of the role he played in his children's lives and the way his life ended with them in Treblinka.

As mentioned above, I had written a memoir. In it, I recall how I, along with my mother and sister, survived the horrors of the Holocaust, how we endured with compassion, love of humanity, and the joy of life. Life should be lived joyfully. Yet, memories continue to linger stubbornly and spin into stories. Invariably, when I sit down to write about a subject that catches my curiosity, I find myself sidetracked and catapulted back to the time and places that shaped who I am, to events both sublime and horrid but that never fail to demonstrate to me that suffering does not have to drive a person to anger and despair. On the contrary, it can teach you to be compassionate and to love more deeply.

In *Hanna, I Forgot to Tell You*, I allowed myself to contemplate history through a third eye — that of fiction.

Acknowledgments

My early readers — my son, Robert; my grandson, Matthew; my niece, Fern Zagor; and my dear friend Sarah Schwarcz — gave me keen insights and necessary courage to persevere. Thank you.

My thanks to my writers' critique-circle friends — Sarah, Brenda, Richard, Barry, Judy, Buzzie, Judith, Lyle, Kathy, Peter, and Kelley — for your penetrating and constructive comments.

My gratitude to Joanna Conrad, Managing Director of Texas Tech University Press, for her interest in my manuscript, and to Travis Snyder, Acquisitions Editor, whose clear-eyed vision helped me shape this book. I thank Christie Perlmutter for her copyediting expertise.

Lastly, my deep gratitude to my sons, my daughters-in-law, and my grandchildren for all they taught me.

Glossary

German terms

aufmachen	open (imperative)
bitte	please
bitte sehr	you're welcome
Du	you
Fraulein	Miss
guten Tag	hello, good day
gnädige Frau	Madame
Hab kein Angst	Don't be afraid
Hunde	dogs
Juden	Jews
Judenrat	Jewish Council
Krautkopf	cabbage head (slang)
schnell	quickly
verfluchte	cursed, damned
Volksdeutsche	ethnic Germans

Polish terms

bardzo mi przyjemnie	my pleasure
bracia	brothers
dziękuję	thank you
do widzenia	good-bye
doroszka	horse-drawn taxi
dzień dobry	good morning
gural	Carpathian mountaineer
Ja nie rozumiem	I don't understand
Jak się masz?	How are you?
kolacja	supper
kochana	dear
laleskzo	little doll
łapanki	roundups
Pan	Mr.
Pani	Mrs.
Panienko	Miss
prosze bardzo	there you go
servus	hello
skurwy syn	son of a whore
Żyd	Jew (pejorative)

Yiddish terms

ketzeleh	kitten
macher	wheeler-dealer (slang)
shefele	lamb
Yekies	Germans (slang)